CLEARLY PLEASING THE EARL WAS OUT OF THE QUESTION

The Earl of Alvescot made it absolutely clear that he considered Vanessa's management of her late husband's estate to be a total disaster.

He made it equally evident that he viewed her methods of raising her children to be a sure prescription for ruination.

He went on to establish without doubt that he believed her treatment of him as a guest to be the height of outrageous insolence.

Vanessa told herself that she should have been overjoyed to have so displeased this man whose departure she so fervently longed for.

The only question was: Why wasn't she . . . ?

A Very
Proper Widow

A Very Proper Widow

by
Laura Matthews

A SIGNET BOOK

NEW AMERICAN LIBRARY

SIGNET, SIGNET CLASSIC, MENTOR, ONYX, PLUME, MERIDIAN AND
NAL BOOKS are published by NAL PENGUIN INC.,
1633 Broadway, New York, New York 10019

First Printing, December, 1982

3   4   5   6   7   8   9   10   11

PRINTED IN THE UNITED STATES OF AMERICA

For Paul, with love

ONE

Cutsdean Hall stood on a slight eminence but it was unobservable from the public road because of the heavy forestation to the south where a visitor turned onto the winding gravel drive. James Montague Damery, Fourth Earl of Alvescot, had visited Cutsdean frequently in his youth, and less frequently in his manhood. He did not relish the visit that lay ahead of him as he skillfully guided the two chestnuts past the Batsford Lodge and through the entrance gates, which were open, he presumed, against his arrival.

The chestnuts were showing some signs of tiring and he admonished himself for not making a longer stop at the inn an hour previously. He had taken the journey slowly so he could have his own pair, with a carriage following to bring his valet, his groom, and his luggage. The possibility that Mrs. Damery would have let the stables degenerate since her husband's death worried him, but he shrugged off his concern. The coachman and the groom would see to his own horses and report to him on any adverse conditions.

Around the sweep of one curve he caught a glimpse of the east front of Cutsdean with its quiet elegance, a large Venetian window and ballustrade above of glistening stone. The west front, he knew, was more interesting, where it was apparent that the house had gone through several stages in its development. There the conical top of the Tudor staircase tower could be seen over the central block, which itself was of Stuart date. The two had been joined less than a century before to form the current building, cleverly united with pediments and pavilions to match the tall south front, which now came into view.

Lord Alvescot was not partial to stucco buildings, preferring the solidity of stone. But there was something compelling about the south front, and indeed the whole house. Its relatively plain exterior disguised a highly decorated interior, several rooms done by Robert Adam himself. Lord Alvescot had not been to Cutsdean since his cousin Frederick had married Vanessa Fulbrook, and he had met her only once, at the wedding. It seemed entirely possible to him that the young lady would have made unacceptable changes in the house itself. She had appeared to him, at the time of their meeting, as a flighty sort of female, but again, it might simply have been her youth and her obvious infatuation with Frederick.

The earl had been in England on leave at the time, as Frederick had, from fighting in the Peninsula, and all of the women (as well as most of the men) whom he met at that time seemed coquettes and empty-skulls, dilettantes and wastrels. He had no patience with their indifference to the fate of Europe, to Wellington's brave bands representing their country without its real support.

As he approached the house he noted with relief that at least externally it appeared as it always had and everything was well tended. The stable block, he knew, was to the southeast, but he was not so much at ease here as in former days, and he headed his pair directly for the front entrance, ignoring the drive which swung around toward the rear. This proved to be a mistake, for if he had paid any attention to the stable drive, he might have caught a glimpse of a young man driving a curricle straight at him, at an unseemly speed for one rounding a corner of the East Wing.

His chestnuts were tired; Lord Alvescot himself was lost in reminiscence of his youthful visits to Cutsdean. The clatter of his own pair on the gravel disguised any other sounds he might have noted at a more observant time. But it is most unusual to find oneself vying for the right of way in front of an elegant country home on a peaceful, not to say languorous, summer day. When one has not encountered another vehicle for the last two miles of one's journey, one hardly expects suddenly to be confronted with a madman twenty feet from one's destination.

Still, that is precisely what happened. There was not ten feet between the two equipages when Lord Alvescot discovered to his horror that he was about to be run down quite unceremoniously by a hooligan driving . . . yes, undoubtedly it was Frederick's own curricle. He would have recognized the scarlet and black vehicle anywhere, with its fanciful D on the body, surrounded by a garland of outrageous thistles. Frederick's joke, which had caused a number of imitators at the time, Lord Alvescot remembered. Though these useless thoughts threaded their way through his mind, they did not hamper him from exerting all his physical control over his horses. He was able to swing them out to the left onto the grass with considerable dexterity.

His adversary, however, was neither so quick-witted nor so skillful in his handling of a pair of wild-eyed bays, and though the two sets of horses barely managed to escape meshing in a tangle of frenzied bodies, the curricles themselves were not so fortunate. The young man's curricle slammed against the earl's with an impact no less than that of a raging bull. There was the horrendous sound of cracking wood, the frantic whinnying of horses . . . and the earl was tossed five feet into the air, still holding onto the reins and possessed of a most astonished expression.

As ordinarily happens in an accident of this nature, the young man who had caused it suffered no such indignity. His vanity always led him, when driving the curricle, to protect his boots from the dust of the road by covering them with a cloth which was draped over a bar he had himself insisted on having installed in the curricle. At the moment of impact he found his toes locked into place by the bar, which collapsed upon them. He might have been embarrassed in having to climb out of the vehicle without his boots, but in settling, the bar once again lifted to free him. The young man was irate at the visitor's carelessness in smashing "his" curricle and he jumped down with flushed face and raised fist.

"How dare you, sir!" he demanded of the poor earl, who was attempting to assess the damage to his body.

Lord Alvescot threw him one withering glance before snapping, "See to your horses, you young fool, else one of them will be impaled on the center pole."

His own horses stood nervously still, the neck collars and saddle pads twisted far to the left because the curricle itself had overturned onto the grass. The earl judged himself to have no more than a sprained wrist and proceeded to climb to his feet where he found, to his chagrin, that the tight-fitting breeches he wore were split from waist to ankle in his impact with the ground. This would not have caused him much concern if suddenly there hadn't been a whole gaggle of people standing fascinated on the entrance porch of the house. One of them disappeared instantly back into the building to return shortly with a driving cloak which she proceeded to carry to him, even as an old man roared at her that she had no right to go offering his cloak to every Tom, Dick, and Harry who had the bad taste to overturn his carriage in front of the house.

Vanessa Damery lifted her eyes heavenward, ignored him, and handed the cloak to the grim-faced earl. Before speaking to him, she turned to the young man who stood glaring beside his horses' heads. "For God's sake, Edward, release the beasts before more damage is done!"

He scowled at her but did as she ordered, muttering a string of ill-natured epithets which apparently applied to the earl rather than Vanessa, since they included "bosky dog" and "rattlepated numbskull."

The earl had shrugged into the cloak while her back was turned, effectively covering the underdrawers and bare leg which had greeted the view of his audience. The cloak came down to his knees, so only a bit of his hairy, muscular shin above his boot was still observable, and Vanessa chose not to glance at it.

"Are you injured?" Her dark eyes scanned his face for any trace of pain, and were met only with a chilling stare.

"So far as I can determine, only a sprained wrist." His lordship barely glanced at the tall woman with her coal-black hair and smoky-brown eyes. If he had, he might have recalled the high forehead and the straight, long nose, but he would not have remembered the lines of care which grief and responsibility had permanently etched into her face. The whimsical girl of twenty had long vanished to be replaced by a mature woman of twenty-five, no less attractive, but lacking that carefree charm she had once possessed. Here was elegance rather than playfulness, but Alvescot was in no mood to analyze his hostess. "Are you Mrs. Damery?"

Surprised, Vanessa nodded.

"Would you mind telling me what that young devil was doing driving hell-bent for leather on the stable drive?" His voice, laden with anger, was nonetheless maintained at a level which did not reach Edward's ears.

"He always drives like that, Lord Alvescot. We saw the entire incident from the Drawing Room and I can assure you no one blames you in the least for what happened. I'm dreadfully sorry. Your horses will have to be checked over, of course, but they appear to have sustained no damage. Your curricle, however. . . ."

The object in question was even now being raised from its reclining position by two stable lads, while a third stood with the horses to calm them. Both wheels were splintered, and the body was so crushed it was barely recognizable. As the horses were released and led away, Lord Alvescot, without another word to his hostess, stomped over to follow the awkward procession to the stables. Vanessa sighed and turned toward the group waiting on the entry porch. Not one of them had moved to be of some assistance.

There was a suspicion of moisture in Vanessa's eyes as her gaze fell on the wreck of her late husband Frederick's curricle, still resting in the gravel drive. The damage to it was irreparable, and made her draw a long breath to steady her ragged nerves. Abruptly, she turned away from the distressing sight and walked slowly toward the frozen group of spectators.

"Everyone can go in now," she announced, feeling extraordinarily cross with all of them for gawking instead of being of any help. "The two gentlemen seem to have received no grave injuries, and the horses will be seen to."

When no one moved, she snapped, "Pray, go inside. There's nothing more to be done."

Edward's mother, Mrs. Curtiss, detached herself from the still unmoving group. "Well, I must say you are a most unfeeling woman, Vanessa! Edward could have been severely hurt by that man's carelessness and you did nothing but bark at him to see to his horses."

"The fault was Edward's, as anyone who observed the accident could plainly see, Mabel. And they are not Edward's horses, nor was it his curricle. I daresay you may not have guessed the identity of the 'man,' but he is Lord Alvescot, whom you are aware we are expecting today."

"Lord Alvescot! Well, no more wonder you defend him against my poor Edward. Now I clearly see how the land lies. My dear child will be blamed so that his lordship's dignity may be kept intact. Yes, that is the way it will be."

Though she showed signs of wishing to continue her diatribe, Vanessa wound her way past the others to gain entry into the house. The butler, Tompkins, gave her a commiserating glance and asked if he might be of any use.

"Yes, I think you might, Tompkins. His lordship will need a pair of breeches if he's to join us for luncheon. See to it, will you? There may be something in the storeroom, in one of the trunks of Mr. Damery's clothes that weren't given away. If not, perhaps one of the footmen is his size. Doubtless his own luggage will arrive shortly. In his present condition he's not likely to come through the Entrance Hall, so have someone stationed at the east door to show him to his room, please."

"Certainly, ma'am. I'll take care of it."

Lord Alvescot, despite the rage he felt at the accident and the destruction of his curricle, to say nothing of the near destruction of himself, found himself carefully studying the stables—their condition, their management, the quality of the horses contained there. His surprise at finding them in exceedingly good order helped to mollify his anger somewhat, though his vexation at having been witnessed by that motley crew at the Hall when he was flipped out of the carriage and then stood up to reveal his drawers and legs through the slit in his breeches remained with him.

His horses were cared for with such punctilious attention that they might almost have belonged to a member of the family. Frederick, he felt sure, would have insisted on the best of stable help, but it would have been no surprise to find them grown slack. Since that was not the case, he determined that Mrs. Damery must be an avid horse-woman herself, and set himself to asking questions which would elicit the information he wished. The lads showed a proper respect for their mistress but were not given to gossiping about her to a stranger, and he learned little beyond the fact that she rode daily.

"And the boy?" he asked. "Has he started learning to ride?"

"Oh, Master John has a pony of his own. Has had since he turned three," a boy with straw-colored hair replied. "Even Miss Catherine is already up in her mother's arms on a horse in the stable yard. Cute as a button, she is."

Assuming correctly that the boy was referring to the child and not her mother, Alvescot nodded and said, "My carriage will be along shortly. Let my groom and coach-man see to the wreckage when they come; you'll have enough to do with the horses. And . . . thank you."

From his former visits, Alvescot knew exactly how to enter the house without going through the main door, and he proceeded to do so, finding to his surprise that the east door was opened even before he reached it. A footman greeted him deferentially and offered to show Lord Alvescot to his room, which turned out to be one of the lesser rooms, of no architectural merit whatsoever. The woodwork was fine enough, the doors, doorframes, skirting, dado rails, window architraves, shutters, and chimney-piece all splendidly carved, but there was little else to commend the room. It was not at all what Lord Alvescot was used to. The mahogany four-poster and the serpen-tine-fronted mahogany chest and bedside commode-table were undoubtedly from Chippendale's workshop, but lacked the setting into which they should have been placed. In short, the room was hopelessly small.

As a boy, of course, Alvescot had had such a room when he visited, might in fact have stayed in this very one, or one similar to it. But he had not, since reaching his majority, been offered an apartment so small, so cramped, so thoroughly undesirable. When he inquired, he found that there was a water closet at the end of the corridor! The footman apparently did not regard his blink of disbelief, but proceeded to hold up a pair of breeches which had been found in storage. A stale odor clung to them, but it occurred to Alvescot that they were probably Frederick's and he silently accepted them.

"If I could be of assistance until your valet arrives. . . ." suggested the footman.

"Thank you, no. I can manage for myself."

"There is generally a cold collation in the dining room at one, milord."

Alvescot drew a timepiece from his pocket and noted he had only fifteen minutes to present himself. "I would prefer a tray in my room if you would see to it," he said.

"Certainly, milord."

Dismissing the footman, Alvescot walked to the window and gazed out over the garden and park. In the distance he could see an octagonal garden house from which a long walk bordered by a stone wall led to a ha-ha, which prevented the cattle from drawing too close to the house. From his vantage point it looked like a sizable herd, but he wasn't close enough to really judge their condition, he reminded himself. As a boy he had admired the garden house with its Adam fireplace and ogival windows, but he turned now to his tiny room with a frown of displeasure.

It had occurred to him that his aunt, who must have been one of the party at the entry porch, had not even bothered to step forward and inquire after his well-being. Not that this seemed out of character. He had never liked his Aunt Damery, whose cold eyes and disinterest in her sole child Frederick had puzzled him from the first time he'd met her. Frederick had never complained of her detachment, but his affection had been given to his nanny, and his father.

Very understandable, Alvescot decided as he kicked off his boots and shed the ruined breeches, wincing at the pain in his wrist. He and Frederick had been much the same build, and he found that the breeches he donned fit admirably. Had Mrs. Damery noted his build, or had she simply given instructions that something be found for him? He shrugged off his curiosity about the matter. Of far greater interest was who all those people on the entry porch had been. At the time it appeared to him that there must have been at least a dozen of them, but on cooler reflection he decided the number might have been smaller, though not by a great deal. She wouldn't have had time to invite all of them here just to meet him, since he'd only written a few days previously of his coming. Which would indicate that they were residents, perhaps even that idiot who had crashed into his curricle. And now he came to think of it, there was something vaguely familiar about the young man, though Alvescot was unable to place him precisely.

By the time his meal came, a tray with a tankard of ale and thick slices of meat and cheese, he had recovered something of his usual aplomb. The accident could not be allowed to put him at a disadvantage with his cousin's widow. He was, after all, a trustee of his cousin's estate, despite the fact that he hadn't seen fit previously to exercise any power in the matter. Vanessa Damery, as the other trustee, had been given rather too free a hand, being actually on the spot, but Alvescot meant now to rectify that oversight. In the two years since Frederick's death at Waterloo a great deal could have deteriorated about the estate and Alvescot meant to see that Frederick's son inherited the land and buildings in good shape. Though Alvescot stood as godfather to both the Damery children, he had seen neither of them. The boy must be four by now, he decided, and the girl just two. Not exactly ages with which he was familiar.

But he felt a certain righteousness in having finally come to take matters in hand. When he had finished his meal and pushed the tray away from him on the small

table, he tilted back in the delicate chair to meditate on
how efficiently he intended to sort out the chaos he was
sure existed at Cutsdean. It was just as he had decided he
would request an immediate interview with his hostess
that the fragile back legs of the chair, unused to such a
weight on their tiny tips, crumpled beneath him to send
him sprawling on the floor, where he gazed in wonder-
ment at the intricate design of the ceiling. His annoyance
at this second accident was so great that he grasped one
leg of the chair savagely, with the intent of flinging it
across the room, but his position was awkward there on
the floor and he succeeded only in further injuring his
sprained wrist and scraping the broken chair leg across
his high forehead.

Hearing the commotion within, his valet, who had just
arrived and was on the point of knocking, hastily entered
the room to find his lordship groaning with exasperation
and pain. Bibury took in the situation at a glance and
carefully schooled his face to show not the least trace of
amusement at the ridiculous scene.

"Don't just stand there gawking," Alvescot snapped.
"Help me out of this stupid chair." When the valet had
assisted him to his feet, Alvescot disgustedly regarded the
ruins of the painted chair, using all his willpower to restrain himself from kicking at it, which doubtless would
only result in a broken toe for his effort.

"I don't know why people insist on having such flimsy
furniture," he grumbled. "As though it weren't bad
enough to be put in the smallest possible bedchamber, she
has to try to kill me with chairs that disintegrate under a
normal-sized man."

Bibury was rapidly gathering up the remains of the
chair, which he calmly pushed out into the hall during
Alvescot's monologue. "Shall I have a look at that scratch,
milord?" he asked when he returned.

"What scratch?" There was a mirror behind him, and
Alvescot swung around to see the reddening scrape across
half of his forehead. The earl was not particularly vain
about his looks, since he didn't think them anything out
of the ordinary, but he considered the garish red abrasion
disturbingly uncouth. He could not recall any instance to

mind, save during the war in the Peninsula, when any gentleman of his acquaintance had appeared in public with such a mark upon his physiognomy. A long, soulful sigh escaped his lips and he met Bibury's eyes in the mirror. "It doesn't need any attention," he admitted, "but my wrist is aching damnably. Have you something to wrap it?"

The little valet nodded and disappeared from the room. Alvescot cautiously seated himself on the delicate bench before the mirror, drawing his uninjured hand through his straight brown hair. He was considering how long it would take the minor wound to heal, and he paid no attention to his own image. His hazel eyes mournfully assessed the brushburn, knowing it would take several days for its traces to entirely disappear. Which wouldn't be so awful, except that he was sure someone was bound to ask him how he had sustained it, since it hadn't been there after the curricle accident.

Well, he would simply ignore their questions, he decided, since he had no intention of detailing his downfall, so to speak. Alvescot felt sure he could turn away any impertinent questions with the simple expedient of a raised brow. Hadn't Frederick teased him often enough about his haughty demeanor? Not that the earl believed for a moment that it was anything more than a joke. He was accustomed to thinking of himself as being unfailingly polite and rather mild-natured in his dealings with his fellow man . . . and woman.

When Bibury returned with the tape to wrap his wrist, he patiently submitted to the valet's ministrations, thanking him when the procedure was finished and asking for a pair of his own breeches. With Bibury's assistance, he was soon returned to some semblance of sartorial acceptability and he went in search of his hostess.

TWO

Alvescot knew his way around Cutsdean without bothering any of the servants. His room was in the West Wing and he unerringly made his way to the Grand Staircase where paintings on the walls followed the slope of the stairs. These paintings did not seem to have changed much since his last visit, though his memory of them was not totally to be relied upon. Certainly they were of the same high caliber as always. Alvescot let himself into the Saloon.

The room was one of Robert Adam's most impressive achievements, a double twenty-five-foot cube with an enormous Venetian window and four great wall mirrors. Here there had definitely been a change, though perhaps a minor one. The furniture, which ordinarily was all placed back against the walls, had been arranged in groups about the immense room, where it obviously stood permanently, rather than being pulled forward only for gatherings. It made the room look less overpowering and austere, but it was certainly not the fashion of the day. Alvescot decided to reserve judgment in the matter.

Mrs. Hortense Damery, his aunt and Frederick's mother, was seated in a rather imposing satin-covered chair near the window. His entry into the room did not gain her attention, as she was speaking with another woman, and he came to a halt only a few feet in front of her before she deigned to recognize him. She had been a beauty in her youth, but rather than fading, her looks had sharpened to almost a caricature of herself. The eyes were sharp, the nose sharp, the cheekbones sharp; he had no doubt the tongue was sharp as well. Alvescot bowed to this straight-backed, dour-looking woman who was his aunt.

"James." Her acknowledgment of his greeting was minimal, and she made no attempt to ascertain his well-being after the curricle accident. Instead, she turned to the woman beside her and said, "This is my sister, Mabel Curtiss."

Before Alvescot could speak, Mrs. Curtiss belied her aging but elegant looks by snapping, "You should have a care how you drive, Lord Alvescot. You could have done serious injury to my son."

"Your son, Mrs. Curtiss, should not have been driving his horses at such a pace around the corner of a building," he said stiffly. "I believe it was he who put both our lives in jeopardy."

"Poppycock! I saw it happen and say what she will, Vanessa is only trying to get on the right side of you by saying you were not at fault. After all, Edward is an accomplished whip and he is accustomed to driving the curricle at Cutsdean. As he says, it was the merest bad fortune you should have been there. We very seldom have visitors here at Cutsdean."

Knowing from experience that it is useless to argue with a prejudiced mind, Alvescot turned back to his aunt. "I hope I fine you well, Aunt Damery."

"As well as can be expected at my age. One does not recover quickly from such disasters as have been my lot." Hortense took a dainty bit of lacy handkerchief from her pocket and pressed it to her eyes, though they showed not the least sign of distress above the hawklike nose.

"Indeed," the earl agreed, waiting patiently for her to inquire after his own mother. When she didn't, he told her that the dowager was in excellent health and even better spirits, a bit of information which appeared to offend his aunt unduly.

"She never did take anything seriously," Hortense accused. "To Lady Alvescot her whole life has been like a magic lantern show, ever a delight, and ever illusory."

Since Hortense barely knew his mother, Alvescot strove not to allow her to wrench a rejoinder from him. Some people considered that age conferred a privilege on them whereby they could be as rude as possible without suffering the consequences, but his aunt Damery was not precisely one of those people. She had always been rude, though in the intervening years since he'd seen her he had almost managed to forget how impossible she was. Under the guise of being "straightforward" she said precisely what she wished, without regard for propriety or for anyone else's feelings. He managed to chat with her for a few minutes, though she never waved him to a chair, before inquiring of Mrs. Vanessa Damery's whereabouts.

Hortense gave a sniff. "She'll be with the children. I don't see what use it is to have a nursemaid if you're going to spend all your time with them yourself. Be sure it's no fit way to raise a child with all that pampering. They should be toughened up to meet with life's adversities, not coddled like a pair of sickly lambs. But she won't listen to me. She has never listened to me. One would think her mother-in-law deserved some deference, but no, she goes about her daily business as though I had never been mistress of Cutsdean, and has all the servants so they refer me to her if I make a suggestion. We never had uppity servants here before she came, I promise you. In the end she'll be sorry."

Undoubtedly she would have continued to catalog her complaints, but an elderly man of military bearing stomped into the room. He halted abruptly when he spied Alvescot standing by Hortense's chair, and surveyed him with a critical eye.

"My brother, Captain Lawrence," Hortense informed the earl. "Perhaps you remember his name from the battle of Trafalgar."

Alvescot had no recollection of ever hearing the name before, but he was willing to concede that with the passing of twelve years the name might have slipped his memory. Nevertheless, the gentleman seemed rather old to have served a mere twelve years ago, surely being beyond sixty.

"You served with Wellington, I hear," the captain growled. "You'd have done better to have chosen a naval career, sir. A much more exacting and professional responsibility."

"But the action was largely on land for some years," Alvescot replied, unwilling to let yet another of these unamiable people annoy him.

"The blockade! You forget how essential the blockade was."

Mabel Curtiss interjected a word presumably culled from her son. "Boring. The blockade was nothing but a bore. All the young men said so."

Captain Lawrence turned on her. "These young puppies don't have the guts to withstand the least discomfort. All the sailors were forever getting sick. Not once did I succumb to a disease on board ship. This generation is a bunch of cossetted ingrates and lily-livered idiots. You didn't find that kind of behavior in my day."

Without waiting for anyone to invite him to sit, the captain did so, and continued to express his opinions of the current youth of England. Alvescot tolerated this for several minutes before excusing himself to find his hostess. She was, a footman informed him, on the nursery floor, but he would be glad to find out if she would see the earl when she was finished there. Alvescot found the assumption that she would come at her leisure a rather unique one in his experience. He was accustomed to immediate attention on account of his rank.

But he refused to feel offended, since that would only somehow put him in league with his sharp-tongued aunt, and he had no desire to share any niche with her. When the footman returned to advise him that Mrs. Damery would meet him in the Library at four, he thanked the man and, not being willing to return to the Saloon, wandered about the ground floor to familiarize himself with any changes that might have been made since his last visit.

Vanessa reached the Library several minutes before their appointed time. Waiting for his arrival that morning had caused her to miss being with the children and she had insisted on keeping to her schedule of being with them in the afternoon. He had, after all, invited himself to

Cutsdean. Vanessa had chosen the Library with its bookshelves built into the walls and its flood of sunlight coming through the bay windows because it was seldom visited by her household, and because it contained her ledgers for the estate, being her office as well. Lord Alvescot, as co-trustee of the estate, had the right to examine her household and estate books if he so desired.

The old pedestal desk dated from the 1720s and Vanessa found it expedient to keep the drawers locked against any unwanted inspection of her records. The heavy mahogany piece was five feet wide with a kneehole flanked by carved corner pilasters so grandiose as to make her feel slightly ridiculous when she sat at it. Despite her unusual height, the desk dwarfed her, making her appear young and vulnerable. Not exactly the impression she wished to give Lord Alvescot, so she pulled a book at random from the shelves and seated herself in one of the red velvet winged chairs which surrounded the room.

At precisely four o'clock the earl appeared in the open door, located her with a quick glance, and stepped into the room.

"You'd best close the door if you don't want everyone to overhear our conversation," she warned him. "I'm not saying any of them would be so crass as to eavesdrop, mind you, but they might just happen to be wandering through the Drawing Room and find a sudden desire to study the portrait right inside the door."

He grimaced and retreated to draw the heavy door tightly closed behind himself. Before sitting down opposite her he made a quick survey of the room. "What are you reading?" he asked as he disposed himself comfortably, crossing one long leg over the other.

"It was just to make me look busy," she admitted disarmingly. "I don't know quite what it is, but I think it's something my mother wouldn't approve of." She laughed and set the book on a table between them, bringing her attention fully back to him, but making no mention of the scrape on his forehead. "I'm sorry for the disaster on your arrival. Of course, I will assume responsibility for the rebuilding of your curricle, though you may not wish to entrust it to our local carriage-builders. Frederick always found their workmanship quite satisfactory."

Alvescot shrugged. "I'll have my coachman check them out. Please don't concern yourself with the matter. It's hardly your responsibility."

"It is, though. I knew how wretchedly Edward drove in the curricle. It makes my blood run cold to think what might have happened."

His brows rose. "I hadn't gained the impression anyone here cared in the least whether I was maimed or killed in the accident."

"I wasn't speaking of you," she said absently, then her eyes widened at his startled expression. "I beg your pardon! Of course we are concerned for your safety, Lord Alvescot. But you sustained little damage, or so you say. I had a mental image at the time of one of the children trampled by the horses. Knowing how Edward rides and drives, I don't let them out of my sight when I have them out of doors, but. . . ."

"Yes, well, I believe mothers are prone to visions of disaster."

It sounded so odiously condescending that Vanessa found it necessary to bite down a sharp retort. Instead, she studied him with cool gray-brown eyes, taking in his artfully windswept brown locks, the deep-set hazel eyes, the disapproving set of his mouth. His coat sat well on his broad shoulders, and he wore a plain waistcoat, unlike the florid style Edward adopted, but Vanessa considered him only passable in looks. There was something too rugged about his face, too unyielding, for the tribute of handsomeness. In addition, she decided with satisfaction, his countenance clearly indicated that he was neither good-natured nor open. Why this should have pleased her, she didn't know, since it was imperative that the two of them should rub along tolerably well as co-trustees of Frederick's estate.

Her perusal was accompanied by a silence which Alvescot made no attempt to break. In fact, several minutes passed with neither of them saying anything, though his eyes narrowed slightly as the time lengthened. Vanessa was aware that he expected her to provide some sort of social chatter, or to query him on his trip, if not his purpose in being there, but she refused as steadfastly as he to be the one to speak first. Eventually, with an exasperated sigh, he said, "I presume Frederick's children are well."

"Very well, thank you."

"I would like to see them."

"Would you? They would be in the nursery at this time of day. Did you want to see them now?"

"No, not immediately. First I think we should discuss the matter that brought me here."

Vanessa acknowledged this straightforwardness with a gentle inclination of her head.

"I have, as you know," he began pompously, "agreed to all the expenses you've recommended during the two years since Frederick's death. Though unaware that he had appointed me a co-trustee in case of his death, I was willing enough to accept the position, since he was my cousin and a dear friend of mine. The responsibility for seeing that his estate comes intact to his son is one I regard as a family duty and intend to pursue with . . ." Here he paused to regard her with a quelling gaze. ". . . resolution."

"Admirable," she murmured, meeting his gaze steadily.

"I have, to this point, been amenable to the large expenses you've entailed on behalf of the estate out of consideration for your bereavement and your position as the mother of the heir to it."

Vanessa interrupted him to say dryly, "You have, to this point, agreed to the expenses because you weren't paying any attention to them, Lord Alvescot. May I ask what drew your notice?"

His lips pursed with irritation. "My solicitor questioned me about them," he admitted. Absently picking up the volume she had laid on the table, he glanced at its title and his eyes widened.

"I told you I chose it at random to look busy. Have no fear that it's my usual reading material, though I must admit," she said, her eyes crinkling with mirth, "that I found the few paragraphs I happened upon most enlightening. I wonder what it is doing in the Library."

Alvescot flipped to the flyleaf of the book and was

seized by a fit of coughing. His attempt to conceal the book during his disgression was unsuccessful, as Vanessa reached out an imperative hand for it and he reluctantly released it to her.

On the flyleaf was written, in a schoolboy's hand, *James Montague Damery, 1801.* "Such bravado," Vanessa remarked, referring to the scribbled notation below: *Very warm but very interesting!* "Would you like it back, Lord Alvescot? I would prefer it not fall into John's hands until he is at least . . . what? Sixteen?"

"I would have been fifteen at the time," he muttered, pushing the volume down in the chair beside him.

"Precocious, probably. Frederick said. . . . Well, never mind. We were discussing the exorbitant expenses I've incurred for the estate."

Trying to recapture the upper hand, Alvescot insisted, "They are exorbitant, Mrs. Damery. My solicitors pointed out to me that a family of three and the associated servants could not possibly incur the expenses you have."

"But as you have seen, we are hardly a family of three. And you should note, sir, that with the exception of Mr. Oldcastle, they are all Frederick's relations."

"Who the deuce is Mr. Oldcastle?"

Vanessa shook her head with barely concealed amusement, making the black ringlets dance wildly. "Well, I guess one would say he is a special friend of Louisa's."

"Louisa," he said flatly. Surely Mrs. Curtiss's name was Mabel. He asked, with his unfailing politeness strained somewhat, "Who is Louisa?"

"Edward's sister. Edward is the one who ran you down. They're both Mrs. Curtiss's children. I would have thought you might have met them when you visited Cutsdean as a child."

So that was why the young man had looked familiar, Alvescot realized at last. He *had* met Edward as a child, and his memories of the fellow were not at all pleasant. There had been an episode when Alvescot was perhaps eleven, and Edward eight, when the younger boy had deliberately lied to get him and Frederick into trouble. There had been several instances of that nature, actually, but fortunately he had only encountered the fellow two or three times on visits, and had gathered that Aunt Damery's side of the family was not particularly welcome at Cutsdean in those days. And now he found them all here—Aunt Damery herself, who had a perfectly good house in Basingstoke, and her brother, and her sister, with two children. Plus the suitor, Mr. Oldcastle. The earl eyed Vanessa with growing suspicion.

"What are they all doing here?"

"They live here, Lord Alvescot."

"But why?"

Vanessa sighed and rose from her chair to pace about the sunlit room. "First Mrs. Damery came, right after the news of Frederick's death. I could understand that, I suppose, her having lost her only child, though she never appeared to care much for him, if I may be so candid with you. She let out her house in Basingstoke and took up permanent residence here. The . . . shock of his death left me a little. . . ." Vanessa waved a hand to indicate her unstable state at the time. "And then she started to gather the others around her—her brother, her sister, Edward and Louisa."

"Why did you let them stay?"

"What else could I do?" she demanded, impatient. "They're family. The captain and the Curtisses haven't enough to survive on and Mrs. Damery saw a way for me to support them rather than she herself. Hers was an impoverished family even when she met and married Frederick's father, and he made an allowance to the family for many years. Recently, Hortense has had to make provisions for them again from her widow's jointure, which doesn't best please her."

Alvescot tapped a finger on the arm of his chair. "They're *her* family."

"She's Frederick's mother," Vanessa countered, adding, "And some of them are very expensive."

"Edward," he guessed. "Do you mean to tell me you're supporting that rattlepate out of my cousin's estate?"

"I make his mother an allowance." Vanessa stopped in front of the earl, shrugging her shoulders helplessly. "Actually, I make all of their allowances from my own jointure, rather than the estate, but the expense of having them live here comes from the estate. There's really no way to separate out the cost of their food and lodging from those of the rest of the household."

"Their allowances are Mrs. Damery's responsibility," he replied, impatient, "not yours."

"And if she says she can't afford it?" Vanessa rejoined. "Am I to let them starve?"

"Obviously, she can afford it. She was doing it before you took over the burden, and she could do it again. You've allowed yourself to be duped, Mrs. Damery. Frederick wouldn't have wanted you to drain your resources supporting a bundle of useless people who are only relations by marriage."

"You can't possibly know that. My mother-in-law constantly points out that *her son* would not have wanted her to suffer on any account in her old age. And she wasn't supporting the Curtisses, you know. They've come here more recently because Mr. Curtiss left them without any funds." Vanessa waved aside the topic altogether. "Besides, it's irrelevant. You have no control over the money I'm using to support them. If you wish to object to the cost of housing and feeding them which comes from the estate, then do so. Work out some equitable figure, and I'll reimburse the estate."

"Which would only further impoverish you."

"I'm not impoverished." She pursed her lips thoughtfully and confessed, "It's not just that, you know. My parents insist that it's my duty, since they're Frederick's kin. Mother is adamant about it. She says that I'm housed and fed and have sufficient pin money for my needs, and that I shouldn't begrudge those who have less. Of course," she admitted, rueful, "they live in Somersetshire and only visit occasionally. Still, my parents are very religious and mother simply goes around tight-lipped and tolerant when she's with them, and my father breathes a sigh of relief when he leaves. Family ties are important to them and they would feel I had disgraced myself if I didn't treat Frederick's kin as I ought. Frankly, I can't afford to set them all up in places of their own and Mrs. Damery insists that the house in Basingstoke won't accommodate all of them."

Alvescot waved her back to her chair. "All right, let's leave that issue for the time being. Let's discuss the exorbitant expenses that have brought me here. I understand the boy has a pony of his own."

"You don't think he should?" Vanessa regarded him incredulously. "His father received his first pony when he was three. Frederick could hardly wait until John was old enough. Unfortunately, he didn't live to see the day."

Alarmed at the possibility of her bursting into tears, or some such womanly display of distress, Alvescot hastened to reassure her. "No, I'm sure the boy should have a pony of his own. But you may be overindulging the children to compensate for their father's loss. It's a common occurrence with widows, I believe."

Her glance was scornful. "I do indulge them—with my time, with anything their position requires, with presents when I feel like it. And I doubt I'm wrecking the estate with a few trifles."

"Then how in God's name are you racking up such incredible bills?" he demanded, impatient. "They aren't imaginary, Mrs. Damery."

"Nor would they be unaccounted for, save that you gave me to understand from the start that you weren't interested in hearing the details."

"I beg your pardon? I'm sure you're mistaken." It was clear Alvescot did not believe her. His brows had risen to new heights in haughtiness and his mouth became a grim line. He settled back in his chair, his fingers intertwined and resting at his waist, the very picture of a skeptical employer interviewing a suspect employee. "Tell me about it, Mrs. Damery."

Vanessa had a brief but fervent desire to slap him. The violence of her emotions surprised and alarmed her, making her rise very carefully from her chair and walk calmly to the desk. The records she kept of estate transactions were thorough and well organized, not only the books but the correspondence. Laborious task that it was, nonetheless she took the time to make a copy of each letter she sent, carefully attaching the reply when it came. There was no problem finding the items she sought.

"Perhaps," she suggested, turning to him, "you would

care to sit at the desk to study the record of our early transactions, Lord Alvescot." When he joined her, she spread out letter after letter for his perusal. "This is your note of condolence, and this is my reply. Here is my first attempt to advise you of my plans for the estate, with your . . . response. You may follow our interchanges straight through to your note advising me of your arrival. If the copies of my letters aren't legible, you have only to ask me to translate them for you. Since they're for my own information, I have a tendency to abbreviate and write quickly. I trust you will be able to decipher your own communications, though I have occasionally had trouble myself."

Vanessa left him to his task, strolling to the bay windows to look out over the gravel drive and the lime avenue beyond it. She didn't turn at his muffled curse but continued to wait patiently until he addressed himself to her. When he cleared his throat some twenty minutes later, she knew he had read every one of the letters.

"I apologize, Mrs. Damery. I can't imagine what possessed me to write such an uncivil reply to your first letter. For a full six months after Waterloo I was not quite myself. Not only was I ill, but I had lost some of my best friends there, including Frederick. But that is only to excuse myself."

He rose and joined her at the windows, standing a few feet from her unexpressive face. "Apparently you tried several times during that period to interest me in your plans, and I was too self-absorbed to show the least concern. Of all people, I should have come to your assistance. Frederick relied on me to do so, else he wouldn't have named me co-trustee."

"Well, after a few months I took hold of things myself. Your advice would have been welcome, but everything worked out for the best." Vanessa offered him a small smile, acknowledging the sincerity of his apology. "Frederick was a soldier, Lord Alvescot. He had no interest in farming, and little knowledge of it. During those years he spent on the Peninsula, things deteriorated at Cutsdean, and I was too busy with the babies to pay much heed. When I realized that little John was going to end up with a sadly depleted estate if something wasn't done, I set about finding a manager to take things in hand. I made two mistakes before finding our current man, and I pay him what you might consider a disproportionate wage, but he is honest, hard-working, and knowledgeable and he relieves me of all worries about running the estate."

The expression on Alvescot's face went through a number of subtle changes, as though he was undecided how to broach his underlying doubt. "I find myself in an awkward position," he confessed at last. "Due to my neglect, you've been forced to make decisions you might have been spared, but they are still decisions which are vital to the management of Frederick's estate, and therefore my responsibility to oversee as co-trustee. The fact of the matter is, Mrs. Damery, that your trust in this fellow may be misplaced. There are the unusually high expenses. . . ."

Vanessa rubbed her eyes wearily. It had been a long day and she didn't have the energy to try to convince Lord Alvescot of her confidence in Paul Burford. What she really wanted was a chance to bathe and rest before dinner. Looking at matters from his point of view, his suggestion was not unreasonable, but Vanessa was tired of trying to see everything from someone else's point of view. She was tired of having her every decision questioned by one or another member of her entourage. If it wasn't her mother-in-law insisting that she coddled the children, or Edward telling her she really needed his assistance (which would best be accomplished by her marrying him), or Mabel pushing forth her incessant menus, then it was the captain deprecating the unmilitary regulation of her household. Vanessa walked to the desk, pulled out several ledgers, and turned to the earl.

"You may take these to your room to study them. I'll arrange for you to spend the day tomorrow with Paul Burford. If, after that, you think it necessary to discuss any change in my arrangements here, I will be willing to sit down and talk with you. I don't want you to interpret that as my saying I will be willing to make arbitrary changes. I'm satisfied with things as they are. But I will listen to your opinions, since you are co-trustee."

"And not because I may know more about the manage-

ment of an estate than you do?" he asked, hackles raised
by her indifference to his position and masculine preroga-
tive in matters of such a nature.

"You can convince me of your expertise," she said
lightly, "if the need arises. Now, if you will excuse me,
Lord Alvescot, I have a few duties to attend to. Please
make yourself at home. Has your valet arrived?"

"Yes."

"Excellent. We dine at six, though generally we gather
in the Saloon about five-thirty. I'm sure you know the
various diversions to be had at Cutsdean and hope you'll
feel free to avail yourself of them."

"Thank you," he said stiffly, watching her lock the
drawers of the mammoth pedestal desk.

"Not at all." Vanessa walked to the door and turned
the brass door handle before she remembered something
she had meant to mention. "I'm sorry about your room.
Ordinarily I would have given you the Chinese Chippendale bedroom, but Mr. Oldcastle was already established
there and I didn't feel I could ask him to move. The only
two large bedrooms unoccupied suffered from some water
damage in the spring and are undergoing repairs. If you
would prefer something larger, I would have to move you
to the nursery floor, which is not the quietest setting." She
cocked her head inquiringly.

"I'll stay where I am."

"As you wish." Her eyes sparkled with amusement. "If
you could induce Louisa and Mr. Oldcastle to quarrel
(which is not a difficult matter to accomplish), I'd be
happy to have you move into the Chinese Chippendale
bedroom when he leaves." And before he could reply, if
indeed he had any intention of doing so, she slipped out
the door.

THREE

Vanessa's hopes of avoiding everyone on the way to her room were not answered. Mabel Curtiss waylaid her in the Entrance Hall before she had a chance to escape up the stairs.

"Now you really must pay some heed to what you give the earl to eat," she insisted, waving a menu frantically before Vanessa's face. "How often do we have so exalted a guest in our midst? I have the very thing, you know; I've been working on it all afternoon. The first course would be soup *à la jardinière,* crimped salmon and parsley-and-butter, plus trout *aux fines herbes,* in cases. Could anything be more perfect? He would rave about it, and I'm sure even your cook is capable of handling that. For the entrees, *tendrons de veau* and peas, and lamb cutlets and cucumbers."

As she made her way through a list of loins of veal, braised ham, roast duck, lobster salad, and raspberry-and-currant tarts, among a multitude of other dishes, Vanessa stood patiently listening. When she got to the nesselrode pudding and the ices, Vanessa said, "Yes, it sounds delicious, Mabel, but a trifle extravagant for us."

"It's not just for us!" Mabel proclaimed. "Do you want the earl returning to London, or wherever he lives, and telling them we don't live in style? Nothing is more indicative of one's position, I promise you, than one's board. I heard my mother say it a thousand times when I was growing up. No less than three courses with two entrees for a party of twelve, and I myself believe it should be three entrees, plus the desserts and ices, of course."

Vanessa held out her hand for the sheet of paper. "Let me consider it, if you please. I suppose we might be a little more elaborate while his lordship is with us."

"A little! My dear child, you can't think to serve him the remains of the stewed veal *rechauffé,* or the John Dory with lobster sauce. It won't do!" Mabel's cheeks grew red with indignation. "Last night we had vegetable marrow and white sauce instead of a pudding!"

"Yes, well, Mrs. Howden is only trying to use what we have to hand, you know. Actually, I found it quite palatable."

Mabel shuddered with distaste. "Just this once you should listen to me. You're quite out of the habit of entertaining, and that Howden woman never knew how in the first place. She listens to no one but the cook on these matters, and Cook is trying to make life easy for himself. You mark my words, Lord Alvescot would despise the table you ordinarily set. Too plain by half!"

"You may be right," Vanessa muttered, edging her way toward the Staircase Hall. "Thank you for going to so much effort, Mabel."

"See that it's not wasted," the older woman called after her.

Vanessa managed to gain her room without encountering anyone further. Her room was the same one she had been given when she first came to Cutsdean as a bride—a spacious bedroom with a smaller sitting room attached. It had been Hortense's room before her, and Hortense had never forgiven her for completely redecorating it. But Hortense was given to a heavy taste in furniture and draperies which Vanessa didn't share and the young bride had suggested Hortense might like to transport her belongings with her to the house in Basingstoke which served as a dower house. Vanessa clearly recalled the old woman's scorn at such a proposal, and the hours it had taken Frederick to talk her around. Wasted hours, demanded by a petty mind intent on disrupting the newly-weds' lives and tempers.

A gown was hung on the front of the wardrobe for Vanessa to wear to dinner, but she ignored the lemon gauze folds and disposed herself wearily on the bed. Her head had begun to ache during the interview with Lord Alvescot and she wished to give it a chance to clear before she descended to meet the whole crowd at Cutsdean preceding the evening meal. The assemblage was always enough to aggravate any slight indisposition from which she might be suffering. And now to have the earl on top of all the others! With him intent, she felt sure, on exerting his authority as co-trustee and potentially interfering with all the plans she had worked out for the estate with Paul Burford. Vanessa's store of patience, never excessive, seemed in danger of being totally annihilated.

Of course, she was aware of the imposition of Frederick's relations! How could she not be aware of it? But Hortense had taken advantage of her grief immediately after Frederick's death, rapidly installing herself and her brother, with her sister following a year later with her two children. By that time, Vanessa had been in control of her life again, but the Curtisses had arrived without her foreknowledge, "to stay for a short while recovering from the shock of losing Mr. Curtiss," as Hortense explained. The biggest shock, actually, was that Mr. Curtiss had gambled away their family estate before putting a period to his own life, and they were literally destitute. From what Vanessa could glean of the situation, there was a suicide note, crammed, according to Mabel Curtiss, with fond endearments to his family and soul-searching recriminations for his own weak behavior. There was everything, apparently, but a body. Since this episode had taken place in London, there were any number of possibilities for a body's disappearance—washed away by the Thames, found unidentified in some rookery and buried without a name, even scavenged by grave robbers. Because Vanessa couldn't blame Mr. Curtiss for wishing to depart this life filled with his acid-tongued wife, his fluffy-witted daughter, and his reprobate son, she was perfectly willing to accept this rendition of the story.

But she was likewise unable to toss the family out of Cutsdean. Unless Hortense would move back to Basingstoke and take them with her, Vanessa could see no possibility of ridding herself of them. Her parents insisted it was her duty to house and finance them in their difficult straits. She who had so much when they had nothing, was how Mrs. Fulbrook was like to describe the situation. And it wouldn't have been so very disturbing, if it had been an unexceptionable family. What didn't settle well with Vanessa were Mrs. Curtiss's constant references to their joint bereavement, to the obligations placed on one by blood ties, and to the possibilities of a match between her son and Vanessa. Apparently, Mrs. Curtiss believed that, in this case, the responsibility of the blood tie was for Vanessa to marry her husband's cousin (on his mother's side) so the money could all be kept in the family. Mrs. Curtiss's entire life was spent making menus and trying to marry her daughter off to Mr. Oldcastle and her son to Vanessa.

Though Vanessa was perfectly happy to see the first goal achieved, she had no intention of falling in with the second. Edward Curtiss, at twenty-eight, was undoubtedly the most conceited, self-involved, and encroaching man she had ever met. Despite the fact that he had not one pence worth of income, he made no attempt to find himself gainful employment, preferring to live on Vanessa's largesse. This, of course, he did not receive in person. No, that would have been too delicate a matter to contemplate. Instead, Vanessa was forced to make his mother an allowance which covered both children, and which she felt confident was spent entirely by the spendthrift Edward. When applied to for additional funds by Mrs. Curtiss (which happened regularly), Vanessa was always tempted not to comply, but she had so little confidence in Edward's character that she feared he would do something unprincipled to obtain the necessary cash.

All of which thoughts did nothing to soothe her aching head, but she eventually drifted into a short nap, dreaming of a day when she and the children would be the only ones residing at Cutsdean.

Strange woman, Alvescot decided when Vanessa left him alone in the Library. On the one hand, she seemed perfectly aware of the imposition on her by her mother-in-law's relations; on the other, she obviously intended to do nothing about it. Quite possibly the same thing was happening with her estate manager, Alvescot thought. Probably a clever fellow who gave the impression of competence, and was robbing the estate blind. Women had such a difficult time learning to turn off the spout of money, which they seemed to think flowed of its own accord. Well, he determined with resolution, he would just have to see that the estate manager was turned off from his position, and a trustworthy man found to replace him.

As he was about to leave the Library with the ledgers under his arms, he overheard the conversation in the Entrance Hall between Vanessa Damery and Mabel Curtiss. That is, he had no difficulty discerning the booming tones of the latter, while the former's more modulated accents didn't quite reach him. Alvescot was not in the least flattered that Mrs. Curtiss, at least, had some regard for his aristocratic position. She made him sound like some superficial, arrogant nitwit to be cajoled with a fine saddle of lamb. Disgruntled, he left the Library by way of the Drawing Room and Garden Room, wandering out through the open doors into the sunny afternoon.

Before him stood a well-tended expanse of lawn with flowering garden beds beyond and a fine stand of timber still further on. There was some activity amongst the trees which he could at first not discern, but by watching for a few minutes he realized that two children were cavorting there with a young woman who was probably their nursemaid. Alvescot decided to join them, despite the cumbersome ledgers. His approach was shortly noted by a sturdy lad of four who came galloping through the flower bed, trampling plants without the least regard to the young woman's admonitions.

"I'm John," he announced in a piping voice. "Who are you?"

"Alvescot," said the earl. "I'm your father's cousin, and your godfather. Do you think it's right to smash down the plants that way?"

John glanced behind him at the crumbled greenery and shrugged. "I was in a hurry."

"Your nursemaid told you to go around."

"It's too far to go around. You have to go all the way to the end."

"Your nursemaid told you to do it. Don't you listen to her?"

There was something in his tone that made John hesitate. "Usually I do," he compromised.

"Has it occurred to you," Alvescot asked, "that someday when you don't listen to her, you will suffer for your disobedience?"

"How?"

"One of her main endeavors is to protect you from harm. Say someday you are playing with a sharp stone and she tells you to put it aside. If you don't listen to her, you'll cut yourself. Even worse things could happen."

John considered this for a moment. "Yes, but I couldn't hurt myself in the flower beds."

"You've trampled flowers that your mother might have used to decorate the dinner table, and that the gardeners worked a long time to cultivate."

"But there are plenty of other flowers," John insisted.

Alvescot brought the full force of his disapproving gaze down on the little boy, who drew back a few steps. "You haven't the right to decide to destroy someone else's property. Not now, not ever, young man. And until you are possessed of enough maturity to make decisions for yourself, you are to obey those who are put in charge of you."

While the earl awaited some reply from him, John shuffled his feet nervously, glanced from Alvescot to the nursemaid who was coming toward them with a girl in her arms, looked toward the house and then across at the Orangery and finally back at the earl. "Yes, sir," he whispered.

"Good. Now, if you would be so kind, I'd like you to show me your pony. You will want, of course, to ask this young woman's permission," Alvescot told him, indicating the nursemaid.

Since John made rather an awkward business of it, Alvescot assumed he was not in the habit of asking permission, but he let the matter rest. Even his mild rebuke had made the boy nervously unhappy, as though he didn't know exactly what was expected of him. But Alvescot could be charming when he chose, and he chose now to put the boy at ease, talking of his own first pony and drawing John out on life at Cutsdean. Obviously the boy's spirits were irrepressible, for he was soon chattering excitedly, his face animated and his hands moving almost as fast as his mouth.

"Did you know my father?" John asked abruptly.

"Oh, yes, very well. He was my best friend. When we were children, I came to visit him here, and he came to my home in Sussex. We went to school together, too."

"Was he . . . very brave?"

Alvescot studied the boy's wide eyes and trembling lips. "Yes, John, he was a very brave soldier, and a good man. I wept when I heard he'd been killed."

"Did you?" The large brown eyes, so like Frederick's, blinked at him. "He never saw my pony."

"No, but he had planned with your mother just when you were to have one."

"That's what Mama said. She said Rollo was a gift from him, too."

A memory stirred in Alvescot's mind, of two little boys riding across the fields of the home farm, and Frederick's youthful voice boasting, "Rollo can do almost anything Papa's horse can do." Alvescot wondered whether Frederick's wife had remembered the name, or if one of the older stable hands had supplied it. Somehow the continuity was impressive rather than sentimental. He doubted if Frederick's mother would have been able to recall Rollo's name.

John rushed over to the loose box where the pony was munching hay. Climbing up on the door, John spoke to him in a very different voice than he had previously used. It was a gentle sing-song, soothing and hypnotic, to which the animal responded promptly, trotting over to thrust his muzzle in the boy's hand.

"Isn't he beautiful?" John asked. "And he's fast as the wind."

Alvescot expressed a suitable admiration, shrugging aside the memories that threatened to disturb him. The threads of the past seemed to interweave: the visits to Cutsdean, the days at school, his first riotous visit to London on his own, the years on the Peninsula, his final farewell to Maria. It was the sultry heat of the late afternoon, he decided, trying to pay attention to the boy, the time of day, the time of year. He had noticed it yesterday at the inn, when the anticipation of visiting Cutsdean again had made him melancholy. There was no recovering the past, and to dwell on it made the present unreal, the future unreachable.

The little boy had asked him something, he realized, but he couldn't recall what it was. "I beg your pardon, John. My mind has wandered back to the days when I was your age. What was it you asked?"

"Shall I show you how I ride? Mama says I get better every day."

Withdrawing his watch, Alvescot shook his head. "I'm sorry. There isn't time before I should be getting ready for dinner. Some time tomorrow, perhaps?"

Disappointed, the boy nodded. "How long are you going to be here?"

"I don't know," Alvescot replied truthfully. "A few days, I suppose."

"I could show you the canal. Mama and I go sometimes to watch the barges. There's a tunnel at Greywell you can see them go in to."

There was an urgency to the invitation that surprised the earl. Was the boy so eager for a man's attention? John was, after all, his godchild, and he had done nothing whatsoever for the poor fellow since his father's death. "That would be famous," he agreed, more heartily than he felt. "Tomorrow I am to go about the estate with Mr. Burford, but the day after should be fine."

"Lucy can have Cook send a basket with us. I'm always hungry if I ride that far," he admitted as the two of them walked back toward the house.

"How far is it?" Alvescot asked, surprised.

"Four or five miles. Rollo doesn't even get tired."

Alvescot watched the boy disappear through the door, waving a small hand as he went. All of five miles, he thought with amusement. With the pony, of course, that could take a good hour. He shifted the ledger books in his arms, stood for a moment gazing out over the park, and

then entered through the Garden Room to make his way
to his minuscule chamber.

A quick count of heads in the Saloon told Alvescot
there were seven other people in the room, including the
young jackanapes who had run him down. Yes, now he
saw Edward close up, he could see more clearly the re-
semblance to the boy he had known so many years ago.
Edward ignored his entrance into the room, but Vanessa
came forward with a welcoming smile, offering to introduce him to anyone as yet unknown to him.

"Edward you have met, more or less. And this is his
sister, Louisa."

Thirty, thirty-two, Alvescot thought, and not too
bright, judging from her vague looks. He didn't remember
encountering her as a child. Louisa smiled and shyly
ducked her head, as though she were an eighteen-year-old
at her first adult gathering. Her blond hair was worn
youthfully floating around her heart-shaped face, but the
lines of passing years were beginning to form there, and
the style looked inappropriate on her. She whispered her
pleasure in meeting him, casting frequent glances over her
shoulder at a solid gentleman who stood vacuously observing the earl. Vanessa gestured to him, and he came
forward wtih alacrity.

Mr. Oldcastle was short and stocky, with a head of hair
already receding rather desperately at the age of thirty-
five. He was monstrously pleased to meet the earl, he
said, and knew they would become fast friends, felt sure
they shared an interest in the same sporting activities, and
believed the aristocracy was what made England such a
great country.

After the tepid welcome Alvescot had received from
most of the Cutsdean residents, the earl was more than a
little taken aback by this rush of friendliness, but he appreciated it no more. It was a maxim with him that he
could recognize a toadeater from twenty yards, and it annoyed him that he hadn't recognized the vacuous expression for what it was, and not merely the vacant look
of a man whose intellect might be questionable. But he
politely disguised his feelings, merely glancing at Vanessa

from time to time to see if he could surprise any evidence of emotion on her placid features. There was none, until Edward approached her, smiling winningly, to say, "Sorry about the accident, cuz."

Since Edward had not appeared for luncheon, it was the first time he had spoken with her about it, and she regarded him with a frown. "I've warned you about your style of driving, Edward. Anyone might have been standing in the drive. The children might have been playing there. If you haven't a care for yourself, you should consider the others who might be harmed."

An angry flush rose in his cheeks. "You're just annoyed about the damage to the curricle," he accused. "I shall see to its repair."

Considering Edward's financial situation, Alvescot could understand the contemptuous gleam that appeared in Vanessa's eyes. The young woman said, "No, Edward, the curricle will not be repaired," in a flat, rebuking tone that made Edward glare at her. In all likelihood he would have made some pungent reply, but the butler, with exquisite timing, arrived to announce dinner at precisely that moment.

Edward stomped away from his hostess so violently that the ceramic figurines on the mantelpiece trembled in his wake. The others, without waiting for Vanessa or the guest of honor, filed through the doors into the dining room. Alvescot glared after the retreating company, offered his arm to Vanessa, and followed the others with a dignity he might have accorded an audience with the Prince Regent. As he seated Vanessa at one end of the table he reflected that he had never seen such a ragtag bunch before.

Their democratic approach to precedence offended his sense of propriety, to say nothing of his inherent good manners. When he saw his Aunt Damery attempt to seat herself at the other end of the table, only to be diverted by Tompkins, he was no longer surprised by her fierce frown in her daughter-in-law's direction. Vanessa ignored her, as she ignored Mabel's exclamations of disgust at the first course, but she smiled rather mischievously at him down the length of the table.

She looked entirely different when she smiled. The lines of worry were instantly wiped away, and the dark eyes held a secret amusement which she seemed to share with him, though he doubted that she meant to. And how could she find her situation so amusing, anyway? Probably it was the wavering light of the candles dancing in her eyes, Alvescot decided, which gave the mistaken impression. Far more likely she was laughing *at* him. He could feel the muscles in his face tense at the idea and he quickly turned his attention to Louisa, seated to his right. But Louisa required very little in the way of concentration, and Alvescot found his mind returning to the younger Mrs. Damery. He could see that, for all she'd allowed her husband's relations to thrust themselves on her, she took her position and responsibilities seriously, and he was not above admiring her for that trait, especially when it was leavened with her own particular type of whimsicality.

It was quixotic of her to harbor such a motley crew, but he was coming to understand her reasoning, and even if he found, as he expected to, that her estate manager was likewise taking advantage of her, he was yet aware that she was doing the best she could, lacking male guidance. Alvescot mentally girded his loins to wade into the fray and take charge. It was the least he could do on account of his longstanding friendship, not to say kinship, with Frederick.

FOUR

When the ladies withdrew, Alvescot found himself in the company of Captain Lawrence, Edward Curtiss, and William Oldcastle. None of them made an effort to speak with him, but drank their port in a sullen silence which Alvescot hadn't the inclination to break after twice venturing a comment intended to elicit some discussion. He withdrew a pipe and carefully tamped some tobacco in it, accepting a taper from the footman with which to light it. The cloud of smoke he exhaled drifted gently down the length of the table, causing Captain Lawrence and Edward to scowl at him and William to cough.

This provided the opportunity Alvescot desired to slip out onto the terrace and have his pipe in peace. He carried his glass of port with him and stood at the railing looking out over the flowing landscape. But he had left the door open into the dining room, and the desultory conversation which followed his departure drifted faintly out to him. The captain announced briskly that he had no desire to join Mabel in one of her interminable card games, that he planned to take a stroll instead. Edward mocked him, enjoining the old man not to fall down in the dark, though it was still quite light out.

"You're bound to trip over your own feet in the spinney," Edward pursued, in a voice that sounded curiously threatening to Alvescot. "You'd best go there before the light fails, no later than nine, I'd say."

There was a grunt from the captain, whether of acknowledgment or scorn, the earl couldn't determine, and he wasn't interested enough to rejoin them and find out. Apropos of nothing, Mr. Oldcastle then declared he would check with Louisa before he decided whether to play cards or not. "If she has a mind to take a hand, then I will of course join her," he said, resolute. "On the other hand, if she has a mind to take a stroll around the grounds, I will accompany her there, though you know that the night air affects me most adversely. She isn't always considerate in these matters, as you know, Edward. Why, only last week when we walked in the shrubbery at dusk I could feel a decided congestion in my chest, but she pooh-poohed the matter. Yes, she did," he insisted, as though someone had contradicted him. "After twelve years, you would think she understood the delicacy of my constitution."

Alvescot heard his elaborate sigh all the way out on the terrace. Twelve years! The earl could scarcely believe his ears. Surely Oldcastle could not have been courting the woman for that long. And yet, on second thought, considering the two people involved, he would not have sworn it wasn't true. How the devil did Mrs. Damery put up with all these fools?

The sound of chairs being shifted in the dining room recalled his attention and he followed the other gentlemen back into the Saloon where Louisa was already seated at the pianoforte in anticipation of their return. Coached by her mother, who regularly seemed to forget her daughter was over thirty years old, she meekly asked Alvescot if he had any preference in music.

Mr. Oldcastle glared at this sign of preferentiality, and Alvescot demurred. "Please play what you like best, Miss Curtiss. I'm sure we'll all enjoy it if it's a favorite of yours."

Louisa took her time deciding. She thumbed her way through a bundle of music sheets, first setting aside one and then another. Finally her mother, exasperated, moved forward, forcefully removed the sheets from her daughter's hands, tapped a finger against one resting on the pianoforte and said, "Play that."

And she did. To Alvescot's surprise, she played extraordinarily well, as though every ounce of her talent was invested in her music. While she played, an idiotic half-smile sat firmly on her lips, no doubt trained into obedience by her mother. But the music she played was expressive and moving; her hands had a life of their own which imbued the strains with feeling one could not have guessed by looking at her face.

"Admirable," Alvescot pronounced when she concluded the piece. "I haven't heard a better performance in months, Miss Curtiss. Would you honor us with another?"

Louisa willingly acquiesced, looking pleased at his tribute. The reaction of the others varied from disdain to surprise. The captain, having no ear for music, barely tolerated any performance at all and sat scowling at poor Louisa, while Mr. Oldcastle, surprised but delighted at this commendation of his (sometime) beloved, thumped a foot in time, more or less, to the new piece she played. Edward slipped out onto the terrace as his mother cast significant glances at Vanessa, clearly indicating her immodest pride in her daughter's accomplishment. Hortense and Mabel then talked to one another in insufficiently lowered voices.

Not waiting for the song to be concluded, the captain stalked from the room. Alvescot shook his head in disbelief at this new evidence of rudeness, but could get no rise from Vanessa, who met his eyes with an impartial gaze of her own. If he expected her to be apologetic for her household, he was far off, he decided, though he felt sure she no more condoned this behavior than he did. Really, he must do something about her intolerable situation—if only for Frederick's sake.

This conclusion was reinforced several hours later, after three hands of boring, bickering-filled whist, when he himself escaped from the company to stroll about the grounds just as dusk was falling. The captain had not returned, nor had Edward, and a certain curiosity drew him to the spinney mentioned earlier. Its existence he remembered well, for it had been the spot in which he had sought solitude as a boy visitor to Cutsdean. The summer night was filled with the gentle sounds of insects and a warm breeze floating over the undulating landscape. Without precisely pinpointing why, he did not approach the spinney in a direct route from the house but circled around by the pebble walk which came from the south and skirted the stand of trees.

As he approached, he knocked his pipe out onto the pebbles and stamped the smoldering tobacco until it was extinguished. And then, because his boots made a crunching sound on the pebbles, he left the path entirely some distance from the spinney to walk through the dew-adorned grass to the first of the trees. His silent approach was almost immediately rewarded by two male voices drifting to him on the night air.

"Did you bring it?" Edward demanded.

"Of course I brought it," he heard the captain reply, angry, "but not the whole twenty-five. I won't have you extort every shilling I own. I have to have at least five pounds to last the rest of the quarter."

"What for?" Edward scoffed. "Did you intend to buy yourself a rowing boat? I can just see you now on the lake in it."

The captain's stubborn voice rose. "Twenty is all you get, you despicable cur."

"All right. All right. Just give it to me." There was a brief pause before Edward continued. "I'm going to take your horse into Basingstoke since the curricle's ruined. Don't bluster at me, old man. I'm not likely to do the beast any damage. There's a good moon tonight and your nag's not likely to get up such a pace as to injure himself." Edward's amused laughter mingled with the captain's ineffectual grumbles of discontent.

Nothing further was said. Alvescot watched through the trees as one man headed toward the stables at a jaunty trot while the other ponderously made his way toward the house. Oh, wonderful, the earl thought, thoroughly annoyed. Blackmail, too. What more could Cutsdean provide in the way of unsavory intrigue? Returning to the house he entered through a side door, since he had no desire to encounter any of the inhabitants again that night, and made his way silently to his miniature bed-chamber.

Breakfast at Cutsdean was served for several hours, entirely at the whim of each of the household members. Vanessa always chose to have hers early because fewer of her guests were abroad then, though she invariably caught the captain finishing his meal. Without fail he would admonish her in the laxity of her arrangements.

"Have them all up by seven, my dear Mrs. Damery. Set a rule that no one is to take breakfast after half past eight, and you would see a more productive group."

Vanessa had no idea what he thought they would produce. More crocheted shawls? More exotic menus? More tatting and lace-covered pillows? The reality was more likely to be more quarrels, more infringements on her time, and more demands on her resources. But she invariably smiled at him, shaking out her napkin and answering the footman's questions on what she wished that morning. If the captain persisted, she would way, "I want each of you to be at liberty to arise when it suits you, Captain Lawrence. We have established hours for the other meals; breakfast should be a little more flexible, I think."

Though he never agreed with her, insisting that the kitchen staff had more work this way, he would soon be finished with his meal, and would bow politely to her before leaving on his brisk morning stroll. Everyone in the household knew better than to join him. He walked for miles without a pause, purposely (or so it seemed) choosing the roughest ground around over which to walk. And if he had a companion, he seldom spoke, unless asked a question, when he would give a monosyllabic response.

But the morning after the earl's arrival, Vanessa found only Alvescot in the Breakfast Parlor. There was evidence that the captain had been and gone, and Lord Alvescot was staring broodingly out the window when she entered. He promptly rose to greet her, a half-apologetic smile on his lips.

"You're an early riser, then," he remarked, holding a chair for her.

"Usually. It's a habit more easily adhered to in the country than in town, I imagine. Have you gotten everything you wanted for breakfast?" She watched him reseat himself and nod. "If you like something special, you have only to ask. There are always cold joints, of course, but if you want particular hot dishes, mutton chops or rumpsteaks, for instance, I should let Cook know in advance."

"No, I found the selection quite adequate, Mrs. Damery." Sipping black coffee and watching her with rather guarded eyes, Alvescot waited until the footman had served her and withdrawn from the room. "I wanted to apologize for my rudeness yesterday. I sometimes speak hastily." He made an expressive gesture with his wide shoulders. "I'm not a particularly patient man and I don't understand how you put up with this bunch of parasites, but that isn't my business, as you reminded me. I promise you my only concern is fulfilling the terms of Frederick's trust and seeing that his son and daughter receive their inheritances in good order. And please believe that I don't for a moment doubt your intentions in serving that purpose."

Vanessa offered him a rueful smile as she buttered a warm muffin. "Thank you. I'm doing my utmost. Have you had a chance to go over the ledgers?"

"Not as yet. I thought it would be more useful after I'd talked with your estate manager."

"Yes, of course. Mr. Burford will put himself at your disposal. I asked him to wait in the estate office for you this morning." Vanessa stirred sugar into her tea, frowning slightly as she met Alvescot's bland expression. "Perhaps I should tell you a little about him. He's not quite what you might expect."

One dark brow lifted skeptically. "I have few expectations."

Vanessa laughed. "I know that, Lord Alvescot. But I'd prefer you didn't embarrass yourself in dealing with Paul."

"Paul? Embarrass myself?" His incredulity was ludicrous, and he assured her stiffly, "I'm not in the habit of embarrassing myself."

"I daresay you aren't," she agreed, remembering him standing dazed by his smashed curricle, with his breeches split. "Paul Burford is a neighbor. You may even have met him when you visited here as a child, though I understand he frequently lived with his mother's family. He owns a small property nearby, but his father drained it, mortgaging it to the hilt before he died. Paul is well-born, Lord Alvescot, but he doesn't cavil at earning his living. I wish Edward would learn a lesson from him."

"I doubt Edward is talented enough at anything to earn a living at it," Alvescot interjected.

"You may be right." Vanessa sighed and continued. "Anyhow, it was Paul who advised me when things went wrong with the first two estate managers. It never occurred to me to offer him the job. He was struggling to make ends meet at Buckland and I didn't think he'd have the time or the inclination to work for me. In the end, he suggested it himself."

The earl set down his coffee cup, studying her face curiously. "I believe you told me yesterday that you pay him what I might consider a 'disproportionate wage.' Did you set the figure, or did he?"

"I set it, and it's considerably more than I paid the first two men. On the other hand, I didn't do it out of sympathy for his situation. Originally I offered him what I'd been paying the previous fellow, and he accepted. When I saw how much he was willing to take on, and how extraordinarily well he was managing affairs, I increased his wage."

"Just exactly how much do you pay him?"

Vanessa told him and his eyes widened in disbelief. She could see the supreme effort he made not to speak with sarcasm when he said, "That's as much as I pay my own man, Mrs. Damery, and Cutsdean isn't half the size of St. Aldwyns."

"No, but it was in twice as bad shape, I daresay. What you must appreciate, my lord, is precisely how demanding the job was, and is. Paul Burford wasn't content to simply see the status quo maintained, as the other two managers had been. Everything was stagnant. No new farming methods had been introduced, no cottage repairs undertaken for the laborers, no attention to the most productive and best-selling crops, no increase in the dwindling herds of cattle. Paul has outlined a three-year plan for renewal and revitalization, and after a year his methods are already paying off. But I can see it won't do any good to try to convince you; you'll have to see for yourself. If you've finished breakfast, I can take you to him now."

Alvescot hastened to his feet and held her chair for her, murmuring, "I'm sure that would be best, Mrs. Damery."

If he weren't trying so hard to be impartial, Vanessa thought, I'd be annoyed with his underlying assumption that I'm out of my mind. She remembered how he'd behaved when she and Frederick were married—polite but withdrawn. Aloof. That was what she'd thought him at the time, but Frederick had insisted that it wasn't so. What was it he'd said? Something about Alvescot being reserved but not haughty. Well, perhaps not with his friends, Vanessa decided, but a stranger could certainly get that impression. She had yet to see him smile anything other than a polite curving of his lips. And, apologies aside, he wasn't precisely accommodating in his attitude toward her, which she assumed might well be his attitude toward the whole female sex. Not that he appeared taken with the menfolk at Cutsdean, either. He seemed, over all, to have decided that everyone residing there was lacking in intelligence and/or good breeding. Of course, with the modest exception of herself and her children, she wasn't sure she didn't agree with him, but she would never be so uncivil as to show it.

But he was not uncivil as they walked to the estate office, located in a building not far from the main structure, which had alternately gone through stages of being a barn, a chapel, and a gothic ruin, if local tradition was to be believed. Alvescot reminisced about its use when he was a boy.

"At the time, no one occupied it. My uncle occasionally spoke of tearing it down, but Frederick always begged him not to because to us it was the perfect spot for a

rainy afternoon. Sometimes it was a ship and we were
sailors battling the elements; sometimes it was a haunted
house and we were searching for the secret of the ghosts
who walked there. I think it may have been used as a
trysting place by the servants because we found some unnerving items of apparel occasionally." For the first time
his eyes really lit with amusement, and he grinned at her.
"That sort of thing always fascinated us as boys."

"I can imagine," she murmured, not quite meeting his
gaze, but pressing her lips together to keep them from
twitching. "They use the Orangery now."

He might have been tempted to ask her how she knew,
but they were at Paul Burford's office and she tapped
lightly on the door. They were bid by a deep male voice to
enter and Alvescot opened the door, allowing her to
precede him into a large room with a gallery at one end
supported by fluted columns. On one side of the room
were traceried, stained-glass windows, but the rest of the
glazing was perfectly standard. A young man rose from
behind a commodious desk and approached them with a
warm smile.

"Lord Alvescot, this is Paul Burford." Vanessa
watched as the two men quickly sized each other up, with
Alvescot still impassive but offering his hand. She hadn't
realized before how much difference there was in their
ages. Alvescot had a good six years on the other man and
was a complete contrast in every way. Burford had a
shock of blond hair and merry blue eyes, standing only an
inch taller than Vanessa, while Alvescot rose substantially
above both of them. The earl's build was more substantial, too, with his broad shoulders and muscular thighs.
Burford had the kind of wiry physique one expected in a
smaller, active man, but Vanessa was inclined to believe
that Alvescot, for all his height, was probably superbly
athletic as well.

Vanessa turned to the earl to say, "I'll leave the two of
you together, unless there's anything further you need of
me. Paul understands that you're co-trustee and have the
responsibility of looking into every facet of the estate's
management and expenses. Why don't you both join us
for luncheon today?"

When the two men agreed, and showed no inclination to ask anything further of her, Vanessa left them, walking quickly back to the house, where she headed directly for the children's floor.

FIVE

The nursemaid, Lucy, already had the two children in the big schoolroom. Not that either of them were old enough for much in the way of lessons, but the room served just as well as a play area, where their toys could be stored in the cupboards and brought out as needed. For a long time John's favorite had been the toy soldiers, but Vanessa had slowly introduced pieces for a replica of a village and farm, with storefronts and tiny animals, a carriage and farm equipment. The soldiers were still available, though he played with them less frequently now. But Vanessa wasn't surprised, somehow, to find him lining up his troops that morning.

John turned to greet her with a solemn face. "That man, Alvy-something, said Papa was a very brave man."

"Yes, he was," Vanessa agreed. "I didn't know you'd spoken with Lord Alvescot, John. He's your godfather, and your father's cousin."

"I know. He told me." The little boy accidentally knocked over one of the soldiers on horseback and quickly set it right again. "I'm going to show him how I ride today, and tomorrow I'm going to take him to see the canal where it goes into the tunnel."

Vanessa wanted to caution him that Lord Alvescot would be busy that day with Paul Burford, since she didn't want her son to be disappointed, but she allowed herself to be distracted by Catherine, who came tumbling toward her with a windmill pull toy. The toy clattered across the floor as Catherine laughed and ran in her own bouncing fashion, tumbling into Vanessa's waiting arms.

"How's my big girl?" Vanessa asked. "Did you meet Lord Alvescot, too?" She really didn't expect a coherent answer from the child, but her eyes traveled over Catherine's head to where Lucy was setting their breakfast dishes on a tray.

"He was in the garden yesterday afternoon," Lucy explained. "We all met him, so's to speak. Then John took him to see the pony."

"Did he like Rollo, John?"

"Oh, yes. He thought Rollo was famous! We're going to take a basket of food with us when we go to the canal." He looked momentarily uncertain. "If that's all right."

"Of course." What was this? Vanessa wondered with amusement. John asking permission? Surely that was something new. But she shrugged off the possible implications, and there was no further discussion of the earl as she sat and played with the children for the next hour. During that time two messages were brought to her by the servants: that Mabel wished to see her and that Edward hoped she would ride with him. The intrusion on her time with the children was exasperating, since both of them knew her habit of spending a while on the nursery floor after breakfast. She instructed the footman to tell Mabel she would see her later and to tell Edward that she had no idea when she would be riding that day. When she was perfectly ready, she left the children in Lucy's care and went to face the demands of the rest of her household.

It was menus that concerned Mabel, of course. Vanessa reluctantly agreed to speak with Cook about the one Mabel had handed her the previous day, mentally chopping it in half to serve for two evening meals rather than one. When she was returning from this errand, Edward waylaid her in the hall.

"Ah, you look charming this morning, Vanessa. Have you been with the children?"

"Yes, Edward, as I am every morning."

He ignored her impatient tone and smiled broadly. "They need a man about the place, my dear. Someone for them to look up to."

Vanessa had difficulty restraining a sarcastic retort, and said nothing.

Deciding it was not the time to press the matter, Edward changed the subject. "Shall we ride now? The weather's perfect and later it may be too hot."

"I have a great deal to do this morning, Edward. You'll have to excuse me, I'm afraid."

"You should make the time for yourself, my dear lady. Surely nothing is so urgent it can't wait for an hour or two."

His expectant face with its engaging grin only served to set up her back. Could he possibly, after all this time, believe his company gave her the least bit of pleasure? The man had a hide as thick as a door! She wished he'd take his flirtatious blue eyes and his curly blond hair and disappear from her life. Fortunately, the housekeeper bustled into the hall as they spoke and Vanessa turned to her. "Mrs. Howden, I need to discuss several matters with you. Excuse me, Edward."

The flash of irritation in his eyes did not escape her as she joined the older woman, but it merely served to reinforce her opinion of his hypocrisy. His great show of affection for her was no more than a ploy to marry her for his advantage. And what money he thought he could get his hands on, she hardly knew. Her jointure was more than sufficient for her needs, but would hardly keep him in style. There was no possibility of his not understanding the trust set up for her son and daughter, so wherein did he think the great bonanza lay? It was just one more of those unanswerable questions Vanessa was constantly forced to set aside as she went about her daily duties, one of the puzzles she occasionally lay awake at night, lonely, considering until she fell into an exhausted sleep.

Even the children could hardly make up for the lack of congenial adult company at Cutsdean. Vanessa couldn't spend the whole day with them, considering the demands of so large a household, and she had to constantly prevent her husband's relations from interfering with the children's rearing: Mrs. Damery with her acid comments on their indulgence, the captain's military commands, Mabel's syrupy cooing at them, Edward's two-faced attention. Really, it was more than enough to deal with.

And now there was Alvescot as well. Did he realize he'd made a promise to little John which the boy expected him to keep? Adults who weren't familiar with children frequently didn't understand how literally their words were taken and Vanessa felt sure Alvescot wasn't familiar with children. Still, she had no intention of broaching the matter to him when the family gathered for luncheon. His frankness of the previous day had been slightly unnerving for her, despite her attempts to laugh it off. Vanessa wasn't comfortable categorizing him with the eccentrics in her household, and consequently could not take his presence with the same indifference. Alvescot had, after all, a great deal of power over her situation, and that of her son and daughter, a power they shared equally under the terms of Frederick's will, but a power nonetheless.

With some expectation that the earl and Paul Burford would have come to a complete understanding of each other during the morning hours, Vanessa was disturbed when they joined the party in the Saloon looking as wary of each other as they had when she introduced them earlier. Not that she had expected them to arrive with mutually glowing reports of their interaction, or slapping one another on the back, but she had hoped for more than the silent neutrality between them. Paul Burford was an outgoing young man, full of enthusiasm, and Vanessa had been sure he would charm the earl in a matter of minutes. But Alvescot appeared thoroughly unmoved by the morning's experience, standing slightly apart from the others and observing them with a carefully schooled countenance.

Vanessa seldom invited Burford to join them for a meal because her husband's relations, though poverty-stricken themselves for the most part, looked on the estate manager as beneath their notice. The fact that he was as well-born as any of them did not, to their minds, make up for his having lowered himself to the status of an employee. Edward especially, she had noted, was insufferable to him, rather than taking a hint from Burford's sensible course of action. Ordinarily, Vanessa would have gone to speak with him, but there was the earl to accommodate today as well, and she cast a speaking glance at Louisa, who, rather surprisingly, drifted over to where Burford stood alone.

Relieved, Vanessa approached Alvescot. "Did you spend the entire morning in the estate office, Lord Alvescot, or have you had an opportunity to ride about the estate?"

"There wasn't time for an inspection if we were going to join the rest of you for luncheon, Mrs. Damery. We would merely have had to cut short to be back here in time."

Determined not to be intimidated by his veiled criticism, she nodded. "True. Well, no doubt you'll have ample opportunity this afternoon to see anything you wish. Has Paul explained his innovations to you?"

Alvescot remained impassive, saying dryly, "Most of them, I daresay. If he's to be believed, the estate was in deplorable condition when he took over. I wouldn't have thought a place could deteriorate so badly in a year."

"We're not talking about a year." Vanessa kept her tone as level as possible, not allowing him to bait her. "You should be as aware as anyone, Lord Alvescot, that Frederick hadn't spent much time on the estate for five years before his death. His estate manager was older and had grown lazy. I pensioned him off almost two years ago, though he hadn't actually reached an age where it should have been necessary."

His hazel eyes studied her enigmatically. "That must have been difficult for you."

"It was," she admitted, not meeting his gaze. "He'd been here for a long time, much longer than I. But it had to be done."

"Yes. Sensibility has no part in the running of an estate. I'm glad you recognize that, Mrs. Damery."

There was an underlying warning in his words and she glanced up at him sharply. "You're still convinced that Paul is a sentimental choice?" she asked, incredulous. "Haven't you been paying attention to him? Every project is thoroughly thought out, every expense documented. How can you be so skeptical?"

"It's not difficult, Mrs. Damery. I've seen all the tricks for hiding illegitimate expenses among the real ones, all the finagling that goes into padding worthwhile projects with unnecessary extras, all the possibilities for bribes in the placing of orders and contracts."

"Paul isn't like that."

Alvescot shrugged. "You may be right." His voice held no conviction and Vanessa could feel a cold frustration building in her when he continued. "But you have to consider the possibilities, Mrs. Damery. He's a young man without resources of his own, attempting to build up his estate. You told me so yourself. It would be so easy to divert a little money to it here and there, you know. An account book cannot prove to me that the seed which was purchased was actually sown at Cutsdean. It could just as easily have been planted elsewhere."

"And how could he possibly prove to you that it wasn't? You're quite wrong, Lord Alvescot. I've known Paul for five years, and he's an exceptionally honorable man."

"I'd like to respect your judgment, Mrs. Damery, and to accept it without question." His gaze moved over the assembled members of her household, coolly taking in a smirking Edward and a stiff, self-righteous Captain Lawrence before he returned his gaze to her. "But I can't. I have a duty as co-trustee to take an unprejudiced look at the situation."

"But you *are* prejudiced," she insisted, "*against* Paul Burford."

"I wouldn't say that. My curiosity is aroused by the large expenses and by what you've told me of his predicament. You have to admit that your friendship may have blinded you to the real circumstances."

"I wouldn't admit anything of the sort," she snapped.

"Then you're . . ."

"A fool," she finished for him when he stopped himself. "Yes, you've mentioned that before."

"That was inexcusable of me. All I meant at the time was that you appeared rather foolhardy to have taken on so many guests." As though he couldn't restrain himself, he added. "And such unpalatable ones."

"The only thing we disagree on there is the matter of obligation, Lord Alvescot. It isn't a case of sensibility." Vanessa turned her gaze to where Louisa stood chatting with Paul Burford. "I want you to promise me you won't take any action about Paul without first discussing it with me. No, more than that. I want you to make some effort not to convey your suspicions to him."

"I'm hardly likely to do that."

Vanessa frowned at him. "You don't understand, Lord Alvescot. Your natural demeanor is suspicious. I'm sure you'll excuse my forthrightness, since you are apparently a frank person yourself, but you would have to make a concerted effort to look other than chillingly distrustful of your fellow man."

His eyes widened, but if he had intended a retort, it was forestalled by the announcement of lunch. In the general exodus, Vanessa was separated from him by hungry guests and he found himself seated, as he had the previous evening, at the opposite end of the table. Vanessa, calmly smiling, put Paul Burford on her right.

Every one of them is crazy, Alvescot decided as he ate his meal in haughty silence. He had thought Vanessa Damery at least had some regard for his consequence. No one had ever told him before that he appeared "chillingly distrustful" of everyone, and he didn't believe it for a minute. These plebians simply did not comprehend the reserve with which a peer of the realm was obliged to disport himself.

Would she have him act like the other "gentlemen" in her household? Smugly complacent like Edward Curtiss, or insufferably priggish like Captain Lawrence. Or perhaps inanely self-absorbed like the perpetual suitor, William Oldcastle? The poor woman had lost touch with civilized society. Probably she didn't even remember Frederick's elegant bearing, his distinguished manners, surrounded as she was with such boors. Obviously, she couldn't recognize a real gentleman when she encountered one!

Which led him to wonder how her poor son—and his godson!—was going to grow up to be one. He had no models on which to pattern himself, with the dubious exception of Paul Burford. Alvescot was not immune to that young man's easy charm, but he was well-prepared to resist it. He'd met charming rascals before, and he'd met men whose values were flexible when their resources were limited. If he was suspicious, he told himself righteously, it was with good cause. And he was not willing to see Frederick's son emulate a man who might turn out to be a scoundrel, no matter what Paul Burford's surface appearance might be to the contrary.

Alvescot remembered, suddenly, that he had promised little John he would watch him ride today, and that he would go to visit the canal with him tomorrow. For a moment he thought of putting the lad off, since he intended to pursue his investigations of the estate management with vigor, but one glance at Vanessa Damery convinced him otherwise. She would consider it callous behavior, no doubt, being the devoted mother she was. Women with children got their priorities confused. It was a wonder she'd noticed the deterioration of the estate at all!

The luncheon was criticized, as usual, by Mabel Curtiss, but Alvescot found it perfectly adequate, though he didn't pay much attention to what he ate. Mabel made it clear to him that he had a treat in store that evening, because she had herself prepared the menu. One would have thought she was preparing the meal itself, from the way she gloated. He did no more than offer her a civil nod and a few distracted and unintelligible words, so caught up with he in brooding about Frederick's son. Was it his duty to take some part in the boy's upbringing? Surely John was too young to need much more than physical care at this point. Later, perhaps, he would have the boy to visit him for a few weeks each year, over a school holiday or during the long vacation. And it would probably be best for him to introduce the lad to London when the time came. Nothing was worse than a woman's thinking she could undertake that task, or for a young man to attempt it with other empty-headed school friends. No, that was his responsibility; Frederick would have wished it.

Because he wasn't sure Vanessa Damery would go along with his mental schemes, he found himself devising arguments to persuade her. They were reasonable arguments, with which no rational woman could possibly find fault, but he found that in his mind, she did. And he plotted ways in which to convince her, dialogues in which they occasionally crossed swords, with him always prevailing, of course, by saying something like, "You may be an attractive woman, and you're not without intelligence, but you have no concept of the intricacies of society, my dear Cousin Vanessa." He wasn't sure how he had become that familiar with her, but she was always won over in the end.

"Was there something further you required, Lord Alvescot?" Vanessa asked from the doorway.

Alvescot looked up from his distracted study of the salt cellar to find that he alone remained at the table. No one else was in the room at all, except his hostess, who stood with amused eyes and a wide grin waiting for him to come out of his trance. He rose swiftly to his feet, very nearly knocking over his chair, and muttered, "I was considering some rather serious matters, madame."

"I'm sure you were, and I wouldn't have interrupted you except that Paul didn't know whether to go to the estate office or wait for you. I sent him on, but I thought you might wish to join him soon."

"Well, yes," Alvescot agreed, feeling rather foolish. Why the devil was she always catching him at some disadvantage? His long-legged stride had already brought him abreast of her and he scowled at the mischief in her eyes. "There is, of course, the matter of your son. I promised to watch him ride today. Perhaps you could suggest the most convenient time. I shouldn't like to disappoint the lad."

Now her face softened to a warm smile. "I'm so glad you remembered. Why don't I have Lucy bring him to the stables about four-thirty? Then you'd have time to spend a few minutes with him before changing for dinner."

"That sounds an eminently sensible arrangement," he said stiffly, stepping past her to open the door. But before he actually twisted the handle another thought worked its way into his sluggish brain. "Ah, there is the ride to the canal tomorrow. Did he mention that to you?"

"Yes."

"And are you agreeable?"

"Certainly, but I should just mention that he may not actually know how to get you there. His sense of direction is not well developed as yet."

Alvescot cleared his throat. "Would you care to accompany us in that case, Mrs. Damery? I'm sure you're familiar with the location."

"I thought perhaps you might be yourself, Lord Alvescot." When he shook his head, she said, "Then you'll need a guide. I'd be happy to come."

"Thank you. John seemed to wish to take a picnic basket with us."

"Yes, he asked if he might."

The earl nodded his approval. "Shall we leave at noon then? Or should you be here to have your meal with your . . . guests?"

Vanessa made a gesture of reckless abandon. "Let them fend for themselves this once," she said with a teasing laugh. "Noon it is."

SIX

The afternoon was warm, but not hot as expected, and Alvescot rode over the estate with Paul Burford quite comfortably. He made some effort to appear interested rather than suspicious as Burford explained the changes that were being made—the new cottages for the laborers, the changed rotation of crops, the attempts to breed a better stock even as they expanded.

Evidences of the deterioration were still observable and Burford explained that he planned to take several years to entirely complete the task, so that capital expenditures wouldn't absorb all the new income. There was nothing wrong with his plans, Alvescot admitted to himself, but they weren't necessarily the whole story. Cutsdean could conceivably have absorbed all the expenditures claimed for it . . . or it might not have. It was almost impossible to tell without a thorough inspection of the books and some side investigations into suppliers in the neighborhood. Alvescot was also highly interested in seeing just how Burford's own estate was being revitalized.

"Are you making the same type of improvements at your home?" he asked casually.

Paul studied him for a moment, a wry twist to his lips. "Some of them. Whatever I can afford. There's been no new building as yet, but I've seen to repairs. My concentration has been on the crops and the livestock. When they produce enough income, I'll see to upgrading the structures."

"I'd be interested in seeing it one day."

"Whenever you wish," Paul agreed, turning his horse

back toward the Hall. "I live there, of course, and you could come over any morning before I leave for Cutsdean."

His willingness to show Alvescot his property did not necessarily reassure the earl. There would be no way of telling when improvements had been made, or how much they cost, but Alvescot stubbornly believed that he would be able to tell from the man's behavior whether the innovations were made at Mrs. Damery's expense. No denying, certainly, that Burford had been progressing nicely at Cutsdean. His grasp of the latest methods was excellent, his plans for the estate prudent and thorough. In light of the friendship between Burford and Mrs. Damery, Alvescot wondered if he had any more personal plans. Like marriage. To her.

This thought would not necessarily have entered Alvescot's head except for one thing: Burford reminded him somewhat of Frederick. Not in his looks, but in his personality. There was the same openness and good nature, a similar enthusiasm, though here Frederick's recklessness was tamed down to a more manageable level. That recklessness in his cousin was the one thing that Alvescot had always dreaded. The impulsiveness that came from high spirits had also led him into scrapes as a boy and a young man. But it was such an appealing quality. Even more appealing, Alvescot decided, when tempered just enough by prudence to keep it in check. Burford reeked vitality, virility, an easy charm. Despite the position he filled at Cutsdean and the consequent snubbing from the members of the household, he was a gentleman, with polished manners and evident intelligence. Alvescot thought he could quite easily detest the man.

His silence didn't affect the estate manager in the least. Burford continued to explain his plans, to discuss the surrounding countryside and the village, to speak of Mrs. Damery's comprehension of an overall project for Cutsdean.

"She's quite remarkably adept at understanding the benefits and disadvantages of every change, of taking a long-range view of the estate," Paul said. "Before Frederick's death she didn't have a thing to do with the farming and confessed that she knew absolutely nothing about it. I gather her parents thought such matters unsuitable or unnecessary for so young a girl when she lived at home. But she wrote her father for advice when she began to see the necessity to end the disintegration here."

Alvescot pressed his lips together in a tight line and said nothing. She had tried first for his assistance, and it had not been forthcoming.

"On her own she made a few mistakes, in the hiring of the first two estate managers. Who can blame her? It wasn't that they weren't reasonably competent men, but they were content to maintain the status quo, and she wanted something more for Cutsdean. I admit I angled for the job myself." Paul grinned at the earl's unyielding face, almost as though he could read Alvescot's thoughts.

"Why?"

"Any number of reasons. I needed the income. Vanessa needed the expertise I could bring. It was convenient. As you can see, I'm not a particularly modest man. I've spent years familiarizing myself with these matters, corresponding with men who've made progress in the field, visiting estates where innovations were taking place. And Cutsdean offered a larger scope than Buckland." Paul frowned slightly at nothing in particular. "I'm experimenting, with someone else's resources. But they aren't risky experiments. They've been proved successful, and all they take is the proper equipment and planning. I intend to apply the most successful of them to Buckland."

"I see." They had reached the stables and Alvescot could see Vanessa coming across the lawn with her two children and the nursemaid. For her benefit he smiled at Burford and extended his hand. "Thank you for the tour. You seem to be making remarkable progress here."

Paul accepted his hand with a look of surprise. Possibly he hadn't gotten the impression that Alvescot wholeheartedly approved of anything he'd done, but he, too, had seen Vanessa coming toward them. "Just let me know if you have any further questions." With a final nod, he swung his horse away, waved to Vanessa and the children, and rode off toward the West Gate.

The group approaching Alvescot was in high spirits,

with John running ahead and Catherine tumbling along
on the grass. Vanessa wore a peach-colored walking dress
with a triple fall of lace at the throat and a white striped
lutestring spencer. She swung a leghorn hat with a wide
brim in her hand, laughing as she spoke with the nursemaid. Alvescot was slightly disappointed she hadn't worn
her habit, but she had probably already had her daily
ride, and the dress was certainly flattering to her tall, slen-
der form.

The boy reached him first and stopped abruptly in
front of Alvescot. "How do you do, sir?" he asked politely, looking up to where the earl still sat his horse.

"Just fine, John. Will you ride your pony for me?"

As he scampered off to get Rollo, Vanessa came up to
the earl. "And how did your afternoon go, my lord? Was
Paul able to answer all your questions?"

Alvescot started to dismount, but she insisted he not
stand on formality. "Mr. Burford," he said with studied
equanimity, "was extremely helpful. Not only did he show
me over the entire estate, but he explained what he had
been doing and what he plans for the future."

"Good. And you have the ledgers to go over. One or the
other of us should be able to answer any questions you
may have."

"I'm sure you will."

Vanessa reached down to pick up her daughter so the
little girl could pat Alvescot's horse. Instead, Catherine
held out her arms to the earl and declared, "Want to ride."

His face was a picture of bewildered consternation.
Catherine looked very small and fragile to him, despite
her energetic roundness. He didn't know how to hold her
so she wouldn't wriggle from his arms and take a desperate fall.

"No, no, love," Vanessa admonished with a laugh.
"You can only ride with Mama, or Mr. Burford, and I'm
not dressed for it now."

"Want to ride," insisted the little girl, turning her large
brown eyes on Alvescot. "Pease," she added, to propi-
tiate this giant.

If Burford could do it, so could he, Alvescot decided.
There couldn't be anything all that difficult about holding

on to a two-year-old, for God's sake. And he wouldn't have Mrs. Damery laughing at him, either. "I'm perfectly willing to let her ride with me," he said firmly. Catherine beamed at him as he reached down to claim her.

Reluctantly, Vanessa allowed him to swing her up in front of him on the saddle. "She doesn't sit still," the anxious mother cautioned. "You'll have to keep one arm firmly about her waist."

Catherine giggled and bounced up and down as he did so, crying, "Go! Go!"

There was an unnerving moment when his high-strung horse took exception to her little heels thumping into his flanks with such exuberance. The horse took an abrupt step backward and prepared to buck while Alvescot one-handedly reined him in with cool determination. "Young lady, if you wish to ride with me you will behave yourself," he ordered. "*I* will decide when we're ready to go."

Though he couldn't see her face, Alvescot soon became aware that his harsh tone had frightened the child. She became limp in his arm and her little body shook with sobs. "Oh, for God's sake," he muttered, aware that Vanessa was regarding him with troubled eyes. In his exasperation he demanded, "Don't either of your children have any concept of discipline, Mrs. Damery?"

"I'll take her," Vanessa replied softly.

Alvescot ignored her. Instead, he turned his attention to the little girl. "Catherine, look at me, please."

Hesitantly, she twisted around, lips quivering and eyes brimming, slowly raising her gaze to his. Alvescot, still holding her securely, asked, "Do you realize that you could have caused an accident, Catherine?"

". . . Yes."

"You don't know my horse, and he certainly isn't used to little girls who bounce about on his back without any respect for his nerves. He's used to people who give clear, firm instructions, and he responds to them. He's not a toy; he's an intelligent animal, and I expect him to be treated that way. Is that clear?"

Catherine bowed her head. "Yes, sir."

"Excellent. Now we're going to ride around the stable yard and I expect you to sit quietly on Satin." His tone changed slightly as he urged the horse forward. "Do you know what the different paces are?"

Alvescot never glanced at Vanessa during the ensuing lesson. Until John came out of the stable on his pony he rode around with Catherine, letting her call out the changes in pace. John looked momentarily taken aback when he saw his sister with Alvescot, but the earl's steady gaze warned him not to make a fuss about it. The earl brought his horse to a standstill to pay strict attention to John's performance, praising him and offering one or two pointers. The boy really was quite good for his age, Alvescot thought. Fearless, and remarkably in control for a four-year-old. And his pride in his pony was touching.

"Isn't Rollo wonderful, Lord Alvescot? Tomorrow you'll see what good bottom he has, too. He can go forever."

Catherine plucked at Alvescot's sleeve. "Can I go tomorrow?"

"I'm sorry, my dear. You're too young." She looked as though she would dissolve into tears again and he said sternly, "Catherine, behave yourself."

With a tragic sigh she said, "I want to get *down* now."

"My word, do they start that young?" he demanded of a grinning Vanessa.

"Of course," she said, taking the child from his arms. "It's the only real power females have, as a rule."

"Well," he said, disgruntled, "I hope she learns to use it with discretion."

"She will. She already does."

Alvescot wasn't at all pleased with the way Catherine kept her face turned away from him when her mother told her to thank him. But what could he say, when the child did obey her, in a sad, disillusioned voice? He wasn't going to let some two-year-old mite twist him about her finger. These children of Frederick's needed to learn that you couldn't have everything or do everything you wanted, just because you were well-born and people felt sorry that you'd lost your father. Or because your mother doted on you, he firmly reminded himself. Mrs. Damery wasn't doing them a favor by indulging them. So he merely said, "You're welcome," to the little girl's back, and sternly repressed the desire to promise her some other treat in exchange.

As John and Alvescot were about to return their mounts to the stable, Edward rode into the stable yard on Captain Lawrence's horse. The beast was lathered and winded, his eyes rolling with fatigue and pain. Vanessa regarded him coldly.

"The captain won't let you use his horse again, Edward. That's a criminal condition in which to return him."

Nonchalant as ever, Edward swung down from the saddle. "Oh, he'll let me use the nag again, Vanessa. Have I seen that dress before?" His eyes wandered over her figure. "It's enormously becoming, you know."

"Please see that the horse is taken care of immediately." She turned away without another word to him, asking Lucy to stay and wait for John.

"I'll bring him," Alvescot offered.

"Very well. Thank you." Her quick smile barely disturbed the anger in her eyes. As she walked off with Catherine and Lucy, Alvescot was reminded of his intention of the previous night to discover the source of Edward's blackmailing of the captain. He couldn't think why the matter should have escaped his memory all day.

Mabel had not stopped complaining since the ladies left the table. "I don't understand you, Vanessa. I spent hours devising a perfect menu, and what did you do? Serve *half* of it is what you did. What good is half? You might as well have put your usual fare on the table! We're a party of eight sitting down to meals. There can't have been enough left over to provide for the servants! Do you want to look positively shabby in front of the earl?"

"I thought it was a delightful meal," Vanessa said quietly. "Cook did your choices proud, and everyone seemed to enjoy them."

"But there weren't enough!"

Hortense Damery glared at her sister and grunted, "Fiddlesticks! You'd have everyone stuff himself until he couldn't rise from the table, Mabel. I sat beside the earl." Her nostrils flared at her own reminder that she'd been displaced from her seat at the foot of the table, but she continued in icy tones. "He found more than enough to eat, I assure you. Two servings of the *tendrons de veau* and peas. I don't know how he managed to enjoy the braised ham after that. And he remarked that the nesselrode pudding was the best he'd ever had."

This slight word of praise did nothing to ameliorate Mabel's disgust at Vanessa's underhanded scuttling of her culinary plans. The full glory of her menu had been destroyed, corrupted, and she wasn't impressed that Lord Alvescot had two servings of the veal or especially liked the pudding. She turned to Vanessa with undaunted anger. "Well, you shall not have my services in future, young woman, to prostitute in this manner. Devise your own menus if you can! I wash my hands of the whole affair."

Her mention of prostitution and affairs apparently struck a chord in her own mind, for she immediately added, "You won't believe what I heard in the village today. It is whispered everywhere."

Vanessa mentally groaned. Mabel was about to relate the latest gossip, one of her favorite activities. At least, Vanessa thought with some gratitude, this time she was not indulging her habit in front of the gentlemen. Ordinarily, Mabel seemed to relish their discomfiture, and would probably have waited until the gentlemen joined them, except that she was so eager to impart the latest scandal.

"You won't credit this," Mabel assured them with a coy look about the assembled women, "but Mr. Tormarton and Miss Clevedon are to be married!"

Her audience did not seem at all surprised by this announcement. Mr. Tormarton, the local innkeeper, had been courting Miss Clevedon, only daughter of the village greengrocer, for several months.

When there was no gasp of astonishment, Mabel said with some asperity, "You don't understand! They were found in a Compromising Position!"

Her daughter regarded her blankly. For a woman of thirty, Louisa was remarkably naive, Vanessa thought, watching Louisa's brow pucker in confusion. "What's a compromising position?" Louisa wondered aloud.

Mabel regarded her daughter with long-suffering exasperation. "You cannot be that stupid," she insisted. "The vicar came upon them behind the church—the church, mind you!—in a most embarrassing posture. Miss Clevedon was not," Mabel announced with relish, "fully clothed!"

"I don't approve of gossip of that nature," Vanessa remarked. "There is doubtless not the least foundation to it. No vicar worth his position would spread such a tale, and you may be certain the couple involved would not. More likely the couple has simply announced their engagement and the local gossips had to make some sensational news out of it."

"But," Louisa interjected, "if it were true, why would they have to marry just because Miss Clevedon was not fully clothed?"

A stunned silence followed her question. Louisa, hard as it was to believe, actually did not understand, as was evident by her bewildered expression. Vanessa took pity on her, praying that the gentlemen would not choose that moment to erupt from the dining room into the Saloon. "Because of the possibility they had been intimate, Louisa, that they had behaved as a married couple." This explanation did not wholly clear Louisa's face, and Vanessa struggled on. "Married people engage in intimate behavior responsible for making babies."

"Oh," Louisa said, just as Vanessa glanced up at a movement near the door to find Lord Alvescot observing her with a spreading grin. Drat the man! she fumed inwardly. If he's not embarrassing himself, he's embarrassing me. To Louisa she muttered, "If necessary, I'll explain more to you later, Louisa. The earl is here now."

Alvescot made no mention of the subject under discussion, politely seating himself next to his aunt, the grin gone and a civil demeanor replacing it. Hortense, however, growled a few semicoherent phrases about dimwitted females before she managed to divert her acid tongue to the matter Alvescot introduced.

It was some time before the other gentlemen joined them and Vanessa could see they were, as usual, at outs with one another. Edward immediately excused himself for the rest of the evening, while Captain Lawrence con-

tinued a diatribe apparently begun at the table about Edward's treatment of his horse. This went on long after
Edward left the room, and was attended to by almost no
one. William Oldcastle sought out Louisa, who regarded
him with a peculiar expression that caused Vanessa a certain amount of alarm. But when Louisa suggested that
they walk in the shrubbery, William declined on account
of his feeling sure that he had a cold coming on.

Mabel Curtiss, obviously annoyed by Vanessa's strictures against her gossip, urged her daughter to play for
the company. On this occasion she approached Lord
Alvescot to learn of his particular favorites and the earl,
remembering that Louisa was quite an accomplished
musician, did her the honor of being frank. While he sat
mesmerized by the music, Mabel speculatively eyed him,
turning over in her head the possibilities of a match between her daughter and the Earl of Alvescot. There was
no denying that he was enchanted with her accomplishment. Mabel wove a tidy daydream of the earl and Louisa
in the evenings at St. Aldwyns, his country seat, where
her daughter played for the appreciative fellow, and Mabel herself, as mother-in-law, sat in splendor regarding the
whole with an indulgent eye.

Why not? Though Louisa was thirty, she had lost little
of her looks, and surely the earl was a few years older.
Louisa was still capable of having children—though it
was possible she didn't understand the mechanics of
conceiving them, since Mabel had never bothered to instruct her. Alvescot was by far a better match than
William Oldcastle, and Mabel felt sure she herself would
enjoy Sussex a great deal more than Suffolk.

"Her talent is remarkable, is it not, Lord Alvescot?"
she asked while Louisa played.

"Yes," he agreed, annoyed at her lack of consideration
for her own daughter.

Undismayed by his brevity and his blatant concentration on the music, Mabel continued, "Louisa is so fortunate to have both looks and talent. So few young women
have both, you know. And some, of course, have neither." A pitying glance at Vanessa accompanied her

words, which fortunately were not loud enough to reach her hostess.

Alvescot didn't deign to make a reply.

"And her age, too, is in her favor, I think. So many gentlemen marry misses just out of the schoolroom and find them irritatingly immature. It's a great mistake to be taken in by the first blush of youth, for it's accompanied by a lack of polish which takes years of experience to acquire. If it ever can be. Some gentlemen see promise where there is none, alas. You mustn't think Louisa has spent her life in the country! No, no, that is not the case at all. We lived exclusively in London from the time she was fifteen until last year when my husband . . . passed on. So regrettable."

A bare nod acknowledged her insincere sorrow.

"Of course, she's had more suitors than Mr. Oldcastle, but I think he has frightened them off with his ardor." Mabel offered an artificial laugh and a sly glance at the earl, who regarded her with astonishment. "Mr. Oldcastle is very wealthy, you know, and comes from a distinguished family, but I worry about his health. One would not wish to see one's daughter married to a man who would leave her widowed in a year or two. I know the anguish of being a widow, and I cannot bear to think of dear Louisa suffering it at her young age."

Louisa finished playing her second piece and rose from the stool with an absent smile in the direction of the earl. Her mother grudgingly decided that perhaps she had given enough of a hint for one evening and sat down to cards with the others, instructing her daughter, who didn't play cards, to entertain Lord Alvescot. Since the earl was already deep in conversation with Vanessa, Louisa found this a rather odd request and paid no heed to it, seating herself beside William Oldcastle without a second thought.

This was her usual procedure of an evening at Cutsdean, so she was monstrously surprised when her mother followed her to her room later for the sole purpose of berating her for her behavior.

"I told you to converse with the earl, Louisa," she said

sharply. "Do I have to write everything down for you in order that you understand it?"

"But the earl was already speaking with Vanessa," Louisa protested. "I couldn't very well intrude on their exchange."

"Certainly you could have! What would he want to spend an entire evening with her for? Lord, I don't know what you use for a brain. He's absolutely besotted with your music, and what do you make of it? Nothing. Positively nothing. Do you intend to let this opportunity pass you by?"

Bewildered, Louisa asked, "What opportunity?"

"The opportunity to nab an earl, my girl. Oldcastle is nothing compared with him! This is your chance to make a splendid match."

"Mama, whatever are you talking about? It is Mr. Oldcastle with whom we wish me to make a match. You have said so often enough yourself." Louisa was feeling grievously wronged and she tossed her reticule on the bed before flouncing down beside it. "You have told me again and again that I must bring Mr. Oldcastle to the sticking point."

"That was before the earl made his appearance," Mabel told her with exaggerated patience. "Can't you see that Lord Alvescot would make a much more suitable match?"

"No, I can't. I don't know him, and I don't think I could come to like him so well as I like Mr. Oldcastle. He's awfully big, you know, and rather stuffy, I think. Oh, he's polite enough, I suppose, but he hasn't said above a dozen words to me."

"He would if you gave him the opportunity, you silly child. Don't you understand that his wife will be a countess and will have position in society as well as every luxury she wishes?"

Louisa stared up at her mother's angry face. "I don't want to be a countess and Mr. Oldcastle has plenty of money. You have said so. Lord Alvescot wouldn't want to marry me, anyway."

"Why not? You still have your beauty and he's quite taken with your music. Louisa, listen to me. Mr. Oldcastle has had twelve years in which to ask you to marry him, and he's never come to the sticking point. You cannot, at your age, afford to pass up a chance to attach the earl. Do you want to die a spinster?"

"I suppose not."

"Then heed my advice, young lady. Men are fools for beautiful women, and if there is one thing I can say for you it is that your beauty is still remarkable. But in this instance you have another virtue which could hold the key to his affection. It is obvious to even the most undiscerning eye that Lord Alvescot loves music, and he is knowledgeable enough to recognize your superb talent. Think of it, Louisa! In the evenings at St. Aldwyns you would play for him, you would soothe his savage breast."

Startled, Louisa gasped. "Savage? Surely he is not a cruel man! I had no idea."

Mabel lost her temper. "What's the sense in trying to reason with you? Just do as I tell you, Louisa, and don't question my decision. You are to have nothing further to do with Oldcastle. He's a waste of time. If he were going to marry you, he could have done it any time these last twelve years. I will *not* let you pass up a chance to attach an earl. You are to speak with Lord Alvescot at every opportunity; go riding with him; ask him to take you for a drive in his curricle when it's repaired; walk with him in the shrubbery. And most especially, Louisa, you are to play for him at every chance you have. Do you understand me?"

Louisa stared unhappily down at her clenched hands. "Yes, Mama, I understand."

"Good. I'll be watching to see that you obey." Without another word Mabel turned and walked from the room.

SEVEN

Both Vanessa and Alvescot were surprised to find Mabel
Curtiss and her daughter at breakfast with them the next
morning. Neither woman had appeared at such an early
hour on any previous occasion, and Louisa at least had
difficulty stifling her yawns. Mabel was convinced that this
sleepy condition gave her daughter a sultry allure that was
lacking at other times of the day, and made a point of
drawing Alvescot's attention to her.

"Louisa is adorable so early in the morning, is she not,
my lord? Like a kitten, really, all cuddly and soft." Mabel
chose to ignore the difficulty her daughter had keeping
her eyes open but urged a cup of coffee on Louisa. "She
thought you might like to go for a ride after breakfast."

Alvescot saw no possibility of Louisa's staying on a
horse in her present condition and glanced over to where
Vanessa was watching the interchange with unholy
amusement gleaming in her eyes. "I think," the earl eventually said, "that you will have to excuse me, Miss Curtiss, though I hope we'll be able to ride another time. This
morning I had planned to continue my inspection of the
estate."

"Then perhaps this afternoon," Mabel said firmly, completely overriding her daughter's comment of, "Oh, that's
quite all right."

"This afternoon I am taking John to see the canal."

"Louisa could accompany you," Mabel assured him.

Vanessa set down her piece of toast. "I'm afraid that's
impossible. You know very well Louisa wouldn't like to

be on horseback for that long, Mabel. John's pony can't make the trip in under an hour each way."

"I suppose *you* are going with them," Mable rasped.

"Yes, I am."

Mabel snorted. "I might have known. It's not enough that you have Cutsdean and two children. Oh, no, you have to have more. Greed is an ugly vice, you know."

"Yes," Vanessa said with a sweet smile, "I know."

Alvescot felt extremely uncomfortable during this exchange, not so much for himself as for Vanessa. But she was apparently untouched by it, picking up her piece of toast and meeting his gaze placidly across the table. If she wasn't embarrassed by Mrs. Curtiss's remarks, he would have at least expected her to be angry, but she showed no sign of it. Why did she put up with these meddling fools?

Turning her attention to Louisa, Vanessa made an effort to put the woman at ease. It was Louisa who was most affected by her mother's rudeness and interference. Her usually pale cheeks were flushed with distress and she sat staring down at her untouched plate. Much as Louisa would have liked to show her appreciation, Vanessa's kindness drew forth only brief answers. At times such as these, Louisa found her throat locked with mortification, unable to think of some social discourse to smooth over the unpleasantness.

When she realized the hopelessness of the task, Vanessa directed her attention to the earl. "Do you think our pasturage could support any more cattle, Lord Alvescot?"

"Not many. Mr. Burford has explained the limitations of the drainage system and I'm sure he's right in planning to improve it, for both the crops and the animals. The acreage should come first; there will be plenty of time to build up the herd over the next few years."

"Mr. Burford," announced Mabel, "should be kept in his place."

Vanessa regarded the woman with cold eyes. "I'll decide what Mr. Burford's place is at Cutsdean, Mabel. He's as well born as you or I, and I can only respect him for making an honest effort to repair his fortunes. There are those . . ." But she stopped herself before finishing the sentence. Provoked as she was, she refused to go so far as to point a finger at the wastrel Edward.

Instead, she pushed back her chair, saying, "Excuse me, please. The children will be waiting." And hostess or not, she felt not the least guilt in leaving the three of them to one another's company.

The earl watched her go with some trepidation. He was perfectly willing to snub Mabel Curtiss, but her daughter was another matter entirely. Though it was true that Louisa was not very bright, she was also exquisitely shy and prone to suffer agonies of embarrassment at her mother's gauche behavior. Alvescot had no desire to further her discomfort, but he had no wish to further Mabel's schemes, either. His compromise, agreed to with a certain stoicism, was to listen to Louisa play a few melodies after breakfast before he started his rounds of the estate.

Shortly before noon, Vanessa picked up the picnic basket from the kitchen and joined her son in the Garden Room. John could barely contain his excitement and eagerly reached for the basket.

"It's too heavy for you to carry," Vanessa admonished.

"I don't want to carry it. I just want to see what Cook gave us!"

So much for a wholesale change in his behavior, Vanessa thought, regarding him with indulgent eyes. He was only four, after all, and there was plenty of time to instill a more thorough consideration for others into his makeup. It was not that he was thoughtless, really, but simply that he had a child's natural inclination to think of himself and his pleasures first. But there were entirely too many adults in her household who acted in precisely the same manner for Vanessa not to be concerned that the child learn consideration as soon as possible. Surely there were too many influences around him that could keep him from developing into the kind of man his father had been.

And sometimes, though she scarcely admitted it to herself, Vanessa didn't like to look too closely at even Frederick's character. Oh, he had been charming and vital, kind and open, but self-indulgent as well. Not in material matters, at least no more than would be expected of a man of his wealth. Frederick's self-indulgence had run to doing precisely what he wished, with little regard for the responsibilities he had taken on in marrying and producing children. Fortunately for him, his actions could be viewed as patriotic, as doing no more than his duty for his country. But Vanessa suspected that had there been no war in Europe, he would still have led a reckless life, gallivanting about the country looking for sport and amusement. She didn't doubt that he had loved her, but it was a love he held separate from the rest of his life.

Which was only to be expected, she scolded herself as she walked with John toward the stables. Gentlemen were reared to consult only their own wishes, to assume that their pleasure was the object of a faithful wife. Any resentment she might have felt at his seeming indifference to her when they were apart—the paucity of letters, the infrequent attempt to gain leave—had been washed away in the very real agony of losing him forever. During the three years of their marriage she had spent exactly ninety-three days with him. Barely three months, with memories that had to last her for a lifetime, that had to serve as the foundation of her tales to John and Catherine.

Frederick had never even seen Catherine, though Vanessa had been assured that word of her birth had reached him before Waterloo. Then why couldn't he have been a little more careful? she thought rebelliously, as she had hundreds of times since his death. Unfair, she knew, but the question continued to return no matter how often she thrust it aside. Why had he agreed to go to the Congress of Vienna rather than stay at Cutsdean with her? All those months he could have been with her and John, wasted, for the excitement of the peace negotiations, followed by the horror of Waterloo.

Lost in her thoughts, Vanessa was only aware of Lord Alvescot speaking to her when he lifted the basket from her hands, asking, "Are you all right, Mrs. Damery?"

"Of course," she murmured, looking away from his concerned hazel eyes. "I just had a few things on my mind."

"If you'd prefer not to go, I could get instructions from your groom."

"No, I want to go." She glanced around for John, who was nowhere in sight.

"He's gone to get his pony. Has something happened to disturb you?"

Vanessa met his eyes. "Not a thing, Lord Alvescot." What *had* brought on this bout of self-pity? Probably John had chattered to her all the way to the stables and she hadn't heard a word he said. Really, for her to be thinking *he* showed a lack of consideration. . . .

Since her attention seemed to have drifted off again, Alvescot turned his to seeing that the horses were saddled and the picnic basket tied securely on his mount. Vanessa allowed him to hand her up onto her horse without really paying any heed to him, smoothing down the voluminous skirts of her forest green riding habit as she watched John lead out his pony. She smiled when her son offered to guide the party.

"Very well. Let's see if you know the way."

Rollo started off eagerly enough, frisking about as John attempted to bring him under control. Alvescot rode beside Vanessa in the hope that she had shaken her distraction, whatever it might have been. The thought did occur to him that she had somehow stumbled on Edward's blackmailing of the captain and he said cautiously, "I've noticed there's some friction between Captain Lawrence and Mr. Curtiss."

Her smile readily appeared. "How very observant of you, sir. Actually, there's some friction between each of the members of my houseparty. I hope you'll pardon the little scene at breakfast. Not that I can promise you it won't happen again."

"Mrs. Curtiss suggested that her daughter might play the pianoforte for me after you left."

"At eight in the morning?" Vanessa didn't bother to suppress her gurgle of laughter. "She's a determined woman."

"So I noticed."

"Louisa . . . well, there's no vice in her. Any untoward conduct is entirely at her mother's instigation, I assure you. Louisa is actually rather sweet, except when her brother provokes her."

Sweet, simple, and musically talented, Alvescot summed up mentally. How could her mother possibly think I would be interested in the woman? But it was far from the first time some totally ineligible female had been urged on his notice and he said nothing.

"Have you had a chance to look at the ledgers?" Vanessa asked.

"I've started going over them. It will take me some time."

"There's no hurry." Vanessa watched a goldfinch flutter from a thistle at the side of the lane, the flash of its yellow wingbars bright in the noontime sun. "If I've seemed inhospitable, I'm sorry. I can't entertain any suspicions of Paul Burford, but you have the right to make any investigations which seem appropriate to you. And I'm grateful for your attention to the children."

He regarded her with a slightly raised brow. "Even if you do think I'm hard on them."

"I was thinking about that on the way to the stables. Not about how you handle them, actually," she confessed, "but how important it was for them to learn to be considerate of people. I've seen too many adults who aren't."

Alvescot sternly instructed himself not to take the remark personally. She could as easily be referring to her household. More easily, he decided. The thoughtful expression had returned to her face and he studied her without her awareness. The breeze tossed her black curls against the wide-brimmed bonnet and her eyes looked suddenly sad. Her clear skin was a shade too pale and her lips, in repose, turned slightly down, enhancing the impression of sadness. And yet he could visualize the change a smile wrought on her features, giving them animation and a subtle beauty. Alvescot felt a strong urge to make her smile, to remove the burdens she carried, at least for the moment, but before he could choose a subject to lighten her mood, she turned to him and said, "I've never known exactly how Frederick died. Would you tell me?"

The question startled him. For a moment he was silent, debating the wisdom of relating so unhappy a tale. Finally, slowly, he spoke. "Wellington had lost most of his officers by dusk. For hours, things had looked hopeless, but Colborne had taken a risk and moved his battalion out of the line, taking the Imperial Guard by surprise. There were heavy casualties for the Imperial Guard and they broke and fled. While the French army's units recoiled, the British Light Infantry inclined to the right toward La Belle Alliance. Around them, scattered units of British and French cavalry charged and countercharged in heavy smoke. Frederick was one of them. His horse was shot out from under him but he was only slightly injured. It was while he was trying to capture a loose horse that he was cut down. I wasn't there. One of his men later relayed the information. I arranged for his body to be brought here, but I was injured and it was some time before I was strong enough to leave Brussels."

"I see. Thank you, Lord Alvescot. I had a letter from Wellington himself, but it only expressed his regret and not the circumstances. You must think it perverse of me to want to know."

"Not at all," he assured her, his voice gentle. "I would have written more myself if I had known your desire."

"I don't think, at the time, that I did want to know. But one day John will ask, perhaps even Catherine. Wellington was very clear about Frederick's courage and resourcefulness."

"No one could have asked for a braver officer." Alvescot tried to draw on some memory that would please her. "He sought me out the night of the Richmond ball to announce his daughter's birth. We drank to your health and Catherine's."

Vanessa nodded in acknowledgment but showed no desire to continue the conversation. Ahead of them, John's pony had slowed to an ambling pace and their horses soon came up with the boy. At the crossroads John looked up in some confusion, admitting that he didn't remember which road to take. Vanessa laughed and tousled his hair. "Some guide you are, dear boy. What landmark do we look for at this crossroad?"

Allowing his gaze to wander down the two lanes, John

caught sight of a barn in the distance. "The barn with the red door! I forgot."

As they made their way toward the canal, one adult on either side of the boy, Alvescot kept up a running dialogue with John, including Vanessa from time to time, but her distraction had returned and she seemed content merely to listen to them talking. When they reached the bank of the canal near where it entered the tunnel, Vanessa took charge of spreading out their picnic while the earl and John floated twigs on the water in miniature boat races. Their laughter and groans drifted back to her and she turned to watch them, John running along the bank while Alvescot crouched down, one hand shielding his eyes from the glint of sunlight off the water.

Vanessa hadn't really looked at Alvescot before. Not as a man. To her he had been only her husband's cousin, a nuisance at best when added to her other burdens. And she wasn't in the habit of considering a man in quite the way she found herself doing now. Not for years, at any rate. Perhaps it was his kindness to her son that sparked this sudden interest, she rationalized as she found herself unable to withdraw her eyes. But it was an unacceptable solution. Paul Burford was good with John, too, and she had never felt this stirring of her senses with him. She had never had the slightest desire to feel the texture of his hair or touch the curve of his cheek. Never once had she wondered what it would be like to kiss him, to be held in his arms.

Good Lord, she brought herself up abruptly, I'm losing my mind. Still, she sat for some time watching him, troubled by her reaction but unable to deny herself the intriguing sensations of physical attraction. His laughter, for instance, had such a deep timbre that she could almost feel it within herself. And his eyes. Even from this distance she was captivated by the way they crinkled with amusement. What color were they? Brown? No, hazel, she remembered, a vague impression returning that they had those remarkable green highlights which seemed so prominent when they narrowed with annoyance.

That was something to hold onto. They often narrowed with annoyance. And with suspicion, and a sort of remoteness, and with a haughty disdain. This was a man of far more complexity than the kindly godfather to her son she was now witnessing. He was a determined man, an opinionated man, and a man who would shortly disappear from her life as swiftly as he had entered it. Well, she told herself as she rose to join them, undoubtedly that was all to the good.

Alvescot was not unaware of her observation, but he could read nothing into it. That in itself he found unusual. Most women in his experience had little control over their emotions, and none over their facial expressions. Vanessa Damery apparently had both. Even when he carefully studied her as he told her of Frederick's death he could detect no change in her countenance. Which might well mean she was simply a cold, indifferent woman, of course, but somehow he doubted that. And it was not that she'd never shown happiness or sorrow, because she had. But when she wished to conceal her thoughts or feelings, she was perfectly capable of doing so. Alvescot had the sudden realization that this might be something eminently important to understand about Vanessa.

"Our picnic is ready," she announced when she came up to them. "And there's a barge coming, John. We can watch it while we eat."

For the rest of their excursion she forced all thought of child-rearing, Frederick, and this unacceptable attraction to Lord Alvescot from her mind. She was accustomed to playing the role of hostess, to entertaining her guests with intelligent and amusing discourse, and she had no difficulty reverting to that role now. Alvescot was somewhat puzzled by her change of mood but quickly adapted himself to it. He was no stranger to playing roles.

EIGHT

Mabel Curtiss was nothing if not persistent. For the next two days she dragged Louisa to breakfast at the same early hour, hounding Alvescot to take her daughter riding, walking, picnicking, driving, and any other activity that happened to come to her mind. The earl politely agreed to some of these activities, but he had no intention of falling into some murky plot designed to place him in a position where Mabel could accuse him of leading her daughter on. Louisa reluctantly followed her mother's direction, but Alvescot could see that her heart wasn't in it. When she spoke, which was rarely, it was usually of her erstwhile suitor—his likes and dislikes, his delicate constitution, his estate in Suffolk which she and her mother had visited on no less than four occasions over the last twelve years.

"I liked it there," she said simply one afternoon as they drove through the countryside around Cutsdean in Alvescot's newly repaired curricle. "It's very peaceful and his sister is a dear girl. She's rather ugly, I suppose, and is not expected to marry, and I think she must be very lonely living there alone while William is so often with us. I should like to be her friend; we go on very well when we're together."

Envisioning some poor ugly duckling of a schoolgirl, Alvescot asked, "How old is she?"

"Meredith? Why, something older than William, I would imagine. Perhaps thirty-eight or thirty-nine. She does a great deal of good in the village, for the poor people, you know." Louisa sighed and regarded her hands which lay lightly clasped in her lap. "I would do something for the poor people, too, if Mama did not insist that my share of the allowance go to Edward."

The blackmail still occupied Alvescot's mind, but he had not as yet devised a plan of attack and he thought Louisa unlikely to be of any assistance in the matter. Still, it could do no harm to sound her out on Captain Lawrence, and when he did, she said, "Oh, he's a rather crotchety old man, isn't he? He treats little John like a cabin boy, barking orders and snapping about everything the poor lad does. And the boy is only four! I do think retired sailors are the worst of the military, don't you?"

"I hadn't actually thought about it," Alvescot admitted.

"Yes, well, we had one in our neighborhood, where we used to live," she said sadly. "His name was Beningbrough and he did nothing but talk of ships and naval actions and rascally powder boys who were rapped on the sconce—whatever that may be. Captain Lawrence only talks of the diseases his sailors got and prides himself on never having had them himself. Which was only because he didn't have to suffer their horrid conditions, you may be sure! He's not a very sympathetic man, Captain Lawrence. I don't think he likes anyone at Cutsdean. I can't think why he stays!"

Alvescot felt sure he knew, and it didn't make his feelings toward the captain any more kindly. Someone of the captain's age should have laid by for his later years, and certainly could have done so with the prize money he frequently mentioned having received. The self-righteous old stick should have practiced what he preached about economy and ordering one's life. But the earl merely nodded gravely to this extraordinarily long speech of Louisa's and said nothing except, "He must have had a rather distinguished career."

His companion frowned slightly. "I suppose so. One day Edward was teasing him—about publishing his memoirs, you know—and the captain got all white and stomped out of the room. People do that, though—publish their memoirs—don't they?"

"Frequently."

"Well, I haven't read anything of that sort myself, but I

was sure they did. I can't imagine why it upset Captain Lawrence. Perhaps he doesn't approve of that sort of thing."

Directing his pair back toward the estate, Alvescot looked thoughtful. "Perhaps not."

Louisa fell silent for the duration of their drive. What she was thinking, the earl couldn't tell, as her face became blank when she wasn't being directly addressed. That it had something to do with William Oldcastle he felt reasonably confident. Mr. Oldcastle had become rather a problem. The more time Louisa spent with the earl, the more sulky William became. If Louisa made any effort to conciliate him, her mother was always there to scotch the attempt. Now, Alvescot wanted Oldcastle's bedroom, feeling more and more confined each day he spent in his miniature chamber, but he owned to a certain fastidiousness about acquiring it in such a way, especially since he had no interest in Louisa.

There were times, when William happened to mention the hangings of Chinese painting on silk or the mirror paintings, when Alvescot was almost tempted to overlook his principles, but he resisted the temptation, steadfastly refusing to precipitate an out and out quarrel between the pair. If Oldcastle had the perseverance to remain in view of Mabel Curtiss's obvious attempts to rid Cutsdean of him, more power to the man.

Alvescot had observed the famous squabbles during the first two days he spent at Cutsdean, but since Mabel had made her strategy clear, William was saying very little. He sat in a corner and glowered at Louisa, and at Alvescot if he happened to be speaking with her, but he spoke only when spoken to. Vanessa had taken pity on him, seating him next to her at meals and engaging his attention in the evenings. In turn, he treated her with a rigid formality, though there were occasional bursts of heavy-handed flirtation tossed in at random, as though he had some intention of making Louisa jealous.

From her sour and stately vantage point, Hortense Damery watched the farce develop with disgusted eyes. Alvescot had heard her berate Vanessa about the conduct of her guests, an attack which the younger woman gracefully ignored. It was difficult to tell whether Frederick's mother had any interest in the conclusion of the various stratagems. If she sided with Mabel in wishing to see Edward win Vanessa's hand, it was impossible to tell by her consistently cold aspect. The earl had finally come to the conclusion that Cutsdean was a hotbed of partially hidden problems and worrisome emotions, but as he readied himself for bed that night he decided he was wasting his time in not acting on the most apparent to him: that of Edward's blackmailing Captain Lawrence.

Unfortunately, without the curricle, Edward was spending a great deal of time on the premises. His treatment of the captain's horse had left that poor beast in no fit shape to ride for several days and Vanessa refused him permission to ride any of her horses until he learned to treat the animals with some respect. This move on her part was actually thwarting Alvescot's plan to search Edward's room, and he was unhappily considering the desperate measure of offering the young man one of his horses as he snuffed his candle and climbed into bed.

In the darkness, however, he found that his thoughts drifted to his hostess rather than to schemes for ending Edward's blackmail. His original annoyance with Vanessa had long since passed, replaced at first by a kind of sympathy for her plight and more recently by some more ephemeral emotion. It had nothing whatsoever to do with his feelings of guilt for not having come to her assistance more quickly than he had. Alvescot didn't waste emotion on things that could not be changed, except perhaps in the case of Maria.

And he realized, almost with surprise, that he hadn't thought of her in days, save that once on his arrival. Well, it was about time he came to terms with that loss, he congratulated himself. Her death could have been no more final than her marriage. But there had been those two years when some sort of hope had seemed to remain, more wishful thinking perhaps than anything with a solid foundation. She might have convinced her parents to change their minds; no unexceptional suitors might have come along. Both highly unlikely, but they had served as the basis of his hopes for a long time.

The night was warm and Alvescot had left the window open slightly. A sultry breeze wafted the curtains but there was no moon and the darkness without was as deep as within. The earl was once again contemplating the smallness of his room, his eyes grown accustomed to the dark, when he was severely startled to hear the handle of his door turn. His first thought was that the intruder would be Edward on some nefarious mission which included the stealing of a few crowns from the pockets of his breeches, or in search of some incriminating evidence with which he could blackmail the earl. Alvescot would immediately have sprung from his bed to confront the young man, but he was sleeping in the buff and it did not appeal to his sense of dignity to be caught at such a disadvantage. So he lay still watching the door inch open.

A head was thrust through the opening and a soft voice called, "William?"

Alvescot was too surprised to answer.

The door was pushed a little wider and Louisa slipped into the room. She had on nothing—no nightdress, no wrapper, not even a pair of slippers, but she carried a wavering candle. Stunned, Alvescot lay blinking at the vision of white nakedness.

"William?" she called again, slightly louder.

Finally recovering himself somewhat, Alvescot said in a strangled voice, "This isn't William's room."

"Oh." The single syllable oozed disappointment. "Do you know where his room *is*?"

It was a well-known fact at Cutsdean that Louisa had a difficult time finding her way around the rambling old structure. Mabel had once complained that Louisa wouldn't be able to find the staircase if she weren't within sight of it. Neither mother nor daughter admitted to the latter's short-sightedness, but that was only part of the problem. Louisa had absolutely no sense of direction.

"Yes," Alvescot said shortly, "I know where his room is, but you aren't going there, Louisa. You are going back to your own room and you're going to stay there." He felt trapped in his bed, but he thought it his gentlemanly duty to clothe her in something, anything, and he pulled out the sheet which covered him and wrapped it about himself before climbing awkwardly out of bed. He was reaching for his dressing gown when he realized that there might be a certain amount of explaining to do in the morning if it was found by Mabel, or even one of the maids, in Louisa's bedroom.

Instead, he picked up one of the blankets he had kicked off the bed and approached her with it, trying not to let his eyes wander to the naked body which Louisa was making no attempt to cover.

"Here," he said, draping the blanket around her shoulders. "You can't walk about the halls naked, Louisa. Someone might see you."

Her long hair, ordinarily so youthfully displayed about her face, was pulled back severely into one long braid. The style was surprisingly appropriate to her, making the wide eyes appear more serious and less vacant. But her eyes were filled with tears now and she clutched the blanket tightly about her shivering frame. "I must go to William's room," she insisted.

"Is he expecting you?"

The coolness of Alvescot's tone did not penetrate her preoccupation. "Oh, no, but I think he would be glad to see me, don't you? He's so terribly hurt by my avoiding him all the time. I don't do it on purpose, you know. Mama won't let me so much as say a word to him without dragging me away."

"Yes, well, you can't go to his room, Louisa. It wouldn't be proper." The earl found it unnecessary to add anything about her nakedness.

A gleam appeared in her eyes, which if Alvescot hadn't known better, he would have called sly. She smiled and said, "Yes, I know it would be improper. In fact, it would be . . . compromising, wouldn't it?"

Something clicked in his mind. That second evening the ladies had been discussing neighborhood gossip when he entered the Saloon after dinner, something to do with compromising positions and the supposition of intimacy between two people. He regarded Louisa with wonder. "You intend to trap William into marrying you?"

"Well," she said, defensive now, "I really think he would like to marry me, you know. He's very unhappy without my attention. Everyone can see that. Mama is hoping that he will go away, but I don't want him to." A tear splashed onto her cheek. "I . . . I'm very fond of him."

"I see. Still, Louisa, I think it would be better to give him an opportunity to offer for you in the ordinary way. He might resent being *forced* to marry you, even if he really wants to."

"But he's had twelve years!" she wailed.

Alarmed by the piercing nature of her cry, Alvescot had visions of being descended upon by some member of the household or staff, who would not think it at all amusing to find Louisa wrapped in only a blanket standing in his room. He said soothingly, "There, there. He'll come about. Perhaps I could have a word with him. Nothing blatant, of course! Just say a little something that would point him in the right direction."

"Mama has tried everything," Louisa said stubbornly. She tugged more firmly at the blanket but only managed to accidentally uncover one small, heaving breast.

Alvescot quickly twitched the blanket back into place and turned her toward the door. "Let me have a crack at it. Man to man, you know." He put a great deal of confidence into his tone. "Can you find the way to your room?"

"I suppose so," she said doubtfully, squinting out into the hall as he opened the door.

It would be too much, Alvescot decided, to be discovered in the hall with her, he wrapped in a sheet and she in a blanket. But there was really no alternative. If he let her leave on her own, she might end up anywhere. She might even decide to have another go at finding William's room. An exasperated sigh escaped him. Really, Cutsdean was more like a madhouse than a placid country home. It would be in his best interest, he felt sure, to pack his valise in the morning and disappear, never to return again. When he thought of all the complications staying meant. . . .

"I'll take you there," he murmured, closing the door behind him.

Every step of the way he listened for the sound of other footsteps or voices. When Louisa started to say something, he hushed her rather brusquely. At her door he whispered, "Go in and take off the blanket. I'll carry it back with me so there won't be any question in the morning."

Really, she has no conception of modesty, Alvescot mused in amazement as Louisa took him literally at his word. Without closing the door behind her she allowed the blanket to drop at her feet before picking it up and handing it to him. "I'd be very grateful if you could convince William to marry me," she said, once again standing there without a rag on her body. "He needs someone to look after him, you know."

He isn't the only one, Alvescot mentally amended as he took his leave. Before he had gotten many feet up the corridor he considered going back to warn her not to mention the episode to anyone, but thought better of the idea. Even Louisa wasn't likely to be that naive, and she would probably only open the door again to him in all her pale nakedness. Dear God, talk about your child of nature!

Disgruntled, Alvescot managed to reach his room without further mishap, but it was some time before he was able to fall asleep. Incredible as it may seem, the question his mind continued to debate for some time was whether a woman of such naiveté would ultimately make a better lover than a woman with a highly developed sense of social and religious values. On the one hand, there was that total natural response in Louisa (look at her astonishing performance on the pianoforte!) while on the other there was the restrained self-confidence of Vanessa Damery. Though Alvescot reproached himself for thinking of his hostess in such a light, he found himself altogether incapable, at that particular moment, of doing otherwise. He told himself, repeatedly, that it was an academic question, having nothing personal to do with either of the women. And since his own experience had been only with assorted mistresses, whose profession it was to please a man, it was a subject which suddenly fascinated him— from a theoretical point of view. And a thoroughly more interesting study than that of the estate books which awaited him in the morning.

The next day he rose later than usual and found himself alone in the Breakfast Parlor, much to his relief, actually. He had an opportunity to eat a leisurely meal before he set himself down to the accounts. And when, an hour before luncheon, he felt he had enough questions to justify an interview with his hostess, he sought her direction from one of the footmen.

"She's in the Morning Room, milord," he was informed.

"Then I shall join her there," Alvescot remarked, remembering that he hadn't as yet set foot in that particular room since his arrival.

The footman's face grew concerned. "Begging your pardon, milord, but no one is allowed to join Mrs. Damery there without her specific permission, and she only gives that to the children. But I can take a message to her and have her join you in the Saloon or the Mirror Room."

For some reason this annoyed Alvescot. Certainly it was sensible of her to have some place where she could not be interrupted by her bothersome guests, but he didn't like the idea of being excluded himself. It was on the tip of his tongue to say that she would make an exception for him, and to simply barge in on her. His good breeding was not what stopped him; it was the thought of her reaction. He had no difficulty envisioning her look of surprise and annoyance, her carefully controlled voice saying, "Did you wish to see me, Lord Alvescot? If you will wait in the Saloon I will join you shortly." And what could he do but obey her? Alvescot hadn't the least desire to make a fool of himself again.

"Never mind," he told the footman. "I'll speak with her at luncheon."

Disappointed, he wandered out onto the East Terrace, slowing walking to the southernmost end of it, where two windows from the Morning Room overlooked the flagstoned surface and the shrubbery beyond. The green velvet curtains were partially drawn against the morning sun and except for the broad bands of light which pierced the room, it wasn't possible for him to see into its depths without coming a great deal closer than a casual stroller was likely to do. He stood for some time at the stone railing near one of the windows, hoping to hear some murmur from the room. It was not from within that voices reached him, however, but from the shrubbery to his left.

"Come now, my sweet lady," Edward's voice said persuasively. "How am I to prove that I can care for an animal if you won't let me ride one?"

Vanessa answered after a short pause. "Edward, you've wrecked the curricle and damaged the captain's horse all within the space of a few days. I cannot, with a clear conscience, allow you to mistreat my animals any further. If you wish to prove your good intentions, go and help them in the stables. Put poltices on the captain's horse; groom some of the animals; help with the feeding. Do anything, but don't expect me to believe in your change of heart. How many times have you promised me you wouldn't race the horses, or drive them beyond endurance? I have only to be out of sight for you to forget your glib words, and you don't seem to understand that I don't have to *see* you mistreating them to know on your return that you've done it."

"For God's sake, Vanessa, horses like to run! I've never had one drop dead under me."

Alvescot could hear her sigh. "In time you will," she retorted. "And I don't want it to be one of mine."

"You know I can't afford one of my own."

"If you stopped spending all your time and money in Basingstoke, you could save up for one, Edward."

There was a distinct change in his tone when he spoke. Alvescot had moved from the end of the terrace to a spot closer to the shrubbery, but he couldn't see the two of them, owing to a bend in the walk. Still, he felt sure exactly what sort of expression Edward wore and it made him grit his teeth.

"My lovely Vanessa, I wouldn't spend so much time in Basingstoke if you would give me the least sign of encouragement." His voice was soft, insinuating. "You know I want to spend every minute, *every minute,* of the day and night with you, but, alas, you offer no hope. Do I detect the tiniest evidence of jealousy in your annoyance with the time I spend in Basingstoke? You have but to say the word, my angel, and I will never set foot in the stupid town again."

"Go there as often as you like, Edward," she returned, "but not on my horses."

Her voice had abruptly become louder, and Alvescot decided this was not caused by her raising it, but because she had turned toward the house. He quickly retraced his footsteps to the door of the Saloon, hesitating for a moment to hear if Edward replied. All he heard was the slight whisper of shoes on the gravel walk before Vanessa came in sight, swiftly negotiating the stairs to the terrace with her long skirts held up to avoid tripping on them. He noted that she had remarkably well-turned ankles.

At sight of him she dropped her skirts and attempted a noncommittal smile. "Good morning, Lord Alvescot. Were you about to take a stroll?"

"Actually, I was hoping to find you, Mrs. Damery. There are a few questions I'd like to ask about the estate books."

Vanessa glanced up at the sky, as though the answer were written there. Apparently it was, for she said, "It's a little close to luncheon to have some uninterrupted time. Would afterward be as convenient?"

"I'm at your disposal, ma'am. Don't you go to your children then?"

"Usually, but I can delay that."

"Please don't. Perhaps we could meet at three in the Library."

Vanessa nodded her agreement and waited while he opened and held the door for her. Alvescot would have liked to tag along but decided there was no point to it. "I think I'll just walk for a while before luncheon," he said.

When she disappeared into the house, obviously finding his statement of purpose of little or no interest, he strode over to the stairs and down into the shrubbery. He surprised Edward scowling at a statue of a nymph.

"Moronic-looking thing, ain't it?" he demanded of Alvescot.

The earl had never taken a close look at the statue and gave it only a cursory glance now. "I suppose it is," he agreed, indifferent.

"Don't know why anyone wants such rubbish in their gardens," Edward complained. "If this were my place, I'd chuck it all."

"But it's not your place," Alvescot reminded him.

Edward gave him a measuring look and appeared satisfied that no scurrilous meaning could attach to the words. "I say, I wonder if you'd let me have one of your horses to ride into town this afternoon. There's rather an urgent matter I have to take care of and without the curricle. . . ."

If he thought to play on Alvescot's sympathies, or even some latent guilt for the curricle accident, he was far off the mark. A smarter man would have noticed the way the earl's jaw clenched, the way his eyes narrowed, but Edward was only listening, half hopeful, and what the earl said was, "You may take Satin, if you think you can do so without damaging him. However, I should warn you that he's a little difficult to manage and any rough treatment will earn you my absolute enmity, which is nothing to take lightly, Mr. Curtiss. Handle him properly and he'll behave; handle him poorly and you'll be lucky to make it back to Cutsdean."

With a flush of anger, Edward turned away. But he was not one to take offense where it would inconvenience him. "I'm sure I can handle your horse, Lord Alvescot."

"I hope so," the earl replied grimly.

NINE

Since Edward's absence provided the opportunity Alvescot needed to search his room, the earl waited only until he saw Edward ride off on Satin before setting to work. He had previously ascertained that the young man had a bedchamber in the South Wing, something called the Tapestry Bedchamber, which Alvescot did not recall from his youth. Possibly he had simply never heard of it; possibly it had been renamed; possibly one of the two Mrs. Damerys had outfitted it since his last visit to Cutsdean. In any case, he was uninterested in its origins, only in its contents.

Edward shared a valet with Captain Lawrence (and Mr. Oldcastle, when he was in residence), and Alvescot wanted to explore Edward's room while the valet would be at his meal with the other servants. The maids, too, would be finished with the bedchambers and at luncheon if he proceeded there directly after the family ate, so he ruthlessly detached himself from Mabel Curtiss and her daughter, mumbling something about correspondence he simply *must* take care of, and went directly to the first floor.

There was no one in the corridor as he approached the Tapestry Bedchamber. Without the least hesitation he walked up to the door, opened it, and let himself in. It was an enormous room, probably a combination of two smaller ones, as the Library below obviously was. Though not originally the master suite, it had for some years served that purpose with its sitting room comfortably furnished with a desk, bookshelves, and several winged chairs, and the bedchamber beyond appointed with every conceivable amenity. Why the devil did she put him here? Alvescot wondered, frowning at the needlework hangings on the four-poster bed. Beyond doubt it was the most prized bedroom of the lot, excluding Vanessa's own suite, which had been Hortense's. Momentarily, Alvescot considered the order in which the various relations had descended on Mrs. Damery and been assigned to their bedrooms. Deciding that didn't explain anything, Alvescot shrugged off the unimportant matter and looked about himself.

There was no way to tell what he was looking for, or if there was anything in the room itself which would give him a clue. It seemed reasonable that Edward had learned some unsavory secret in the captain's past which he was using to extort money, but it wasn't necessarily anything which would leave a tangible trace in Edward's room. Nonetheless, Alvescot was determined to have a thorough look about him. Captain Lawrence might not be the only victim. It was possible Vanessa tolerated Edward's presence because of some sort of pressure on her, a thought that left Alvescot feeling an icy anger. He didn't really believe it, but he didn't want to take any chances.

The bedroom itself was devoid of everything except Edward's personal toilet articles, clothing, and some old editions of the *Turf Remembrancer*. Alvescot felt some distaste in going through the drawers and looking in every conceivable hiding place, but then he felt some distaste at the idea of Edward's nefarious activities as well. When he had finished with the bedroom, he started to work on the sitting room, running an eye over the books on the shelves and through the contents of the desk, which were minimal. Edward apparently undertook little correspondence. The letters he had received Alvescot did not peruse, since they would not likely have any bearing on Captain Lawrence. But when he had finished with the desk there was no place else to search. He stood for some time absently staring at the bookshelves, not really seeing them, while his mind tackled the problem of where to go next for some solution to the problem.

As in each of the guest chambers, there was a selection

of reading material on the bookshelves. Alvescot doubted that Edward had ever touched any of the volumes, though they were well dusted and neatly organized on the shelves. It was the usual collection—some volumes of sermons and other uplifting reading, some historical works and biographies, a few light novels by Mrs. Smith and Mrs. Maria Edgeworth, poetry of Pope and Byron. Alvescot couldn't see titles on all of them but he doubted there was anything here he wished to read. No, it was something about the symmetry, or the lack of it, in one particular row which drew his cursory attention.

One book appeared overly plump, wider at the back than the front, so it left a small gap between it and the books on either side. Alvescot absently reached out to tighten the arrangement but, finding this didn't work, took out the book to see wherein lay the problem. As he lifted the book from the shelf something slid to the floor, leaving him with only the binding in one hand. Glancing down, he was surprised to find that an entire volume lay there, and not just the interior pages. Curious now, he picked it up and turned to the flyleaf, which announced it to be the diary of Captain Charles Lawrence for the years 1802 to 1808. Most decidedly what he was looking for, else why would it be in Edward's room?

A fair amount of time had passed by now and he heard some movement in the hall, but he was intent on restoring things to an order that wouldn't attract Edward's attention. The empty binding which he held in one hand turned out to be for Ned Ward's *The Whole Pleasure of Matrimony*. Trust Edward to destroy that for his hiding place, Alvescot thought, and not to do it well enough to escape detection.

Choosing a smaller volume on herbals, Alvescot inserted it in the empty binding and carefully replaced it on the shelf. He slid the captain's diary under his coat, holding it tight to his side with one arm as he opened the door silently and checked the hallway. At the far end a maid was polishing a sconce, but she had her back to him and he slipped from the room, closing the door soundlessly, and headed in the opposite direction. When he turned the corner into the West Wing, he glanced back at the maid, who gave no sign of having noticed him.

In his room he set the diary on the bedside commode-table and rang for his valet. Bibury appeared in a matter of minutes, a faint question in his eyes.

"I hope I didn't interrupt your meal, Bibury. If possible, I'd like to have a word in private with Captain Lawrence. Do you think you could find him and bring him here? It's not a matter I'd like to discuss in any of the public rooms."

The valet nodded. "Yes, milord. I saw him on the terrace only a few minutes ago."

"Don't approach him if he's with anyone, Bibury. If I can't see him now, I'll see him later."

While the valet was gone, Alvescot paced about his small room trying to decide exactly how to handle his knowledge and some resolution of it. He did no more than glance at the diary sitting on the commode, though his curiosity was roused. Just what was in it that gave Edward such power over the old man? Alvescot wasn't fond of Captain Lawrence: he was opinionated, uncivil, self-righteous, and overbearing. But the earl liked Edward even less, and he hated the kind of extortion by intimidation that the younger man was using. There was something naturally repulsive about it which Alvescot wouldn't tolerate, no matter what Captain Lawrence's failings or the possibly petty amounts of money involved.

There was a soft rap at his door and Bibury entered to announce Captain Lawrence, who stalked into the room muttering, "What is so important that I must see you in your bedchamber, Lord Alvescot? Surely if you wished to speak with me you could have sought me out yourself?"

The earl waved Bibury off with a nod of thanks and only spoke when the door had closed behind him. "I'm sorry I can't offer you a seat, captain. As you see, my room has only the one chair and I have reason to doubt its sturdiness. As for why I invited you here, I thought we needed the utmost privacy for our discussion, which concerns Mr. Curtiss's blackmailing of you."

A flush of color rose to the captain's sallow cheeks.

"Has the little rat made you privy to his allegations, sir? I would have thought you above such slimy dealings."

Alvescot successfully concealed his annoyance. "On my first evening here I overheard the two of you in the spinney, where he extorted most of your quarter's allowance, I gather. I have no idea on what basis this blackmail is based, but I want it stopped. Mrs. Damery has enough on her hands without such goings on at Cutsdean." Turning away from him, the earl walked to the window where he said, "I searched Mr. Curtiss's room a few minutes ago and discovered one of your diaries hidden inside another book. It's there on the commode-table and I hope you will take it with you and make some effort to conceal it from him should he try to recover it. I haven't looked at it, but I presume it contains damaging material."

Captain Lawrence drew himself up to his full height and said harshly, "Only a snake such as Curtiss would find it damaging. He threatened to read it out to the company one evening if I didn't hand over any money I had. And having the diary back won't prevent him from making a to-do about it. He doesn't have to read it to make those silly women believe him." Nevertheless, the captain picked up the diary and rammed it into the pocket of his coat, glaring at the earl as he straightened. "Your retrieving the diary won't do the least good."

"I'm delighted that you appreciate my efforts," Alvescot murmured.

"I'd have appreciated your minding your own business."

"Then you intend to keep on supplying Mr. Curtiss with money forever? Supplying him with money from Mrs. Damery?" Alvescot's voice had taken on a sharp edge.

"It isn't only Mrs. Damery's money," the captain protested, indignant. "I have an income from the funds that supports me as well. There were plenty of years when I put my prize money in the funds to provide for my old age."

"Then what are you doing leeching from Mrs. Damery?"

"My income isn't sufficient to live in such a style as

prevails at Cutsdean. She supplies me with an income because of the services I render as an experienced older man: the guidance I provide and the protection she receives from my residing here."

Alvescot regarded him with astonishment. "Can you really believe that? Is it truly possible to delude yourself so thoroughly? And why do you think Mrs. Damery houses and provides an income to your two sisters, and Mabel Curtiss's children?"

"I haven't the slightest idea, and I'm sure I could care less," the captain retorted. "She's doing me no favors, young man. I could hardly be further from the sea, where my real interest lies. I stay here only because she has need of my presence. One could hardly consider Edward Curtiss a satisfactory male protector. He's more likely to lead the ravaging hordes over the place than protect it from them."

"Mrs. Damery has servants to protect her from the ravaging hordes, if there were any about to menace her," Alvescot snapped. "She houses her mother-in-law and you and all the Curtisses out of a feeling of family obligation. Nothing more. You are all a vast drain on her widow's jointure and your interference in the rearing of her children is unwelcome."

The captain stared him straight in the eye and growled, "I don't believe you."

"Ask her." Alvescot felt a stirring of doubt as soon as the words left his lips. Vanessa was not likely to be so rude after all this time as to tell Lawrence the truth. He made a slight tack in direction. "And I'm sure she wouldn't wish you to stay here under threat of being exposed by Edward. She's not a woman to ask such a sacrifice from you or anyone else."

"I told you, there's nothing to expose, save the interpretation of a few passages in the diary."

"And yet you are alarmed enough by the thought to pay Edward for his silence."

Captain Lawrence lifted his shoulders in an unsuccessful attempt at indifference. "There are a lot of vindictive people here who would be pleased to believe the worst of me. I prefer that they not be given the opportunity. What a man writes in the privacy of his own diary is not meant for the consumption of others. We all have doubts and I'm of the opinion that it does one more good than harm to express them in some form. Only a consummate villain like Edward would use them to his own advantage."

"So what do you intend to do about it?"

"If what you say is true—which I don't believe for a minute—I shall leave Cutsdean," the captain said disdainfully. "I have never intruded where I'm not welcome. On the other hand, if she wishes me to stay, I shall continue to placate the little weasel in the interest of maintaining my authority here, since without it I could not be so effective."

Effective at cowing little boys and stomping out of pianoforte performances? Alvescot struggled to keep his temper under control. "I'm to see Mrs. Damery at three in the Library. Why don't you join us there?"

"Very well." Lawrence turned on his heel without so much as a farewell nod and stomped from the room.

Alvescot considered the wisdom of trying to reach Vanessa before the confrontation, but decided there was not the time to explain himself properly. He knew she was going to be extremely angry with his presumption and interference; he also knew that she would be at a disadvantage being presented with so delicate an issue without warning. And he decided that her confusion was possibly the best means of accomplishing his end—getting Captain Lawrence to leave Cutsdean. Unfair to put her on the spot that way, of course, but potentially beneficial. Alvescot wasn't precisely proud of his reasoning, but by concentrating on the efficacy of his plan he was able to rationalize it almost to his satisfaction.

When the earl entered the Library to find Vanessa bent over some ledgers on the desk, he had grave misgivings. She looked tired and vulnerable, sitting there with her chin propped on her hand, lines of worry distorting the wide forehead. His awareness of her increased each time he saw her. At first she had seemed just another burdensome duty, a rather prickly young woman who continually had him at a disadvantage. Even then, he had noted her wry sense of humor and her unfailing sense of responsibility.

But recently (and aside from his ponderings of the previous evening) he had started to see her somewhat differently, as a woman alone in need of some human warmth. Her children provided it, of course, he reminded himself. And there was Paul Burford offering his friendship. So why did he think she needed him? He had only the advice of an experienced estate-owner to give, and he wasn't sure she was willing to accept his judgment on such matters—especially if it amounted to doubts of Burford. Alvescot flirted briefly with the idea that she was a stubborn woman, but his growing understanding of her wouldn't allow the concept to take root. She was determined, not obstinate. And she was lonely, though not alone. The earl didn't wish to consider the possibility that she still missed Frederick.

To halt the dirction of his thoughts he stepped into the room, causing her to glance up from her work. Before she could say anything, he spoke. "I've asked Captain Lawrence to join us."

"Captain Lawrence? I thought you wished to discuss the ledgers."

"I do, but this matter is just as pressing." He could already hear footfalls in the Entrance Hall and felt a sense of impending disaster. "Believe me, I regret handling the problem so you had to become involved. I——"

His words were cut off as the captain, holding himself with precise military bearing, entered the room, nodded coolly to the two of them, and closed the door firmly.

Alarmed now, Vanessa glanced at each of the men's grim faces and rose. "We'd do best to sit in the alcove," she suggested, leading the way.

When they were all seated, no one spoke and she folded her hands in her lap. This was no problem of her making, and she had no intention of being the one to probe for the wound. Eventually, Alvescot cleared his throat preparatory to speaking, but the captain rushed in first.

"This *gentleman*," he said, making a derogatory gesture toward the earl, "informs me that I am a drain on your widow's jointure and an interference in the raising of your children."

Vanessa felt sick. How could Alvescot do this to her?

But the captain wasn't finished. "He discounts the value of my guidance and protection. And he says you house me only out of a feeling of family obligation."

The quietly folded hands in her lap had become clenched and she stared accusingly at the earl, who immediately volunteered his defense.

"I'm afraid Captain Lawrence is speaking out of context, Mrs. Damery. The fact of the matter is that Edward Curtiss has been blackmailing him on account of something in one of his diaries that Edward had gotten hold of. I managed to recover the diary and restore it to Captain Lawrence, but he insists that Edward would still have this power over him, and he intends to continue allowing himself to be fleeced of his allowance as well as his income from the funds."

"That's my business!" the captain bellowed, slapping one hand down against his knee. "I can do what I like with my money."

The earl glared at him. "Mrs. Damery makes an allowance to Edward. If she wanted him to have more, she would give it to him herself, not expect you to deliver yours to him."

"Please, gentlemen," Vanessa begged. "I'd like to have a clearer understanding of precisely what's been happening here. How did you learn of this scheme, Lord Alvescot?"

"I overheard the two of them in the spinney the night of my arrival."

"And, Captain Lawrence, why is it that Edward could still blackmail you, even without the diary?"

"Because he could tell them what's in it," the captain muttered. "You don't have to have proof to defame someone's character."

Vanessa's brows rose. "Surely you don't think I would allow Edward to speak disrespectfully of you with or without the diary."

The captain scowled at her. "You wouldn't have anything to do with it. He could tell them at any time, and he probably will, now the diary's been removed from his room." He turned his scowl on Alvescot. "I'd have been better off if you'd never interfered."

Alvescot was surprised by Vanessa's vehemence. "Nonsense!" she exclaimed. "I won't have such things happening at Cutsdean. One word from him to anyone and he leaves here immediately. In fact, for his villainy I'm afraid he'll have to leave anyhow, though I can't think what I'm to tell his mother and his sister."

"Don't do that!" The captain looked shaken. "If you make him leave, there will be nothing to keep him from telling them."

Impatient, Vanessa shook her head. "I can't let him stay and continue to blackmail you, Captain Lawrence. I have no choice."

"There is one possibility," Alvescot smoothly interjected. "If Captain Lawrence were to leave Cutsdean and settle elsewhere, I doubt Edward would make the effort to follow him or harass him in any way. Edward's lazy. He only chose to extort money from him because he was close at hand. I would have a word with Edward and you may be sure not a breath of scandal would leave his lips if he wished to remain here."

Neither of his companions welcomed the suggestion, to judge by their hostile expressions. Vanessa's cold eyes positively froze him, but she was the first to speak.

"I think, Lord Alvescot, that if you were to leave us alone, the captain and I might reach some understanding."

Being dismissed like a schoolboy was not exactly the disaster Alvescot had foreseen. Embarrassment, tears, conciliation on Vanessa's part were more what he had had in mind. He rose, stiffly formal, bowed to the two of them, and left the room. There was no one in the Entrance Hall and he stood undecided for a moment. What he really needed was a ride to work off his spleen, but he couldn't make himself leave the house. He wanted to have an opportunity to explain to her, as soon as possible, that he had done what he had in her best interests.

After a while he wandered out onto the East Terrace, but not before he had stopped Tompkins, the butler, to inform him where he would be if his mistress should seek him out. Alvescot sat on the stone railing for half an hour, his long legs dangling almost but not quite to the flagstones. The weather had cooled, the wind had risen. Overhead clouds were beginning to gather, forerunner to a summer storm. Maybe she had no intention of allowing him to explain.

"Lord Alvescot." She was standing in the open doorway of the Saloon, frowning. "Could I see you for a moment?"

"Of course." He stepped down from the railing and followed her, to his surprise, to the Morning Room, her private sanctum. If he had bothered to picture it, the room would have been much as he found it—cozy, comfortable, sparsely furnished. Vanessa hesitated before taking a seat on the small sofa. Alvescot joined her there, knowing she had done it purposely to make their talk more informal, less abrasive. Which only let him know how truly annoyed she was.

"Captain Lawrence will be leaving," she announced, choosing a spot somewhere to the left of his head to address.

"I think it's for the best."

"I realize that's what you think, Lord Alvescot. And I realize you believe you acted on the most worthy of principles." She allowed her eyes to meet his. "Would you be interested in hearing how I feel the whole affair should have been handled?"

Since she had effectively taken the initiative away from him, he could see no option but to agree.

"Well, let me see. First, there is the matter of your overhearing the conversation between Captain Lawrence and Edward which led you to suspect what was going on. If you had been a visitor in Frederick's home, you would doubtless have taken the matter to him to sort out, rather than charging ahead on your own. You never for a moment considered approaching me, did you?"

"No."

"And yet I am mistress of Cutsdean. You were a new arrival and hardly knew how matters stood here. If you had brought the matter to my attention, I would have spoken to the captain to find out what was going on. If he refused to assist me, I would have approached Edward. I'm not afraid of any of these people, Lord Alvescot. They may be fools or worse, but they are my household and I expect to arrange affairs in my own way. I don't need to be protected."

Her words were spoken not with anger but with sadness. The rebuke held all the more power for being so gentle. Alvescot automatically reached for her hand, giving it a gentle squeeze and continuing to hold it. "I'm sorry. The business was so unsavory and you had so much to do already, I didn't want to bother you with it. It wasn't that I thought you couldn't handle it, Vanessa, but that I didn't want you to have to."

She stared at her hand in his, now resting on his thigh, but made no effort to retrieve it. And he had called her by her Christian name. "I . . . I have to learn to handle everything, the pleasant as well as the unpleasant. Otherwise, people *will* take advantage of me, as you think Paul is doing."

"No one else knew about this. I didn't intend to usurp your authority. I just wanted to help."

"By telling Captain Lawrence I didn't want him here?"

Alvescot grimaced. "I only did that because he was so incorrigible, Vanessa. He was wretchedly ungrateful for my efforts to free him from extortion, and then he had the nerve to tell me you made him an allowance because you wanted him here for his guidance and protection."

"Perhaps he believes that."

"If he does, he's a fool."

They glanced at each other and Vanessa chuckled. "All right, but you shouldn't have told him," she insisted. "It was vastly awkward for me to handle."

"How did you?"

She sighed. "I told him some of the same things I've just told you—that I don't need guidance and protection, that Cutsdean is my responsibility, that I appreciated his assistance, but that he shouldn't stay here on my account. And then I told him about a neighbor of ours in Somerset, an old seadog like himself. The name was familiar to him and he said he'd consider settling in that area, where he'd have someone to talk with about the old days, and the water close by. He's to go there for a visit. My parents will make him welcome."

"Surely you didn't say he could stay with them!"

"No, I told him about the local inn but suggested he call on them. He wants to tell his sisters only that he's going for a visit. If he decides to settle there permanently, he'll write to tell them and have me ship whatever belongings he doesn't take now."

"So you've found a way to help him save face." He pressed her hand again, though he hesitated to meet her eyes. "Would you let me speak to Edward?"

"Thank you, no." A faint smile appeared. "I'd prefer that Edward knew I was aware of his rotten behavior, Lord Alvescot."

"James. And I could tell him."

"In this instance, I will positively enjoy doing it myself. You saw the way he treated Captain Lawrence's horse. I have very little sympathy for him."

"I let him borrow Satin this afternoon."

"You must be mad!"

His engaging grin appeared. "Thank heaven we don't stand on ceremony with one another." But the grin faded and his face became almost stern. "Satin won't stand for any of Edward's sloppy riding habits. I'd be surprised if Edward didn't take a fall or two if he tried them."

"Edward isn't a fast learner," she admitted, her eyes amused. Reluctantly, she withdrew her hand from his. "Shall we discuss your questions about the estate? We seem to have come rather far from the original purpose of our meeting."

The rapport between them was broken. Alvescot could see that she was already preparing to ward off any damaging blows he might deliver. Not that she had become defensive, exactly, but now she was wary, businesslike. This was not a time for friendship to intervene. Was that what they had exhibited while they sat there with her hand in his? A sort of cousinly camaraderie? Neither of them was willing to examine it too closely, he assumed as she moved to her desk and indicated a chair across from her. Now they were co-trustees of Cutsdean, where personalities and emotions didn't intrude. He took a list of questions from his waistcoat pocket and put it on the desk between them.

"First, there's the matter of the drainage," he began.

TEN

Vanessa sat alone in the Morning Room for some time after Alvescot left her. His questions about the estate management had been probing and she had found it necessary to give them her whole attention. Not that they had raised any doubts in her mind of Paul Burford's honesty or his expertise, but they had made her concentrate on matters in hand to provide the right answers. She felt she had helped acquit Paul Burford in the exchange, that Alvescot was coming to believe her evaluation of the estate manager almost against his will. It would have justified his trip to Cutsdean to have found the place a shambles and taken over the obligation of setting matters right, but Vanessa thought he was open-minded enough to accept the real state of affairs.

His interference in the blackmailing she found understandable, though upsetting. Vanessa would not have liked to handle it herself, but she thought she should have. It was a great nuisance having all the obligations of a man laid on you, when you suffered from all the restrictions of a woman. Her upbringing had not prepared her to take charge of more than the household. Directing the servants, ordering the meals, planning entertainments—for all these she had received instruction from her mother. But no one had bothered to explain the more involved affairs of an estate—the expenses and income, the laborers and their cottages, the tenant farmers and the rotation of crops, the number of livestock which a field could support, the essential matter of drainage.

All these things she had abruptly come to deal with af-

ter Frederick's death, when she saw that the estate was
daily deteriorating under the old estate manager. No decision in her life had been more difficult than that to turn
the man off, and to have to repeat that depressing duty
twice more. Did men find such chores a burden to their
minds and their hearts? Old Fletcher had regarded her so
incredulously when she spoke to him that she had found
herself tripping over her own tongue. She had worried
about damaging his self-esteem, taking away his liveli-
hood, and only by steeling herself with thoughts of her
obligation to the children was she able to go through with
the unhappy task.

Vanessa sighed and turned her gaze to the park beyond
the terrace. The scent of newly mown grass wafted in on
the slightest of breezes and she could hear the murmur of
the gardeners' voices further along the terrace where they
tended the riot of summer blooms which she daily
gathered to liven the various rooms of Cutsdean. The
Morning Room was her favorite of the public rooms and
she had insisted, with great effort, on keeping it unin-
fringed upon by the other members of her household.
Why had she so easily allowed Alvescot to join her here?
She had steadfastly ignored the murmurs of discontent
over her arrangement which came from the others. After
all, there were rooms enough at Cutsdean to supply the
other residents with perfectly acceptable alternatives.

And she never skimped on the fires in cooler weather.
If someone felt an urge to use the Library, even when
there were fires in the Saloon and the Velvet Drawing
Room, she never objected to another fire being laid.
Sometimes, when she considered the expense of having
fires in each of their bedrooms, and any public rooms to
which their whimsy might take them, she felt exasperated
to the point of outrage. One would think the lot of them
came from luxurious households where no measure of
economy had ever been taken.

It had not occurred to Vanessa, until Alvescot came,
that perhaps she shouldn't accept her parents' decree on
the "guests" without questioning it. Oh, she did feel a certain amount of obligation to Frederick's relations, when
she had so much and they so little. Except for Hortense.

There was no way Vanessa could include her mother-in-law in the category of penurious relations. And now it had turned out that the captain, too, had resources of his own. But Mabel and her children had nothing, literally. No home, no income.

And they were doing nothing to better their position, unless you considered Edward's blackmailing a step in the right direction. Mabel's plot to encourage Alvescot for Louisa was patently doomed to failure, and in the meantime poor William Oldcastle was being further and further alienated from the woman who really *should* be his bride, after twelve years of courtship. Vanessa was inclined to believe that Oldcastle and Louisa were actually quite right for each other, everything taken into consideration.

With Captain Lawrence leaving, Vanessa took the opportunity to reassess her position. Decidedly, there was no need for Hortense to remain at Cutsdean. In spite of what the elder Fulbrooks said on the subject of kinship and charity and a vast number of other virtuous subjects, Hortense had a home of her own in Basingstoke and an income to more than manage it. Her continued presence at Cutsdean was entirely a matter of prestige. The old woman had presided here until Frederick's marriage, and she would wallow in Cutsdean's glow for the rest of her life if she were not prevented. Allowing Hortense to take advantage of her was not, Vanessa determined, a virtuous duty but a criminal mistake. She would have to go.

Pulling open a drawer of the delicate Pembroke desk, Vanessa drew out a sheet of paper and scratched a memo to herself: *Find out when lease on Basingstoke property expires.* Surely that was the first step to take, and she (not Alvescot!) would be the one to take it.

Then there were the Curtisses. They were a much trickier proposition. If she hadn't promised the captain otherwise, Vanessa would have liked to tell Edward to pack his bags and get out. He had forfeited any claim on her generosity by his underhanded doings. But he would have to stay, at least for the time being.

The point to concentrate on was Louisa. If Louisa could be married off to William, it would remove at least three people from Cutsdean. Edward might or might not go, of his own accord, but Mabel would undoubtedly follow her daughter into Suffolk. And how deliciously far away Suffolk sounded right now! On her list, Vanessa wrote: *Get Louisa and William engaged*. She had no idea, as yet, how she was going to accomplish this, but she was determined to do it.

Captain Lawrence's departure would mean that the Blue Velvet Bedroom would be vacant for Lord Alvescot to move into. Vanessa was sure he would appreciate the added space and wondered, briefly, if his interference had had anything to do with this goal. And holding hands with her! Vanessa felt a self-mocking grin twist her lips. The poor man was only trying to work his way into her good graces so she'd give him a better room! *That* she had no difficulty believing. Vanessa was willing to admit to herself that she liked the earl, liked him perhaps too well, but there was no denying he had a decidedly high concept of his own consequence. He was, of course, above her touch, a fact of which her parents would be willing enough to remind her, but there was no reason not to strive for his friendship. As co-trustees, they shared a large responsibility and if they could work together on it amicably, so much the better.

Vanessa shoved her short list back in the drawer and left the Morning Room in search of the housekeeper. Mrs. Howden's office was toward the rear of the main floor, next to a door which led directly out to the stable drive. The door was seldom used by anyone but the servants and Vanessa was surprised to see it open to admit Edward. The curly beaver hat he had worn on leaving was a tattered wreck in his hand, and his clothes were dust-covered and torn in three places that she could see. A sure sign that Satin had thrown him at least once, she observed, feeling a certain satisfaction in the uncharitable thought.

At sight of her, he brushed ineffectually at his buckskins, with no worthwhile result save the cloud of dust that emerged. His blond hair was dampened with perspiration and looked gritty with dirt. He was obviously annoyed to have her see him in this condition, and made to pass her as though she didn't exist.

"I want a word with you, Edward," she said.

"When I've changed," he growled.

"No, now." She opened the door to the plate room on the opposite site of the hall and waved him into it. For a moment he looked as though he would refuse, but the uncompromising light in her eyes decided him to humor her.

The plate room was long and narrow, consisting entirely of walls full of cupboards and a stool on which a footman could sit to polish silver or wipe china. Vanessa didn't bother to seat herself on the stool, but stood in the dim light grimly regarding Edward, who had his back turned toward her.

"What has come to light about you today I find deeply disturbing," Vanessa began. "If I were to act entirely on my own conscience, I would ask you to leave Cutsdean immediately."

Edward continued to keep his back to her, muttering, "What the devil are you talking about?"

"I'm talking about your extortion of money from Captain Lawrence."

He swung around to face her. "What's the old hypocrite been telling you? Not that he was a coward in battle, I daresay," he sneered.

Vanessa eyed him coldly. "The *only* way you will remain at Cutsdean is if you never mention that matter again. One word of it to anyone, and you will leave here permanently, with not a penny from me. Remember that, Edward, because I mean it. I have enough to deal with without your slimy machinations. And be warned that I shall in future keep a wary eye out for any dishonest activity on your part. You would do well to look about you for some opportunity of honorable employment, because I don't intend to support you forever now this circumstance has come to light."

Edward was not convinced as yet that he couldn't bluff his way out of this particular hole. "Would you take that old curmudgeon's word against mine?"

"Yes," she said flatly, "but I'm not taking his word, Edward. Lord Alvescot overheard you in the spinney the first night he was here. Today he searched your room and found Captain Lawrence's diary."

"He searched my room!" A black scowl descended on Edward's face and his fists clenched tightly at his sides. "How dare he?"

"Lord Alvescot does not approve of blackmail any more than I do. He didn't read the diary, nor did I. Captain Lawrence will be leaving for a trip to Somerset immediately, and if you value 'your room' here, you won't mention a word about any of this. That's all I have to say to you, Edward."

Vanessa opened the door behind her and left before Edward could attempt any justification of his actions. Just being in the same room with him made her flesh crawl. But by the time she reached her bedchamber, her righteous indignation had given way to a sort of nervous shuddering. Vanessa had found, on more than one previous occasion, that she felt a sort of repulsion with herself when she looked back on incidents of this nature. From whence did this hardness, this coldness come that she displayed? Her reaction to it was a case of jangled nerves that took several hours to control. And yet, chastising Edward was something she had to do, and in no mealy-mouthed way that would let him think he could get away with the same sort of misbehavior again. Each time, though, she wondered what had happened to the sweet girl Frederick had married, the dutiful daughter her parents had raised. Was she to become a mean, vindictive creature like Hortense? A rude, self-centered woman such as Mabel? The thought terrified her, and she went to the children, where she could be loving and kind, just as soon as her hands had stopped shaking.

Over the next few days, Alvescot spent as much time with Vanessa as he reasonably could, riding out with her, talking in the evenings, sharing anecdotes from his childhood, welcoming any revelations she made about herself. His attachment to her grew, and with it his determination to see that she obtained some sort of peace at Cutsdean. He would be less heavy-handed in his approach in the future, he vowed, but he *would* do something about the crowd that remained at Cutsdean. Captain Lawrence left (and Alvescot got his bedroom), but Hortense and the Curtisses remained, and he wanted to see them removed.

Apparently Vanessa had spoken with Edward, but Alvescot could see no lessening of the young man's jaunty obliviousness to the censure. The earl's only consolation here was learning that Edward had returned from his ride on Satin looking totally disheveled. Edward never requested the loan of a horse from him again, and with Captain Lawrence taking his horse, and Vanessa's edict still in effect, Edward had taken to hiring a dilapidated bay from a neighboring farmer and disappearing for long stretches of time.

Despite Alvescot's nighttime encounter with Louisa, she was totally unembarrassed with him, only cringing at her mother's strictures to ignore William Oldcastle. Alvescot did what he could to promote a romance between them, but Mabel was working equally hard to destroy it, and Louisa's spirits were obviously flagging. Since Alvescot had not spent any time in Basingstoke, he allowed Mabel to push him into taking Louisa one morning in his curricle. The earl considered this a diversionary tactic, a chance to get Louisa's mind off her problems. He also hoped she would help him choose gifts for his godchildren, something which had not occurred to him before coming to Cutsdean. He was, almost secretly, spending a good deal of time with the children, working for their trust and affection. It wouldn't hurt to cement their growing friendship with a few presents, he assured himself.

After being overcast for two days, the weather had cleared and the drive promised to be accompanied with brilliant skies and a warm sun. Louisa had tied her bonnet ribbons securely under her chin before allowing the earl to hand her into the sporting vehicle. "I'll remember your thread, Vanessa," she promised solemnly.

Vanessa, who was at the stables to go riding with John, smiled and admonished Alvescot to drive carefully.

"I will," he assured her. "If our errands take longer than expected, we may have something to eat at the inn, so don't await luncheon for us," he said as his groom hopped up behind and he urged his pair forward.

His tone was light, but Louisa glanced up at him from under the brim of her bonnet, trying to assess the mysterious tension she sensed between the earl and Vanessa. Her uncanny emotional antennae were vibrating with it, and she wondered at his brooding expression as they moved off down the drive.

"Vanessa is a very good person, you know," she informed him. "She has a lot of responsibilities, what with the children and the estate. You're not angry with her, are you?"

Surprised, Alvescot transferred his attention from his pair. "Angry? Not at all. I quite admire the way she's taken charge. Why should you think I was angry with her?"

"I don't know. It was just a feeling," Louisa admitted. "Not anger, necessarily. Just some . . . oh, I don't know, some emotion sort of echoing between you. As often as not," she said with a sigh, "that's anger—in my family, at least. Though this didn't feel quite like that."

Alvescot considered it wisest to change the subject, and he began to relate just what kinds of things he was doing at Cutsdean as co-trustee—the two years' worth of accounts to investigate, his survey of the estate itself, his visits to the farms and his talks with the tenants. He did not actually expect Louisa to be interested in these subjects, but she nodded her head all through his recital, saying abruptly at its conclusion, "My father used to do that."

"I was sorry to hear of his death," Alvescot interjected politely.

Louisa's lips puckered thoughtfully, and then she dropped a small bombshell. "I don't think he's dead."

"I beg your pardon?"

"Well, I know he left a note saying he was going to kill himself, but I think I should have known if he died. You see, when other people have died, I've felt it, even before I heard of it, you know."

When his sophisticated air deserted him, Alvescot looked astonishingly boyish. His brows now sprang up and his eyes widened, the corners of his mouth drooped and the tips of his ears reddened just the tiniest bit. "Do you have some reason, other than your 'feelings' for believing him to be alive?" he demanded.

"Oh, no," she replied simply, adjusting her hands in her lap and gazing out over the fields they passed. "I knew when nanny died, long before the letter arrived. You just feel sort of different about someone when they're dead. I even knew when the dog was run down by the stage."

There didn't seem to be anything for him to respond to her disclosures of being psychic. And it was a truly absurd idea, anyhow! If she was so damned psychic, why did she have so much trouble finding her way around Cutsdean? She could have sensed where William was and imposed upon him in her nude state, and left Alvescot out of the matter entirely!

They drove in silence for some time before he came out of his revery with a start. "I beg your pardon! Would you mind if we went to the inn first? Or better yet, I could leave you at a shop and join you in a few minutes."

"Whatever you wish. I have a number of purchases to make at Newsholme's."

"Splendid!" His enthusiasm was out of all proportion to the simplicity of the arrangement, but he didn't seem to notice. "And I wonder if you would point out Aunt Damery's house to me. I'm not sure I would remember it."

Louisa indicated a charming, older building as they approached, and he realized he couldn't possibly have forgotten it. The property sat slightly apart from the town, on the edge, surrounded by its own lawns and a stone wall with gates. Alvescot slowed his pair as they passed, noting the size and condition. Certainly it was sufficiently large and grand enough for anyone without grandiose pretentions. And convenient, with the shops so close by and a medical practitioner practically across the road. Really, there was no reason why Hortense shouldn't return there, except for her having let it out.

Aside from being an ancient market town with a good trade in woolen and silk goods, Basingstoke boasted few attractions. There was the ancient hospital of St. John

Baptist for aged and infirm priests, and the parish church
of St. Michael, plus the ruins of an old guild chapel in a
cemetery dating back to the early eleventh century. Otherwise, there were only the usual shops, and even those
were not of a type to attract much attention. The earl set
his companion down at Newsholme's, promising to join
her as soon as possible, and drove the curricle to the Red
Lion.

What he had in mind was a private parlor for himself,
where he could write a few lines to his solicitor in London. The innkeeper, a Mrs. Wilstrop, was more than
willing to accommodate his demands for writing paper
and pen, an inkstand, and some sanding powder, but she
provided more. Mrs. Wilstrop proved to be a fountain of
information.

"From Cutsdean, did you say? Why, bless my soul,
you're Frederick Damery's cousin, aren't you? I remember when you were in leading strings! And later, why, you
cut almost as fine a figure as Mr. Damery himself." She
sighed, a whoosh of air that appeared to momentarily de-
flate her substantial person. "Poor lad. Oh, an awful thing
it was, him losing his life that way without never seeing
his daughter. Saw his son, of course, but not all that
much. He was forever away fighting. Hard on Mrs. Damery. His wife, I mean. Not his mother." Her expression
indicated an utter lack of sympathy for the older woman.
"A great pity the old lady moved back to Cutsdean and
invited all her relations to join her."

"Yes, a great pity," Alvescot agreed. "The captain has
just left for Somerset, where he may settle."

Mrs. Wilstrop eyed him speculatively. "Mrs. Damery
has taken hold of the estate now, but it can't be easy to
get rid of all those people."

"No, it's not easy." Alvescot drew his gloves slowly
through his hands, frowning at a slight tear in one of
them, probably a result of his collision with Edward. "Do
you happen to know Edward Curtiss? I understand he's
frequently in town."

Mrs. Wilstrop snorted her disgust. "He has a woman
here, a married woman with a husband who's away most

of the time. And he gambles and drinks. Altogether a wicked man, if I may be so bold as to say so."

"Quite." Alvescot smiled at her quivering indignation as she took his driving cloak and gloves, and led him to a private parlor off the entryway. One window was open and a curtain fluttered in the breeze. Mrs. Wilstrop indicated a small writing desk, scarred but serviceable, in an alcove toward the rear. "You'll find what you need there, sir. Did you want a tankard of ale?"

"Thank you, no." As she turned to leave, he spoke abruptly. "There is one thing, though. Mrs. Hortense Damery's house here in town. Do you know who's let it?"

"A man by the name of Jackson. He don't spend much time there any more." She pursed her lips and her eyes became thoughtful. "I doubt he intends to renew the lease when it comes due next month. The folks hereabouts didn't just take him to their hearts, so to speak. I guess he expected a little more respect for having the grandest home in town. We're simple folk, but not given to toadying to some overblown stranger. He don't use the shops here, and he's nevet set foot in the church. Who needs him?"

Satisfied, the earl nodded. "Thank you, Mrs. Wilstrop. You've been a great help."

His pen scratched quickly across the sheet for several minutes. Even if Louisa's impression was wholly in her head, the strange story of her father's death could bear some investigation. Alvescot might have considered going to London himself, but he found he didn't want to leave Cutsdean yet, and he had confidence that his solicitor would give the necessary attention to his request. When he had finished the letter, he sanded and sealed it before seeking out Mrs. Wilstrop, who, in appreciation of the coins he pressed on her, offered to carry it herself to the receiving office.

At Newsholme's he found Louisa debating between two identical colors of thread which matched the sample she had brought. Alvescot patiently helped her make the decision and trusted to her choice of toys for the children since her childlike delight in them could be no less than John's or Catherine's. He was tempted to buy a charming parasol he saw on display for Vanessa but resisted the urge, only to have it catch Louisa's eye. Her gaze was so whimsically eager that he hadn't the heart to deny her, having seen how few were the coins in her purse. Louisa rushed into a flow of grateful words.

"It's no more than a trinket," he muttered, "in appreciation for your assistance in buying the children's toys."

What Mabel Curtiss would say of the gift he preferred not to imagine.

ELEVEN

When Alvescot had driven away in the curricle with Louisa, Vanessa tried to turn her full attention to her son. It would have been pleasant, she admitted, to have been the one who set off with the earl on his excursion to Basingstoke, but she had been in the Breakfast Parlor when Mabel made the push for her daughter. Vanessa was appreciative of Alvescot's efforts to maintain some kind of peace within the household.

Louisa, she knew, had no interest whatsoever in their aristocratic guest nor could she believe for a moment that Alvescot entertained the slightest thought of an alliance with Louisa. So their excursion was nothing more than the most ordinary errand trip, which would give Alvescot a chance to see Basingstoke again, and Louisa an opportunity to putter about the goods in the shops, a chief delight with her despite her lack of funds for actually purchasing anything.

The overcast weather of the last few days had kept little John close to the stables in his rides, and now he urged Vanessa to ride with him to the far boundaries of the estate on the south. Their direction kept them in sight of Alvescot's curricle for some time, as he tooled his pair along the leafy lane which skirted Cutsdean. Unfortunately, John noticed this as well.

"Why don't we go through the West Gate and ride along with them, Mama?" he asked, eager to force himself on his godfather's attention as often as possible.

"No, love, we wouldn't be able to keep up with Lord Alvescot's pair. Rollo would like our ride a great deal better, I think, if we go down to the stream. There never was such a pony for walking in the water!"

Easily distracted, John agreed that Rollo would especially like going in the stream, but part of his mind was still on Alvescot and he asked, "How long is he staying, Mama? The earl, I mean. I thought he was only come for a short stay."

"Well, he hasn't said when he'll be leaving, John. He and I are trustees of your papa's estate, and he's looking into matters here."

"What's a trustee?"

"A person who looks out for your interests in a piece of property." Vanessa smiled at his look of confusion. "One day Cutsdean will be yours, but someone has to take care of it in the meantime, until you're old enough to do it yourself."

"I thought Mr. Burford did that."

"Mr. Burford makes plans for the estate and carries them out, but I'm responsible, with Lord Alvescot, for deciding what plans to use. I direct the work Mr. Burford does because I'm the one who wants to make sure your inheritance will come to you." The boy still looked uncertain, so Vanessa said, "It's like taking care of you and Catherine. I'm your mother and I'm responsible for your health and happiness, but I can't be with you all the time, so Lucy takes care of you under my direction."

"I see," John said, nodding wisely as his pony jogged across the meadow. "Since Papa can't be here to take care of me with you, Lord Alvescot is sort of a second father for me."

Startled, Vanessa protested, "Only in a *legal* way, you know. But then, he's your godfather, too, which is sort of a *religious* guardianship. And he's your father's cousin, of course, so he's related to you as well."

"There, you see?" the little boy piped. "He's connected with me in every sort of way, so I shall think of him as my . . . my *step*-papa."

Color rose in Vanessa's cheeks and she agitatedly toyed with the reins in her hands. "No, John, that would be inaccurate. The only person who can be your step-papa is a man to whom your mother is married after your father.

You should think of Lord Alvescot as your godfather, since that is what he is."

"Oh, very well." John was tired of the subject and gave Rollo an energetic kick to start him trotting toward the row of trees along the bank of the stream.

Now why should his saying that have upset me, Vanessa admonished herself. Obviously, he's heard the term "stepfather" and simply thought it would fit in this instance. He's a child, and as a child I'm probably lucky he didn't ask me something like, "Well, why don't you marry him, then?" Not that I couldn't have answered a question like that. I would simply have said. . . . Various possibilities came half-formed into her mind, but none of them seemed both appropriate and wholly honest. In the end, as she and John dismounted near the stream, she decided she was infinitely grateful to him for not posing the question, and she would be careful in future to avoid the subject entirely.

John walked along holding Rollo's reins while the pony splashed up and down the stream. The two of them made so much noise Vanessa was not aware of Paul Burford's presence until he had ridden quite close to them. She watched him spring down from his horse and tousle John's hair before approaching her with a smile.

"I thought I might find you here. For the last few days I've wanted a word with you, but there never seemed a good opportunity."

His face was mildly perturbed and Vanessa said, "Come and sit with me. I just want to keep an eye on John so he doesn't do anything outrageous."

Paul tied his horse to a sapling and crouched down near her, brushing at a twig that had stuck to his buckskin breeches. There was a layer of dust on his brown topboots, but he paid no heed to it as he turned thoughtful eyes to her. "It's a little difficult to broach the matter, Vanessa, because I know Alvescot is your co-trustee and he has every right to go into estate records as thoroughly as he wishes. And you mustn't think he's been in any way impolite or condescending to me. That's not at all the case. But he seems to have some bee in his bonnet (so to speak) about my management of Cutsdean."

A fly was buzzing about his head and he swatted at it impatiently, as though the distraction might prevent him from stating his case cogently. "I could understand his suspicion at first. After all, our expenses have been high for the last year, though not out of proportion to what we can expect from the harvest. He's seen all that now, but he continues to go into everything with a fine-toothed comb. At this rate, he could be here a month."

"Yes, I know it's a little nerve-racking." She brushed a strand of black hair away from her cheek. "But he hasn't found anything whatsoever amiss, Paul. Not that I expected him to! I mean, I really believe he's coming to realize that you've done wonders for Cutsdean. He didn't understand the condition into which the land had gotten, you know, or the need for repairs to the cottages. You may be sure he wouldn't allow such a state of affairs to exist at St. Aldwyns. And he was such a good friend of Frederick's that I think it's a bit difficult for him to understand how my husband could have permitted the neglect during those years."

Paul nodded and turned his gaze to John and Rollo, both now well splashed with water. "I don't think Alvescot disapproves of anything I've done here, or my plans for the next few years. What he can't seem to decide is whether I've diverted any of the Cutsdean resources to my own estate."

"Oh, Paul, you mustn't think that. I'm sure he knows better."

"But there's no way to prove it, Vanessa," he said with a shrug. "Of course it would have been the easiest thing in the world to divert a few bags of seed to Buckland, or made off with a few chickens. I wonder if he thinks I tucked them under my coat."

Vanessa was relieved to see a grin transform his face. "Or under your hat," she laughed. "No, Paul, I'm convinced he doesn't have the least doubt of your honesty any more, or your ability."

"Then why does he continue to go into the books and roam about the estate?" Paul asked, exasperated.

"It gives him an excuse to stay." Vanessa regretted her

words the moment they left her mouth. His brows shot up and she hastened to clarify her meaning. "He has taken it into his head that it's his duty to see me rid of all my undesirable guests, you see. On the very first day he came, he assured me that Frederick would not have allowed all of them to settle here, and he considers their imposition an affront to me, or him, or the universe, I'm not sure which. Anyhow, he was behind Captain Lawrence's leaving, and I very much fear he's intent on staying until he clears Cutsdean of the lot of them."

"I shouldn't think that was his business."

"No, it isn't, but he won't admit to that being his reason for staying, and I can't very well ask him to leave. So I'm very much afraid you will have to put up with his wandering around and poking his nose into things for a while longer, Paul."

The young man studied her rather intently for a moment, noting the color in her cheeks and the way her head was turned slightly away from him. There seemed to be more to Alvescot's stay than she was willing to admit, but he hadn't the right to probe further. He rose to his feet without further ado, brushing his hair back with one arm before settling his hat on his head.

"You know I'm at your service, Vanessa, and I'm perfectly willing to answer Alvescot's questions for as long as he sees fit to ask them. I hope you're right that he doesn't really suspect me of any misappropriation of goods. And if he's successful in finding new homes for your guests, all the better."

"It's something I should do myself, if I wish it done," she answered, a trifle stiffly. "I don't know that I am entirely convinced I'm not responsible for some of them."

He gave her a mocking glance as he swung up onto his horse. "They're such a grateful bunch. . . ."

"True charity is its own reward," she retorted, but her eyes were playful rather than serious. Vanessa watched him wave and ride off before she called to John. "We'll have to go now if we want to be on time for luncheon, my love. Don't forget to change into dry shoes when we get home."

Vanessa was coming down the stairs from changing her
clothes when Alvescot and Louisa entered the house.
Louisa was reluctantly closing her parasol, which she had
used to protect herself from the sun all the way from the
stables. Alvescot had offered to leave her at the front
door, but as this provided no opportunity to use the new
trinket, Louisa had assured him she preferred to walk
back from the stables with him.

"Look what Lord Alvescot has given me!" Louisa
cried, once again unfurling the parasol. "Is it not the most
charming one you've ever seen?"

It was, which only made it harder for Vanessa to say
so. "Lovely," she murmured, not meeting the earl's eyes.
"Imagine finding so luscious a sunshade in Basingstoke."

"Yes, that is just what I was telling him. But it was
right there on display, Vanessa. And I very nearly didn't
see it myself, except that Lord Alvescot was so taken with
it."

William Oldcastle was just beginning to round the corner of the stairs, and Louisa called up to him with great
eagerness. "Oh, William, you will be so pleased for me. I
have needed a parasol for the longest time. I daresay you
recall that my own is quite tattered. And look what we
have found in Basingstoke, of all places. Mama always
says you cannot find anything of the least merit at
Newsholme's. But even in London I've not seen anything
to equal it."

It should be noted that Louisa did not actually say, to
William, that Alvescot had bought it for her. In his
present state of dejection, however, he never for a moment doubted it, and the gift loomed large in his eyes.
Over the years he had given Louisa a few trinkets, to be
sure, but nothing which had caught her enthusiasm in
quite the same way as the parasol. Her eyes glowed with
delight and her cheeks were pink with pleasure. The fine,
long fingers that called forth such exquisite music from
the pianoforte were now stroking the polished handle and
the blue silk fabric.

All this caused William a real pang of regret. He alone
was supposed to provide Louisa with such treasures. To
him the gift was a symbol of something more—a sign that

Alvescot was decidedly courting "his" intended. The fact that he had never once, over the twelve years, actually brought himself to offer for her was entirely beside the point. It was *understood* that they would be married, and here was Louisa accepting gifts from a perfect stranger. The very thought made William's choler rise, and he snapped, "I've seen dozens exactly like it in London. It's probably an imitation, though, if you've bought it here in Basingstoke. They do that sort of thing, you know," he added, with a decided air of knowledge.

Louisa was stung by his callousness. How could he try to take the pleasure out of the one treat she had had in the last year? Tears welled up in her vague blue eyes and threatened to spill over onto suddenly pale cheeks. Clutching the parasol tightly to her, she stumbled blindly away from the group in the Entrance Hall and ran awkwardly up the stairs. The sound of a heart-wrenching sob drifted down to the others.

"I say," William protested, guiltily pulling at his neckcloth to ease it about his neck.

"Gudgeon," Alvescot muttered, stomping past Oldcastle and giving only a brief nod to Vanessa before he, too, ascended the staircase.

Neither of the two left, Vanessa or William, was sure whether the earl intended to go to his room or to follow Louisa. It seemed unlikely he would do the latter. In fact, it seemed unlikely (to Vanessa) that in her current state Louisa would even be able to find her own room. Vanessa hesitated at the foot of the stairs, uncertain whether to follow, but decided against it. What could she say?

Though William and Louisa frequently bickered, she had never seen Louisa so overset before. Arguing was one of the ways William and Louisa communicated, and though it was not a method to be recommended for everyone, it often suited their purposes well, since William did not like to be contradicted, and Louisa was not willing to submit to his ideas without expressing her own. In Vanessa's considered opinion, neither of them had any convictions worth fighting for, but she did like to see Louisa stand up for her notions, especially when William's were particularly idiotic.

Vanessa was exasperated with William. If the man didn't intend to marry Louisa, why in heaven's name was he so obstinately refusing to uproot himself from Cutsdean? And if he did intend to marry her, why didn't he act like it? She turned to him now with a frown. "I'm surprised you'd be so unkind as to dash Louisa's pleasure that way, William."

"She shouldn't have accepted a gift from him," William retorted, sulky. "It's not proper. She hardly knows the man."

It was on the tip of her tongue to ask, "How long do you have to know a man? Twelve years?" but she refrained, saying mildly, "They're related, William. They were both cousins of Frederick's. If Lord Alvescot wished to indulge her with such a small gift, I'm sure he had every right to do so, and she to accept. No one else indulges Louisa. She never has a pence of pocket money with Edward so expensive as he is."

"Oh, yes, Edward," the man said scornfully. "He would suck a turnip dry. I have every reason to believe he was extorting money from Captain Lawrence, you know, and I doubt the old gentleman will return here after his visit in Somerset."

Vanessa was staring at him in astonishment. "If you thought there was something amiss, why didn't you do anything about it?"

"I tried to talk to the old fellow," William protested, aggrieved at this new attack. "He wouldn't admit a thing, said I was talking nonsense, as I always did. Well, what was I supposed to say to that, I ask you? It's a great pity Louisa has such a rascal for a brother," he added darkly. "Perhaps Lord Alvescot will like to keep an eye on him, and be constantly pestered for money. The fellow's pockets are always to let and it's his own dissipated ways that account for it. No one else is to blame."

With an abrupt bow to her, William stalked off in the direction of the Saloon. Though it was almost time to assemble for luncheon, Vanessa didn't follow him. Instead, she made her way to the Morning Room where she could have a few minutes' peace in which to reflect on what he'd said, because it seemed very important to her. Here, in a few thrown-away sentences, said in annoyance and probably regretted afterward, William Oldcastle had laid forth a spectacularly valid reason for never allying himself with Louisa in the course of twelve years.

For all his limited insight and his discouraging lack of tact, William was intelligent enough not to be deceived in Louisa's brother. Edward had probably approached William countless times for loans, had possibly even tried to extort money from him over the years. It was one thing to be a suitor; quite another to be a husband. If William married Louisa, he would be taking on the responsibility of Edward permanently.

Vanessa could imagine how large this aspect loomed in William's mind. Edward was likely, given time, to disgrace himself, and bring disgrace on any family with whom he was connected. William was proud of his lineage, too proud to wish to see his name in any way besmirched by the likes of Edward Curtiss. And say what you would, if his wife's brother was a rat, sooner or later it was going to reflect on Louisa and consequently on her husband.

To say nothing of the financial drain. If Louisa married William, her mother would go with her to Suffolk. And aside from Mabel's other annoying propensities, her adoration of her only son was almost an obsession. There was every possibility she would divert every pound on which she could get her hands to her son, whether he followed them to Suffolk or set up on his own somewhere. (Vanessa didn't like to even consider the possibility that he would try to stay at Cutsdean.) So William would find himself in the position of supporting a very expensive, and a very unethical, Edward Curtiss. The prospect was not tempting.

Everyone was assembled for the meal when Vanessa joined them. William stood at the windows looking out; Louisa sat on a sofa with downcast eyes and pale cheeks. Alvescot was impatiently listening to Mabel's sly hints as to the import of his gift to her daughter. Edward was quarreling with Hortense about the cut of his coat. A perfectly ordinary family gathering, Vanessa decided ruefully. Alvescot had once told her he thought perhaps this unpleasant time might be smoothed over by having a few dishes of fruit or nuts placed at their disposal to ward off the hunger they exhibited, but that was before he realized they always reacted this way to one another's company— hungry or full.

At the table she was aware of Alvescot's eyes frequently on her during the meal. His face, though, was unreadable. Even the expressive eyebrows were immobile. Vanessa had begun to distinguish several of his moods by those brows. Raised, lowered, drawn in, askew, they gave information more accurate than his lips, which were as often as not a simple, straight, uncompromising line. Vanessa didn't think the earl was aware of how much the eyebrows gave away, and she had no intention of telling him. But the one thing she wanted to know most was totally inexpressible by the twin fringes. His eyes, the more likely repository of this information, were invariably guarded.

But he sought her after the meal, saying, "I wonder if I might have a word with you. It won't take long; I don't want to keep you from the children."

She led him to the Morning Room, though this time she seated herself in one of the rose damask-covered chairs instead of the sofa. The chair opposite reminded Alvescot forcefully of the one that had collapsed under him in his room that first day and he regarded it with grave suspicion. The sofa had been such a comfortable place to sit, when they had talked there before.

"I hope you won't mind, but I don't trust your chairs," he said apologetically, heading for the sofa. "They're a little fragile for my taste. Won't you sit with me here?"

"Mrs. Howden told me one of the chairs from your room had mysteriously turned up broken in a storage room, Lord Alvescot," Vanessa replied, moving easily over to the sofa to seat herself. "Ah, the scratch on your face that first day. My, it was quite an introduction to Cutsdean, wasn't it?"

"James," he reminded her. "Yes, I cannot say it was one of the most pleasant days I've spent. I didn't know Bibury had put it in a storage room, though I didn't instruct him to do otherwise. I should have had it repaired for you."

Vanessa waved a dismissing hand. "It's of no importance. What was it you wished to discuss with me?"

Alvescot noted that she had her hands clasped rather firmly in her lap, so he leaned back at his ease against the sofa, casually extending one arm across its back, where it just barely touched her hair. She made no effort to move away from him and he began to speak almost immediately.

"I wanted to let you know what I've done today, so you won't think I'm acting high-handedly again. On our drive into town, Louisa mentioned she doesn't believe her father is dead. She can give no other reason than the 'feeling' she gets, a psychic sort of thing, I gather, that lets her know someone is dead. Now, I for one am not prone to rely on that kind of evidence, but it seems to me there's a fair chance that the man *isn't* dead, since no body was ever found. So I've written to my solicitor in London asking him to look into the matter. He's a thorough man; if he finds anything suspicious to follow up, he'll do so."

Vanessa studied his face for a moment before replying. "I can't object to that, of course, but whyever would the man have left a suicide note if he wasn't going to do away with himself?"

"I can think of several good reasons." The earl smiled at her questioning look. "His wife, his son, and his daughter."

"Just as good reasons to kill himself, I would think. And what about his gambling away his whole estate?"

Alvescot shifted his arm so his fingers rested lightly on her shoulder. At her startled look, he asked, "Do you mind?"

If he had said nothing about it, she would probably have shifted away from him. After all, it was not quite the same thing somehow as holding her hand. His fingers felt warm through the light lavender muslin dress, and reassuring. She had wanted some contact with him since that other occasion in the Morning Room, some small sign that he was as aware of her as she was of him. But she met his eyes a little doubtfully as she said, "No, I don't mind."

He nodded, keeping his fingers unmoving on her shoulder. "About Mr. Curtiss's gambling away his estate, I could make a few conjectures. Of course, I didn't know the man very well. I doubt I met him more than half a dozen times in my life, but Edward reminds me of him. Let us say he was tired of the type of life he was living, nagged by a shrew of a wife, impatient with a dull-witted daughter, exasperated by a son as spendthrift as he. Such a man might take his life; I think it far more probable he would disappear. But he would see no need to leave all his worldly goods behind him. Why not arrange his disappearance to look like a death, his fleecing of his own estate to look like a gambling loss? It could be done, by someone unscrupulous enough."

"Where would he go?"

Alvescot shrugged. "Almost anywhere out of England. To the continent, to America."

"But wouldn't someone recognize him?"

"Possibly. He didn't travel in very exalted circles, Vanessa, or I would have run across him a great deal more often than I did." Because he had wanted to do so for some time, he touched her dark curls, never taking his eyes from her face. "You have lovely hair, like a cascade of ebony."

"Th-thank you." She couldn't think of another thing to say and swallowed hard in her nervousness.

"I bought the children some presents while I was in Basingstoke. Louisa helped me choose them. I hope you don't mind my buying her the parasol. She was so pathetically eager to have it."

"Of course I don't mind! Why should I mind?"

Alvescot ignored the question, saying, "I wanted to buy it for you, but I was afraid you'd consider it impertinent of me. You're a very proper widow, my dear Vanessa, and it would seem a rather personal gift, I fear. Now, Louisa didn't view it in that light at all, though I fear William did. What a numbskull that man is! To think of his being in possession of the most delightful guest chamber at Cutsdean. . . ."

His eyes were laughing as he said this, mocking himself for his preoccupation with his sleeping accommodations.

Of what interest could they possibly be to him now, when they were the one room in the house in which there was not the least likelihood of encountering this charming young woman?

But his mention of William had given her thoughts a new direction. Not that she was unaware of his hand on her hair, gently twisting a curl about his fingers, but she had no desire to comment on that, or on his gift to Louisa, so her former thoughts on William seemed an absolute inspiration.

"Do you know," she said earnestly, "I believe this impossibly long courtship of William and Louisa's is directly related to Edward? Something William said in the Entry Hall gave me pause, and I've decided his hesitation is not with Louisa at all, but with marrying into her family. Think about it, L . . . James. Edward is likely to bring disgrace on himself and anyone connected with him, to say nothing of his incredible spending habits. I would certainly not want him to be *my* brother-in-law. He's certain to keep turning up like a bad penny for the rest of his life. If he weren't Louisa's brother, I daresay William would have married her years ago!"

The arrested expression on Alvescot's face was not caused by this simple theory, but by the endearing eagerness of her delivery of it. He was struggling to gain control over his bizarre desire to kiss her when there was a discreet tap on the door. Vanessa guiltily rushed to her feet, forgetting that his fingers were still entangled in her hair.

This caused her a certain amount of pain, which she felt herself most deserving of for her improper conduct, no matter what Alvescot said. You did not just sit on a sofa in a private room and allow a gentleman to entwine his fingers in your hair, if you hadn't some idea of his intentions. And she most decidedly had no knowledge of his intentions.

"Come in," she called, in an unnecessarily loud voice.

The footman who entered never once glanced at his lordship, who remained seated comfortably on the sofa showing not the least sign of distress. His mistress, he thought, looked a little flushed, but it might have been the warmth of the day. In any case, it was not his business, and he delivered his message from the nursemaid without hesitation.

"Oh, yes, the children," she murmured disjointedly. "No, tell Lucy not to put them down for their naps yet. I was coming directly." She turned to Alvescot with a trace of embarrassed impatience. "You'll excuse me, I know. I always go to them straightaway after luncheon."

The earl rose gracefully to his feet. "I didn't mean to detain you so long, ma'am. I had thought what I had to say would only take a moment."

"Yes, well . . . in any case, I must go now," and she hastened off without awaiting his reply.

TWELVE

Alvescot decided to give his presents to the children later in the afternoon. Since Vanessa had not invited him to go along with her, he assumed she had forgotten he, too, had an errand in the nursery, and he chose not to embarrass her by appearing there on her heels. The afternoon loomed rather long before him as he left the Morning Room, and he decided to take a ride around the estate. Of course, by this time he knew every inch of it, and he was beginning to be a trifle uncomfortable about the excuse of looking into estate matters. The earl knew Paul Burford was becoming a little impatient with his ever-ready questions and his continual appearance where he wasn't wanted or needed. Suspicion of Paul Burford had gradually diminished to the point of nonexistence, but Alvescot was not willing to let go of the one reason he had for remaining at Cutsdean.

This was the matter that most occupied his mind as he allowed Bibury to help him into his riding boots. The little valet was babbling away about something—the torn driving glove, perhaps, which had split further on the drive back—but the earl was not attending. Soon, very soon, he was going to have to admit that he no longer doubted Burford's complete expertise and honesty in managing the estate. Really, his admission was past due, but he couldn't very well say he wished to stay on so he could spend more time with his hostess. And waiting for a letter from his solicitor, which might literally take weeks to arrive, could hardly serve as a substitute reason.

That Vanessa had accustomed herself to him, had in

fact come to like him, he felt fairly confident. But there was a great deal more to the matter than that. She was his cousin's widow, the mother of two children whose home was Cutsdean. Little John should be raised on his own estate, should feel that link with the land and that affinity with the neighborhood which would make him a responsible landlord in his adulthood.

And Alvescot was not quite sure of himself yet, either. It was only recently that thoughts of Maria had ceased to plague him. Did one switch allegiance so easily? Granted, he had hung onto his memories of the Spanish beauty for longer than was healthy, or reasonable under the circumstances. But was this fiercely independent young woman—so different in every way from the dutiful Maria—the right sort of match for him? His mother, he felt sure, would not object to her birth, though it was well below his own, and he himself was not in the least troubled about that. She would have no trouble adjusting to the position of a countess, though it might not best please her. Her particular brand of dignity was a personal one, and would never derive from marrying into a title. The precedence, the formality, of life as a countess might even irritate her.

In the stable, he found Edward leading out the nag he hired from a neighboring farmer. Edward had been cool toward him since the incident involving Captain Lawrence, which didn't bother Alvescot in the least, but getting Edward away from Cutsdean seemed among the most pressing of his obligations and he stopped now to speak with the younger man.

"Are you headed in any particular direction? I thought I'd ride toward the South Gate, through Compton Wood," he said by way of invitation for Edward to join him.

"I'm going to Basingstoke," Edward replied, at his most unpleasant.

Undaunted, Alvescot suggested, "You could easily go by way of the South Gate."

"But I'm not going to." With which he mounted the tired-looking beast and rode off without a word of farewell.

As Alvescot waited for Satin to be saddled, he reflected that the whole experience at Cutsdean had been one of severe disregard for his consequence, unless you could count Mabel's angling for him to marry her daughter, or William's fawning obeisance (when it suited him). Vanessa treated him with respect, but hardly the awe one was most used to encountering among people of lesser birth. Hortense acted as though he were obliged to her for his daily bread. And certainly Captain Lawrence had not shown him any deference. Alvescot shook his head ruefully as he swung up onto his nervously prancing thoroughbred. What a collection!

The reason the earl chose to ride toward the South Gate was that he had some grounds for believing Paul Burford would be in quite another direction overseeing work being done there. Now Burford was someone who treated him properly. Not with any undue servility, to be sure, but as a gentleman of rank and intelligence. This only made it more difficult for Alvescot to keep up the sham of suspecting anything amiss with the estate management.

Sun was filtering through the leafy branches of the trees in Compton Wood as Alvescot cantered along the wellworn path. It wasn't a thick wood, nor a deep one, but it was pleasant with the dappled light and the fresh earthy smell of the undergrowth. The only thing that detracted from his enjoyment of it was the rider coming toward him, whom he identified without hesitation as Paul Burford. Since he couldn't very well simply tip his hat at the man and pass by, he drew Satin up slowly as they came abreast.

"Beautiful afternoon," he remarked, unable to think of anything else suitable to say.

"Delightful," Burford agreed. "I've been checking the cattle in the south pasture but I'm on my way to see how they're coming with the drainage tiles. Would you like to join me?"

"Thank you, no. I'm convinced you have everything well in hand," Alvescot admitted under the man's calm, straightforward gaze. "Everything."

"That's kind of you to say, Lord Alvescot." Burford smiled widely in acknowledgment of this long-awaited tribute.

Once he'd begun, Alvescot decided he should, in all fairness, complete the compliment. "And I believe you'll make quite a success of Buckland over the next few years. Mrs. Damery is fortunate to have acquired your services for Cutsdean."

"She's an excellent employer to work for—open-minded, intelligent, concerned. It's been an opportunity I wouldn't have wanted to pass by."

The man admired Vanessa, there was no doubt about that. Alvescot could not help wondering, however, as he had that first morning, if there was anything more on either side. He found it difficult to believe that any reasonable man who knew Vanessa would not be attracted to her, for who could ignore her elegant carriage, her subtle beauty, her proud determination? Alvescot assured himself he had seen no signs of Vanessa's having a *tendre* for Paul Burford, despite the man's various appealing qualities. He would not have denied a close friendship between them, nor even the suitability of a match once Burford was wholly on his financial feet again, but there was no *evidence* of any such attachment. This might have meant more to Alvescot if he had not remembered his own observation that Vanessa was entirely capable of concealing her emotions. . . .

The two men chatted amiably for a few minutes before parting. The earl continued on his way through the woods to the South Gate, more for the exercise now than for the beauty of the scenery. His thoughts were mere repetitions of those he'd been having all afternoon, running through his head like a chant. No decisions were made, and no flashes of inspiration came to him. He was going to have to leave Cutsdean sooner or later, and he far preferred later, but his excuse for staying had run out. Vanessa was unlikely to press him to leave, certainly, though she might make assumptions about his staying that were not completely warranted. As he let Satin out for one last stretch of gallop before he reached the stable, he chose to put off any decision for a few more days.

But the decision was taken from him as he rode into the stable yard. A liveried groom from St. Aldwyns was awaiting his arrival there, with a sealed letter in his mother's writing.

"Trouble, Tom?" he asked as he hastily dismounted and extended his hand for the missive.

"I'm afraid so, milord. Your brother's taken a bad tumble and her ladyship sent me off to bring you post haste."

Fear instantly clutched at Alvescot's heart. He was inordinately fond of his younger brother Charles, though twelve years separated them in age and their temperaments were so entirely different. Charles was a scholar, and rather shy and retiring. A good sort of lad.

Alvescot broke the seal and hastily scanned the contents of the letter. Oh, Lord, there was a fair chance the boy might die! His mother wrote that Charles had been coming home from a friend's house the previous evening when his horse had stumbled in a hole and thrown his rider, or so they assumed. Charles had apparently hit his head against a tree in falling and had been discovered after his horse returned to the stables alone. The doctor had come immediately, but Charles remained unconscious, his breathing slow and irregular, with very little the doctor could do but wait to see what transpired.

"Alert the others that I will be leaving within the hour, Tom. I'll take the curricle, with post horses after the second stage. Stay here the night and follow with the carriage in the morning at a reasonable pace. Bibury will come with you; I won't need him if I drive straight through." Alvescot turned to go, but paused. "And thank you, Tom. You've ridden hard. They'll make you comfortable here."

"Yes, milord. I'm sorry about Mr. Charles."

The earl nodded. "Is my sister back from visiting in Kent?"

"Got back just two days ago, milord."

Well, that was something. Janine would be a great support to his mother during the trying time. Alvescot tried not to think about what might have happened since the groom left St. Aldwyns. His mother's note was marked nine o'clock in the morning; they had waited to see if there was any change before sending someone to fetch him. With luck, he could be home some time before midnight. It would depend on how quickly changes could be made at the posting houses, how good the posting horses themselves were. His long-legged stride carried him rapidly to the house where he asked a footman to find Mrs. Damery and send her to his room, if she would be so kind.

Bibury was just arranging some cravats in the drawer of a mahogany bureau when the earl entered. He knew there was something amiss by the stricken look on Alvescot's face, but waited to be told.

"Charles has taken a bad fall and hasn't regained consciousness since last night," Alvescot informed him briefly. "I leave immediately. You can follow in the carriage with the others in the morning. I won't need to take much with me—a driving cape, an extra pair of driving gloves, a carriage rug. I'll leave money for you to take care of the vails, if you will."

"Certainly, milord. But you'll not be wanting to stop for food and drink on the road. Let me get a parcel from the kitchen for you to carry with you."

"If you wish," Alvescot answered absently as he perused the letter once more and carefully folded it to place in his pocket. He allowed his gaze to wander over the Blue Velvet Bedroom, trying to clear his mind enough that he didn't leave something behind that he'd need for the journey or immediately upon his return to his own home. Bibury had set aside his toilet articles for him, and glanced up from the pile of correspondence on the writing table with a questioning look. "Yes," Alvescot said, "I'd best take all that with me. I don't want to have to sort it out now."

There was a tap on the door and Bibury went to answer it. Vanessa stood there somewhat uncertainly, her eyes taking in the preparations for departure before coming to rest on Alvescot.

"Please come in," he offered. "Thank you for coming.

My brother's had a dangerous accident and I have to
leave immediately. Will you give these to the children?
I'm afraid I won't have time to see them before I go."

Vanessa accepted the two packages, though she felt a
little numb. "I'm so sorry about your brother. How did
you learn of it?"

"My mother sent a groom from St. Aldwyns. I hope
you won't mind my people spending the night here."

"Of course not! I wish there were something I could
do." He had spoken of his brother once or twice and she
knew he was fond of the young man. Her hands were
filled or she strongly suspected she'd be wringing them.

Alvescot turned to the valet to say, "If you would just
get me a parcel from the kitchen. . . ."

"Certainly, milord."

When Bibury had left, prudently closing the door behind himself, Alvescot stepped closer to Vanessa,
reaching out to touch her pale cheek with a gentle finger.
"Don't worry, my dear. Charles is a hardy lad. I have
every confidence he'll pull through. But he's been unconscious since last night and I really must go home. I . . .
had intended to stay a little longer."

"Well, that's out of the question now," she said sadly.
"I think, though, if I am not mistaken, that you are
wholly convinced Paul is handling matters well."

"Yes, I told him so today." At her look of surprise, he
confessed, "I couldn't very well do otherwise. The poor
fellow must already think I'm particularly slow-witted. We
met in the woods when I was riding."

Vanessa stared down at the packages in her hands. "I
will, of course, continue to advise you of any matters that
would concern you as co-trustee. I hope you'll let me
know how your brother does."

"Yes, and any reply I have from my solicitor on Mr.
Curtiss." He rested his hands lightly on her shoulders. In
his current state of worry over his brother's condition he
wished to make no statement which would be misunder-
stood, but he *could* not leave her without saying something. "Vanessa, I greatly admire the way you've taken
hold here. Frederick would be no less impressed than I

am. I know you'll press on in trying to get rid of your
guests; I had intended to help you. I learned in Basingstoke this morning that Hortense's property could be
available soon. The fellow who rents it doesn't come there
much any more and the lease is almost out. Insist on her
going back there, my dear. I know it's not what your
parents want you to do, but *you* know it's right and I
trust you to follow your own conscience in the matter."

She smiled bleakly. "My conscience or my inclination."

"Either is valid. Cutsdean is for you and your children."

He dropped his hands from her shoulders and paced
toward the window, stooping to pick up a pen that had
rolled off the writing table. Outlined against the window
he already looked a distance removed from her. His voice,
too, seemed to have changed when he spoke.

"You have two lovely children, Vanessa. Sometimes I
think they need a slightly firmer hand, but. . . ." He
shrugged and the rueful twist to his lips was hard to discern against the background of brightness outside. "With
your example they can scarcely go wrong."

"Thank you," she whispered.

"As to the others," he remarked, his tone becoming
firmer, "I would do everything in my power to push William and Louisa together. When I'm gone, Mabel should
see the wisdom of seeking a marriage in that quarter again.
And in their own way, I think they are quite fond of one
another."

"Yes."

"Don't let Edward stay if the others leave. I don't like
to think of you here alone with him."

"No, I won't." It was easy enough to promise with him
standing there. She could absorb the confidence and courage he naturally exuded. But what of when he was gone?

Alvescot stepped away from the window, setting down
the pen before he approached her. "I don't mean to dictate to you, my dear. These are just my thoughts on your
situation and I could hardly leave without sharing them
with you."

"I realize that."

"Good." He stood close to her now, so close his arm touched hers and his breath whispered in her hair. "You're quite a remarkable woman, Vanessa. I wish I could stay longer."

"Yes, I do, too."

They could hear the sound of footsteps approaching in the hall and he quickly leaned to kiss her. She was so surprised she hadn't time to respond before he had straightened and called to the valet to enter.

Alvescot guided her past a curious Bibury and out into the hall. "Give my love to the children, and tell them I'm sorry I had to leave so abruptly. As to the others . . . well, you will know what to say. Good-bye, Vanessa."

She was very aware that he had not said he would be back, soon or ever. Forcing a smile to her lips which almost reached her eyes, she said, "Good-bye, James. We've enjoyed having you. I hope your brother will be well soon." And then she turned away from him and walked purposefully down the hall and around the corner.

Though she would have preferred to go to her own room for the chance to be alone, she headed instead for the schoolroom. There were the packages she still carried to be delivered to the children, and the schoolroom window looked out over the stables.

For John, there was a country landscape operated by sand, and for Catherine, an elegantly dressed doll which she clasped so tightly to her Vanessa feared she would break it.

"Why didn't he bring them himself?" John asked, disappointed.

Vanessa explained, adding, "I thought we might watch for him from the window and you could wave good-bye."

"He won't see us way up here. If he's in a hurry, he won't think to look up at the schoolroom." John's little face trembled with hurt.

"He'll think of it," Vanessa replied firmly, gathering the children in her arms to stand at the window.

It was several minutes before they saw Alvescot's tall form striding toward the stables, but his curricle was ready and it took but a moment to stow away the few items he was taking with him. His groom hopped up behind and Alvescot urged the horses forward. Perhaps remembering his arrival, he kept them at a decorous pace along the drive, giving them his full attention. As the carriage drew closer to the house, Vanessa began to fear that he would not, after all, think to look up at the schoolroom.

She could feel the nervous anxiety of her son, wriggling in her arms, and the bubbling excitement of her daughter, already waving frantically at the preoccupied man. And then, almost at the last moment when it was possible, Alvescot raised his gaze to the house, looking directly to the second story where they stood. He touched his whip to his hat in a wide gesture of farewell, smiling broadly at the children's flapping hands and glowing faces. Vanessa's arms were full and she could only watch him pass by, rounding the curve of the house to disappear from her life.

In a choked voice she said, as she set the children once more on the floor, "You see. He didn't forget you."

"Will he be back soon?" John demanded.

"No, I'm afraid not, my love. He was here on business and his business is finished now, but he won't forget you. You're his godchildren and he told me once that he will always take an interest in your welfare. When you're older, John, you will go to visit him sometimes at St. Aldwyns, just as he came here when he was a boy. Would you like that?"

The child's eyes rested seriously on her face. "Would you go with me?"

"Oh, no. This will be when you're old enough to travel alone, when you're a big boy and don't want your mother tagging along on your adventures."

That time was not yet really within John's comprehension and he looked doubtful. "Well, perhaps I shall like to go alone one day. I would rather that we all went together to visit him there. Don't you want to go?"

Vanessa bit her lip. "Yes, I'd like to see St. Aldwyns one day. Will you show me how your landscape works, John?"

They were so easy to distract when they were young. Catherine was already deep in conversation with her doll and John willingly led the way to his new toy. Vanessa stayed with them until it was time to dress for dinner.

THIRTEEN

"He's gone?" Mabel asked, incredulous. "You must be mistaken, Vanessa! He cannot simply have left. Why, only this morning he presented my daughter with a most extravagant parasol. A very telling gift, I assure you. He cannot simply have left without speaking to her."

Vanessa repeated the explanation she had just given, trying to be patient.

"I see how it is!" Mabel exclaimed. "He will return at the first possible moment to speak with Louisa."

"Lord Alvescot did not mention returning at all."

"But he shall, of course. He shall return and make good on his implicit promise to Louisa."

Her daughter sat twisting her long, shapely hands in her lap, unable to meet anyone's gaze, but saying as forcefully as she could, "There was no promise, Mama. Lord Alvescot bought me the parasol because I had helped him choose presents for the children. His present to little Catherine is no sort of promise. Nor was his present to me."

Hortense snorted, glaring at the entire company in turn. "You're fools, all of you. That's the last we'll see of the man, and good riddance. He did nothing but disrupt the household from the day of his arrival. He was not particularly agreeable even as a child, and as a man he suffers from too great an opinion of his own consequence."

"But he's an earl," William almost yelped. "An earl *is* of the highest consequence. Well, perhaps not the highest, but certainly quite high. Above a viscount or a baron, you know." This defense of Alvescot's nobility had nothing to do with his own feelings for the man, for he continued angrily, "Of course, he was presumptuous in quite another way, imposing on his relationship with certain members of this household by giving them gifts. That is another matter altogether. One cannot think it was prudent for a man of his standing to be toying with the affections of a well-bred young woman when he had no intention of offering her marriage."

Edward regarded William with an ugly, sardonic curl to his lips. "And you, of course, are far above that sort of thing, are you, Oldcastle? Your prudence is your most remarkable virtue, I swear."

William flushed hotly at this barb, but said nothing, turning aside from the group to shamble toward the windows. The others continued their bickering while Vanessa observed them in a remote kind of way. Without Alvescot there to add some dignity to the gathering, she was seeing all of them in a much harsher light than she was used to. Before he had come, she had considered them her responsibility, her family obligation, her duty to Frederick and her own parents. Now they all stood out in glaring relief as an uncommonly trying lot of people.

But she didn't know if she had the courage to rid herself of them. Her mother-in-law, wrapped so successfully in her *grande dame* attitude, would not be easy to convince that it was time her "visit" ended. And if they were all to leave, miraculously, wouldn't Vanessa be left almost too much to her own devices? Somehow the thought of taking meals in the enormous dining room alone, of wandering through the house without running into another soul, was rather unnerving just now. Quarrelsome as they were, they did manage to keep the loneliness at bay for her—when she was with them. It wasn't easy to concentrate on your disappointments when one or another of them was constantly impinging on your thoughts. They did, after all, serve some small purpose at Cutsdean.

It was all very well for Alvescot to tell her to get rid of them—and then take off for his own home. Vanessa felt guilty about resenting this, especially when his brother was dangerously ill, but if he had wanted to, he could have said he would be back. No, he had purposely said nothing, of that she was sure. He may have found her pleasant, or even attractive, but he had no intention of pursuing the acquaintance beyond what his connection to her dictated.

Later, as she lay in bed, she wasn't sure how she made it through the meal and the long evening. She could see that her guests were gradually coming to terms with Alvescot's departure. Hortense was smug; Mabel was indignant but beginning to understand the consequences. Louisa was relieved, though William was not as yet prepared to forgive her for the earl's attentions. And Edward. Edward was sure this reopened the possibility Vanessa would pay some attention to him, perhaps even be won over by his charm. Couldn't any of them see that his leaving was the worst thing that could have happened?

Cutsdean, which had seemed to come alive for her during his stay, was suddenly flat once again. In fact, it would seem almost intolerable, except for those hours she spent with the children. How she would miss him! The evenings, when he wasn't there to talk with her, or the mornings, when there was no one to spar with over breakfast. She remembered the rides when they had laughed together, but always her mind came back to those two times in the Morning Room when they had actually been in physical contact with one another. Strange, what that had done to her.

Vanessa was not in the habit of thinking of men in quite the physical way that those two occasions had prompted her to do. Not that there was anything overtly sensual in those two innocent touchings. Holding hands could hardly be considered a great intimacy! Compared with her marital relations with her husband they were as a drop of water to the ocean. But like the drop of water, they were of the same substance. Else why that surprising, fleeting kiss?

Her bedroom seemed to have grown stuffy and Vanessa slipped out of bed and padded in her bare feet over to the window. She was pleased to see there was a full moon. That surely would have made his drive safer. And even in his haste he was sure to drive carefully, remembering the pall under which he made the journey. There was a fresh breeze, too, as she pushed the window open more widely to allow the air to cool her, to drift past her tied-back hair and swirl the folds of her cotton nightdress. Frederick had teased her about her nightdresses, saying, "You shouldn't bother with them, my love. They're too lacy; I got my toe caught in one of them the other night. And the buttons are far too small for my clumsy fingers."

His fingers *had* been a bit clumsy. In his eagerness and arousal, he had twice torn her nightdresses, and she had secretly repaired them herself, not wishing one of the servants to get a mistaken impression. But Frederick had been very direct in his desires, and a nightdress had only stood in his way. He had been home so seldom during their marriage that when he was there, he seemed unable to have enough of her.

After dinner, when it was perhaps only eight o'clock, he would break off in the middle of telling her something about the campaign in the Peninsula, his eyes suddenly opaque with desire. "Let's go upstairs now," he would say, grasping her hand with an urgency she couldn't quite understand. He would follow her directly into her room, dismissing her maid with a cheerful, "You won't be needed," and proceed to undress her himself. Delicate gowns had been discarded in a heap on the floor, her underclothing tossed onto the nearest piece of furniture. His only intent was to disclose her naked body. He was entranced with her firm young breasts, occasionally sucking so hard on the nipples that she winced.

Sometimes he was too impatient to wait for her to draw back the bedhangings and the bedclothing but would take her standing up, pressed back against the wall, moaning with his desire and pleasure as he hungrily fit his body to hers. The movement of his body would cause her bare back to rub against the wall, which was hardly a comfortable position. He never noticed, and she didn't tell him. It had seemed enough that he was with her, holding her, after long months of absence. Wasn't it sufficient that he loved her so desperately he could hardly restrain himself?

Vanessa shivered at the open window. No, it wasn't sufficient. She had been too young and naive to realize that she should have spoken up. That she should have made him understand that he handled her a little too roughly. His eager invasion of her body had usually come as something of a shock, damping down any flame of her own which might have consumed her. But not always.

There had been the mornings. Frederick would awaken her several times in the night to consummate their love, and in the mornings he was frequently a little spent. Those were the times when she had most enjoyed their lovemaking. He was drowsy, half drugged with sleep and satiation, but not willing to admit he had had his fill. Then he would take his time (for himself, she later suspected), his hands roaming less greedily over her body, almost in a dreamlike way. Those were the times she could feel the flame growing, spreading through her sleep-softened body. Those were the times she had learned what desire was, when his lips were remarkably gentle on her lips and her breasts, and in fact all over her body. Then the tingling of first touch turned into the aching of longing, the drifting current of pleasure into a tide of passion. Those were the times of fulfillment.

Fascinating that he hadn't seemed to notice the difference in her reactions to his lovemaking. But then, he had not been a particularly sensitive man. He had been exuberant, full of laughter and life, giving pleasure to those around him as a natural offshoot of his own great joy in living. Everyone had loved him. You couldn't help but love him. Vanessa had loved him. She had also come to see his shortcomings as a husband and father, but they had paled against his charm. He was intemperate in his thirst for life. And he was dead.

The night seemed cooler now and she pushed the window back down to a small crack of an opening. Her warm spot in the wide bed had grown cold and she huddled under the single light blanket. In this bed, always her bed, she and Frederick had lain together. Never once had she been in his, and he only slept in it himself when he had had a little too much to drink. How few nights it seemed now that they had shared a bed, and how long ago. Those mornings of splendor were long gone, and, until recently, she had scarcely thought of them. There had been too few of them to set against the less pleasurable times when he had simply taken her and she had felt nothing. But her memories stirred as her body reawakened.

Alone in her bed she could feel the tension in her as she recalled the three simple encounters with James. Her hand in his, his fingers in her hair and on her shoulder, his lips on hers. They were nothing compared with the complete intimacy of a married couple, but they were enough, now in the dark of night, to arouse her body, to send waves of anticipation through her veins, to make her breasts ache to be touched, her empty womanhood to be completed. She did not fight her fantasies. What harm could they do? Only she would ever know of them, of the vision of Alvescot coming into her room, coming into her bed. He would be gentle and loving. She could almost feel his hands on her, his body held close, his whisper in her ear, his manhood filling that aching void in her. She could feel how it would be, did feel it, all of it. A solitary tear slid from the corner of her closed eyes and wandered down her temple into her ebony hair.

He had left and he wasn't coming back.

Vanessa lay awake for long minutes thinking, but she could not recall any occasion when Frederick had sat and simply held her hand, before or after they were married.

FOURTEEN

Everything seemed to settle into its old course the next morning. No one mentioned Alvescot at all, as though he had never come and influenced their lives. Mabel and Louisa slept until their usual late hour, and Hortense took her breakfast in her room. William and Edward didn't speak to each other when they came into the Breakfast Parlor, but each directed comments to Vanessa, who was just finishing her meal.

"How about letting me use one of the horses today, Vanessa?" Edward asked. "They need the exercise, and that nag of Harley's is too old to hobble around much longer."

Vanessa thought it more likely Edward would go away if he didn't have horses at his disposal. On the other hand, there was really nowhere for him to go, without money. His consistent abuse of her animals, however, had not ceased to annoy and upset her. If she granted the privilege again, there would only be more of the same. "Have you made some effort to help in the stables, Edward? None of the grooms has mentioned it to me."

"You can't expect me to be mucking out stalls, Vanessa! I'm a gentleman, not a peasant, for God's sake. Besides, you have more than enough people to do that kind of thing. I won't have your grooms snickering at me behind my back when I'm up to my ankles in filth! And I haven't a pair of boots I'd be willing to ruin that way. You're treating me like a child."

The charge was true, of course. It was the sort of action she would take to instill some respect for animals in

John. But how did you convince a grown man he could not mistreat your horses and continue to be permitted their use? Alvescot had sent Edward off on Satin with the comforting knowledge that his horse wouldn't tolerate such abuse, but Vanessa's mounts were not so highly strung. And they *were* in need of exercise. Rather than let Edward ruin them, Vanessa contemplated selling one or two. Surely the pair for the curricle should be sold; they would be of no further use. She would speak to Davies about it.

"Well?" Edward demanded, impatient with her air of absent reverie.

"No. I'm afraid not." She met his angry eyes calmly. "I've decided to sell some of the horses and I want them to be in good condition when I do. You should continue to use Harley's horse."

"Don't you worry about *it?*" Edward asked, in a voice laden with sarcasm.

"Frankly, I do, but it is not my responsibility."

Edward proceeded to ignore her, attacking his breakfast with a grim determination. His "cousin" needed to be taken down a peg or two, he decided, and he was just the man to do it. Cutsdean had become his home, and it infuriated him that he didn't even have the use of the stables any longer. It was Edward's intention to make Cutsdean his home permanently and the surest means of doing it was to marry Vanessa. He was not unaware that the estate was only held in trust for little John, but that made no difference.

Any man with a bit of gumption could live luxuriously off a stepson's property with great ease. Edward would have sneered at anyone who thought otherwise. When he maried Vanessa, he would take over control of the estate and use its income precisely as he pleased. Alvescot's visit had been a small stumbling block, with the man poking into everything, but Edward could now see it was a good thing he had been here before Edward took charge of the place. Alvescot was satisfied with what he had found, and he had no intention of returning to question further expenses.

There had arisen in Edward during the visit a suspicion

that the earl was interested in Vanessa, but fortunately this had proved untrue. Alvescot had obviously indicated he had no intention of returning. His brother's accident had been fortuitous, to Edward's mind, because he had to admit that Alvescot's rank would have been of great weight in inducing Vanessa to marry him if the earl had asked. He was aware of his own lack of title, but was convinced that his other merits were more than enough to make up for this deficiency. Was he not exceedingly handsome? Alvescot could not hold a candle to him in looks. Edward's conviction of his own prowess with females, verified by the lovely young woman in Basingstoke, was so great as to exclude any doubts that he could win where he chose. He was, after all, Mabel's son.

Some drastic measure would have to be taken to bring the matter to a head, he decided. Vanessa had come to think of him as merely a member of her household rather than a prospective husband. Unfortunate, but not insurmountable. Edward was convinced he had not given the proper attention to secure his bride, but he was willing, when faced with the thought of Vanessa's selling off some of his horses, to put forth the necessary effort. There was no need to reduce the stables now, only to have to add to them at greater expense in a few months time when they were married. He had been remiss in his courting and he intended to make up for the lost time, but that might not be all that was necessary to jolt her out of her established habits. Something dramatic would have to be done.

He had been paying no heed to the dialogue between William and Vanessa, but he now allowed it to penetrate his mind, though he made a pretense of not listening to them. The old fuddy-duddy was on his usual hobbyhorse about health.

"I happened to note," William was saying, "that your son came home the other day with wet feet. There is no more likely way to catch a cold, I assure you! Wet feet chill the whole body, and walking about in damp footwear is more hazardous than having wet hair, though that is nothing to minimize. I have known strong men caught out in a drizzle to succumb to the most debilitating illnesses, which have occasionally even proved fatal. You must take the greatest care with John. He does not, at his age, have the sense to attend to these details himself." He frowned at the cup he held in his hand. "I don't know how he can have gotten his feet wet. It didn't rain that day."

"No, he was playing by the stream with his pony. It was a warm day, William, and he loves to play near the water. His feet weren't wet for very long and he didn't contract a cold."

"He very well might have. Children are susceptible to colds. I remember when I was a child. . . ." And he was off on a long reminiscence about his youth and his health.

Edward stopped listening and started planning. Oldcastle, despite being a dull dog, had given him the inkling of an idea. You never knew where an idea might come from, Edward had found, and he tended to keep his ears open at all times for the hint of scandal, or an opportunity. Now, it was true that Vanessa was a concerned mother, although she was an indulgent mother as well. John and Catherine were precious to her, no doubt about that. Edward found them a nuisance, but he was willing to concede that their mother, poor lonely widow that she was, put some store in them. It seemed perfectly reasonable to him that if he were to rescue young John from some peril, the grateful woman would fall into his arms without further ado. So he set himself to planning an accident where he could rush forward as the hero, but William's voice irritated him and he found himself unable to concentrate. Edward excused himself.

His hostess would have liked to do the same, but William continued to speak and she politely sat and listened to him. The thought did just run through her head, though, that she was not going to be able to tolerate this much longer. Either William was going to have to marry Louisa and take her away, or he was going to have to go away himself. When his voice began to run down, she asked, "Are you and Louisa going for a ride this morning? It's perfect weather."

"I haven't spoken with Miss Curtiss this morning," he announced primly. "She will in all probability wish to parade about the garden with her new parasol."

Vanessa lost patience with him. Ordinarily she was a remarkably patient woman. She had to be to put up with all the disagreeable people who resided in her home. But having Alvescot leave had put her nerves on edge and she very unfairly snapped at William. "What are you doing here, William? Why are you at Cutsdean? Do you know you've been at Cutsdean for nine of the last twelve months?"

Tactless people are often very sensitive to slights themselves. William was offended by her questions, mostly perhaps because he couldn't think how to answer them, but for his dignity as well. He sulked. "You said I was welcome here."

"Well, I've changed my mind," she retorted, unrepentant. "When you first came, I believed you to be Louisa's suitor. I thought her happiness was dependent upon your visiting and making her an offer of marriage. But it never comes—the offer, that is. You come, and you stay and you stay and you stay. We aren't related, William, and I can see no reason to feed and house you, to say nothing of your horses, for endless periods of time, if you are unwilling to come to the point with Louisa. I realize it has been difficult for you, with Mabel pushing Louisa at Lord Alvescot, but you should have taken a stand instead of pouting about the house."

"I haven't pouted."

"You're pouting now." Rather than being relieved by venting her spleen, she was growing more exasperated. She leaned toward him, tapping her spoon on the table to make her point. "One week, William. I will give you one week to make your declaration to Louisa. And then, if you don't do it—out. There's no point in this. You're breaking poor Louisa's heart. I don't care if her mother is a pest and her brother a villain. If you want to marry her, you should do so. If you don't, then stop hanging about her as if you meant to. It's unfair to her and it's unfair to me. You have a home to go to, and I want you to go there, with or without Louisa."

William stared at her, wide-eyed. No one had ever spoken to him quite like that before and he was near to expiring with the shock. She had always seemed such a refined young woman. If he hadn't been so attached to Louisa, he might have made her an offer himself. Indignant, he pushed back his chair and bowed stiffly to her. But he had to have the last word and he said, "I shall go to London."

"Go anywhere you please. Just do it before the week is out."

"I shall go today."

"Just as you like," she muttered, tossing down her napkin and rising. She was alarmed that things had gotten out of hand, but she refused to let him see it. "I'm sure, when you're gone, Louisa will be besieged with suitors." My God, she sounded just like Mabel. In order to keep herself from saying anything more of that ridiculous nature, she hastened from the room, leaving him standing there gaping at her.

Vanessa hid in the Morning Room for the next two hours. She had no desire to see anyone, to talk to anyone. How could she have so mishandled the situation? Her embarrassment made the color come and go in her cheeks each time she thought of it. There was no harm in William, any more than there was in Louisa. He had a few annoying habits, and he was no brighter than he needed to be, but that was no excuse for blundering into his private life and rudely ejecting him from her household.

And Louisa was going to be so upset. Poor woman! She had spent twelve years waiting for him to propose to her, and now, when there might have been some chance with Alvescot gone and Mabel presumably desperate to see her daughter settled, the opportunity was snatched from within her grasp. Vanessa was not ordinarily given to such dramatic mental images, but all her emotions seemed to be in a chaotic state that morning. She must take hold of herself and act more reasonably. Not so reasonably as to apologize to William, though. That she would not do. Of all of them, he had the least right to impose on her, and a stubborn core of her said that she had every right to ask him to leave if she wanted to.

Eventually, she went to visit with the children. They were a little subdued that morning and she took them both on her lap and read to them. The story was not very exciting, but they cuddled close and listened almost absently. They were nearing the end of the little book when the door burst open and Louisa stumbled into the room.

"He's leaving! Vanessa, William's leaving. All his valises are packed and sitting in the front hall. And he won't say anything to me except that you told him to go." In her distress, Louisa kept wringing her hands and shifting awkwardly from one foot to the other. "I don't understand. What did he do? Did you really tell him to leave?"

The children stared up at Vanessa, puzzled and a little alarmed. She gave them each a hug and turned to the nursemaid. "Will you finish reading this story to them, Lucy? I'll be back after luncheon."

By now the tears were flowing freely down Louisa's face. Vanessa winced, feeling desperately guilty again but knowing there was no way she could retrieve the situation. Her own handkerchief was thrust into Louisa's hand and she put an arm about her waist to lead her from the schoolroom. Looking horribly betrayed, Louisa gasped, "You did tell him to leave, didn't you?"

"In a way, yes," Vanessa admitted, leading her companion to Catherine's room across the hall where they could sit undisturbed for a while. The room was done in yellow and white, looking bright and gay in the summer morning sunlight. Vanessa gently urged Louisa into a striped satin chair and pulled one close so she could speak softly. "I'm sorry this has happened, Louisa. My nerves were a bit on edge this morning, and William made a snide remark about your parasol. I promise you I hadn't any intention of asking him to leave when I went down to breakfast this morning."

"What did he say about my parasol?" Louisa sniffled, not looking at her companion.

"Oh, just that you would probably want to parade about the garden with it. *You* know how he has been. Well, I became annoyed with him for behaving like that, when here was the perfect opportunity to settle things with you, and I told him." Vanessa flushed, but Louisa had her eyes pressed to the handkerchief. "I told him I would give him a week to offer for you, and if he didn't, he'd have to leave. He said he would leave today."

Louisa straightened in her chair, clutching the wet handkerchief against her bosom. "He's leaving because he doesn't want to offer for me?" she asked, despair making her voice shake.

"No, he's leaving because I was so presumptuous as to give him an ultimatum." Vanessa said it very firmly, to ensure its penetrating her unhappy friend's mind, but she could not be sure that it had. "He's miffed that I would bring up the subject at all, and he has no intention of being dictated to by me. And I shouldn't have done it, Louisa, but I felt so very impatient with him this morning. I don't expect you to understand or to forgive me. It was wrong, but on the other hand I won't beg his pardon, either."

"Of course not," Louisa said, pride stiffening her drooping shoulders. She rose, absently dropping the handkerchief on the floor. The tears had stopped abruptly and she reached out to squeeze Vanessa's hand. "You had every right to do what you did, my dear, and I think it is best we know just how matters stand. There certainly is no reason for William to be here if he doesn't plan to marry me. Strange, I had always thought he did, you know. How very odd! Well," she said, forcing down a lingering sob, "I shall just have to accept this turn of events. It is better to know now, than to go on as we have been for the last twelve years. I do wish this had happened a little sooner, though. If I had known he didn't intend to marry me, I would have looked about for someone else, as Mama says it is the only course for a woman—marriage. And I've grown a trifle old to be much in demand. That wasn't the case when I was twenty. But that is bragging! We are all more in demand when we're twenty, aren't we? I don't know quite why it is men think girls are so much more interesting than women. I have never found them so, but I'm not a man. Perhaps William liked me better when I was a girl."

"Louisa, really, you don't understand!" Vanessa protested. "William's leaving isn't a sign that he doesn't want to marry you. It's me he's angry with."

The vague eyes were not quite so vague when Louisa placed a hand on her arm, her head held erect. "It's as good an excuse as any, Vanessa. He cannot bring himself to the sticking point, so he used that to get away. Just think how often he has quarrelled with me for the same purpose. Whenever we were getting too comfortable, there was always some little disagreement. Oh, I know I am guilty of my share, but that was only because he would purposely say something to provoke me and I couldn't resist being provoked. He doesn't want to marry me."

"Nonsense. He does want to marry you; he just doesn't want to marry your family."

Louisa blinked uncertain eyes, then shrugged. "Possibly. It amounts to the same thing in the end, doesn't it?"

There was no good answer, and the question was rhetorical, anyhow. Louisa turned toward the door, fumbled with the knob, and let herself out into the hall. Because she didn't seem to remember in which direction to go, Vanessa quickly picked up the soggy handkerchief and followed her, leading the way toward the stairs. "Are you going to say good-bye to him?" she asked gently.

"No. I would only make a fool of myself. I'll stay in my room until he's gone."

Feeling utterly helpless and not a little responsible, Vanessa saw Louisa to her room. They could hear the sounds of activity in the Entry Hall and Vanessa decided she really should go down and bid her guest farewell. The front door was open and his traveling carriage could be seen standing on the gravel, already piled high with valises. Vanessa had had no idea he had so much with him. To think that now the Chinese Chippendale bedchamber would be empty, after Alvescot had left. It hardly seemed fair.

William was standing on the black and white tiles giving instructions. "That is to go in the carriage with me. No, don't put anything more on the top. Strap this one to the rear. I shall be wearing the cloak to keep off the dirt of the road, even though it is a warm day."

When he heard the sound of footsteps on the stairs, he swung around, but apparently it was not Vanessa he expected to see. His gaze traveled further up to the hall above and then confusedly returned to her. He said stiffly, "As you can see, I'm leaving now. Thank you for having me."

"Of course. I trust you'll have a pleasant journey."

"This is not the type of day I would ordinarily choose to travel," he said petulantly, his gaze once more seeking the upper hall. "But then, I have no choice."

"You had a choice."

He rammed a beaver hat on his diminishing locks, bowed slightly, and moved to the door. Once again his eyes raced up the stairs. In a loud voice he announced, "I'm leaving now."

"Yes, so you said. If you've forgotten anything, we'll forward it to Suffolk."

"I'm going to London."

"Well, if you wish to leave your direction, we'll send anything there."

William scowled at the upstairs hall. "I won't be leaving my direction."

"As you wish. Good-bye." Vanessa was tempted to offer her hand, but he was paying no attention to her. Tompkins stood waiting to close the door behind him, but still William hesitated.

"I haven't left anything behind," he said, stalling. "I was very careful about that. Every drawer, even under the bed. I didn't just trust the servants; I looked myself. You won't find anything, not a trace of me, once I've gone, once the dust has settled behind the carriage. It will be as though I'd never been here."

The thought seemed to depress him. With one more hopeless glance at the stairs, he turned and walked out, his shoulders hunched forward and his hands clasped uneasily behind his back. "Good-bye," he called as he stepped into the carriage. Vanessa could hear his instruction for the coachman to proceed before Tompkins closed the door. And then the crunch of the wheels on the gravel, which quickly faded.

Vanessa could not resist glancing up to see if Louisa had come out of her room, but the hall above was empty.

FIFTEEN

It took Edward several days to devise a scheme which pleased him. He didn't want anything to go wrong. If the child were actually to come to any harm, Vanessa was more likely to boot him out of the house, as she had Oldcastle, than she was to marry him.

Neither Louisa nor Vanessa was willing to talk about Oldcastle's departure and Edward began to wonder if he'd made some sort of amorous advance toward his hostess. Edward had contemplated the efficacy of such a step, but especially now decided it wouldn't do. He had to cover for himself. If he wasn't able to convince Vanessa to marry him, he still wanted to be able to live at Cutsdean and receive his allowance.

There was diversion enough for him in Basingstoke. Edward wasn't particularly interested in Vanessa's body. She wasn't really his type at all, being so tall and dark. He preferred small fair-haired women, feminine versions of himself. Vanessa's sole advantage, as far as he was concerned, was the access she would give him to financial independence. He didn't really like her caustic tongue, nor her understanding of estate matters. When he became master of Cutsdean she would have to slide back into a more properly female role—directing the household and crocheting doilies, planning entertainments and taking her children to visit her parents in Somerset.

Edward decided it would be well to plan the "accident" around his own riding ability, which would down two birds with one stone. Not only would he rescue Vanessa's son, but he would exhibit his skill in the saddle and she would never consider denying him the stables again. The only obstacle to this plan was, of course, that he would be riding Harley's nag, not the most dependable beast he could imagine. Still, he felt every confidence that he could handle the lazy animal. Edward was used to believing all horses lazy and stubborn when he took them in hand.

The conversation at the breakfast table the morning he'd had the idea eventually helped him develop the plan. John and his pony were both attached to the stream on the south end of the estate. Edward had seen them there even before Oldcastle had mentioned John's wet feet and Vanessa had explained. It seemed a simple matter to him to cause the boy's pony to bolt with him into the stream bed. A prickly burr surreptitiously shoved under Rollo's saddle blanket would start him off, and if the boy fell it would be into the shallow water, where he wouldn't hurt himself. Edward would wait until they were actually on the stream bank, blocking the pony's retreat in that direction with his own horse, but close enough to give immediate chase. The bank on the other side was steeper, and it was unlikely Rollo would try to climb it in his panic.

So everything was settled in Edward's mind. The only difficulty he was encountering was that Vanessa never invited him to join her and her son on their rides. She was, in fact, quite adamant about his *not* joining them, saying carelessly, "No, thank you, Edward, we'd rather go alone. John is jealous of my time and he wouldn't appreciate your diverting me from giving him my full attention." So each day they rode off by themselves and Edward was left to kick his best boots against a hapless fence post in frustration.

After a few days, he no longer asked to be included. Instead, he rode out when they did, hoping they would go in the direction of the stream and he could appear there as if by accident. But they didn't head for the stream. The weather was cool for the better part of a week, and Vanessa had no intention of allowing John to play in the stream when there wasn't a hot sun to dry him out quickly. Twice, in fact, she had Catherine sitting up with her on her horse and they didn't go far from the stables at all, just far enough to satisfy John's insatiable need to be regarded as old enough to run his pony outside the confines of the stable yard.

Vanessa would have liked to go for a long ride by herself, but her time was limited and any she could spare for riding was naturally devoted to accompanying her son, and occasionally her daughter. There had been no word from Alvescot or Oldcastle. Each day when Tompkins brought her the post she had to stifle her disappointment.

A hard gallop across the fields might have relieved her of a little of her pent-up restlessness. She was not taking his rejection at all well, she admitted to herself. The placid manner in which she had accepted her household before Alvescot's advent was permanently destroyed. Only with a supreme effort was she able to bear her remaining guests, and even then she was given to speaking her mind more often than she was used to do.

It was time, she knew, to work up the courage to ask Hortense to remove to her house in Basingstoke as soon as the lease ran out. Each day she told herself this would be the day she did it. But each day she couldn't be sure whether she was going to do it because Alvescot had suggested it, or because it was what she wanted. Her parents expected her to continue to house the old woman, and she was, after all, Frederick's mother. What was perhaps more pertinent was that if Hortense went, Vanessa would be left with Mabel. Early on, Vanessa had suggested that Hortense could house her sister and her sister's children at Basingstoke, and Hortense had stared at her with that sharp face and those cold eyes, saying, "You must be mad! There's not room in that house for more than one person. It is a *town* house, my dear Vanessa, not meant for a family at all. There is but one decent bedroom in the whole place, and no acceptable public room at all."

Vanessa knew for a fact that there were four family bedrooms in addition to the servants' rooms, and several comfortable parlors. But there was no use arguing with her mother-in-law. If Hortense wasn't willing to house her own sister, Vanessa wasn't going to be able to convince her to change her mind. No one changed Hortense's mind. The only way to get her to leave was to tell her. Vanessa mentally debated the issue for days before coming to the decision that Hortense had to go, for her own peace of mind. If she didn't act soon, Hortense would search for someone else to let the Basingstoke house and Vanessa would be stuck with her for another year at the very least.

So one afternoon when she had changed into her riding dress but had some time before she was to take John to the stables, she hunted Hortense down in the Saloon, where the older woman was frowning at a letter in her hand. The frown remained when she lifted her gaze to Vanessa.

"It's from my brother," she remarked. "He says he has decided to stay in Somerset permanently. Apparently there's a naval man there who has befriended him, and he prefers his society to that of his own family."

"How nice for him to have found a friend. I'm sure it's a wise course for him to pursue." Vanessa seated herself opposite Hortense, whose eyes had narrowed and were observing her keenly.

"The population here seems to be decreasing rapidly, and I wonder if you are not responsible for the change," Hortense commented with an intimidating glare.

Vanessa steeled herself against the woman's assumption of authority. It would be too easy to gloss over the matter—and neglect to carry out her intention. She clenched her riding gauntlets a little more tightly in her lap. "That's a matter I wished to discuss with you, Hortense. The lease on your house in Basingstoke will soon expire and I think it would be . . . prudent for you to move back there."

"Prudent? What are you talking about? I'm settled here."

"Yes, but this is no longer your home. This is my home, and my son's and my daughter's. You have a home of your own over which you can exercise complete control. Often enough you've objected to the way I run things at Cutsdean and it makes for an uncomfortable situation."

"I'm perfectly comfortable here," Hortense insisted.

"You would be more comfortable in your own home."

"You mean *you* would be more comfortable if I weren't here!"

Vanessa lifted her shoulders in a gesture of resignation.

"Yes, that's true. I can't see any point in your being here, Hortense. You don't approve of the way I raise my children, you don't approve of the way I run my household, you don't particularly approve of me. We don't rub along together satisfactorily. There's no sense in your staying here."

"Cutsdean was my home for thirty years."

"Yes, but it's no longer your home. When Frederick brought me here as a bride, he moved you to the house in Basingstoke."

"He would have wanted me to return here after his death, to see that the family heritage was properly maintained."

Vanessa shook her head. "I'm sorry. I don't believe that's true. Even Lord Alvescot said Frederick would not have intended for you to return here."

"Ah, I see," the older woman proclaimed, her eyes glittering angrily. "It is my nephew who's at the bottom of this. He always was a troublemaker. But it won't do you the least good to try to please him now he's gone, young lady. He's no more possessed of a knowledge of what my son would have wanted than you are. It is my duty to stay and see that Cutsdean and the Damery name are treated with the proper respect."

"No," Vanessa said gently. "You've been here for two years and I can't see that it's done the least good. You wouldn't be happy here unless you were in charge of Cutsdean, and that I can't allow. Cutsdean is my responsibility now. I'm doing my utmost to preserve it for John, and I have to run it the way I see fit."

Vanessa rose, pulling on the riding gauntlets. "The lease on your property in Basingstoke is almost expired. I want you to move back there, Hortense, as soon as it's available. Don't be concerned about your grandchildren; I'll bring them to visit you as often as you wish."

Vanessa waited to see if her mother-in-law chose to respond to this direct instruction, but the older woman sat silent, staring straight ahead of her. There was an arrogant tilt to her head which Vanessa knew well. If Hortense decided to ignore what she'd just said, Vanessa could not picture bodily removing her from Cutsdean.

Well, she had done what she could. Hortense lived by her own code of honor, and if it could incorporate staying where she didn't belong, there was little Vanessa could do.

"Excuse me, please. I have to meet John at the stables," she said, and walked quickly from the room.

Her mind was preoccupied during the ride. John chattered with his usual eagerness and she smiled at him, teasing occasionally, but not with her whole attention. The day was warm again after a cool spell and she agreed that they would go to the stream. When any thought of Alvescot drifted into her head, she thrust it forcefully aside. There was enough to worry about with Hortense and the others. Louisa, according to her mother, was going into a decline.

And it was true that Louisa was more than usually subdued, but Vanessa could think of nothing to divert her mind. She didn't wish to ride, or read, or even play the pianoforte any more than was necessary under her mother's insistence. Edward made fun of her for pining after such a fool as Oldcastle, and Mabel accused her of letting him slip through her fingers.

How good it would be to have them all gone! But it looked more and more as though the Curtisses, at least, were bound to remain. Vanessa determined to try to get Hortense to take them with her when (and if) she left. She was prepared to continue their quarterly allowance, so long as they weren't hanging about her house. Louisa was the sole exception. Vanessa had grown more fond of her over the last few weeks, but it was highly unlikely Louisa would remain if the others left. And, of course, it was highly unlikely that they would leave. . . .

When Vanessa and John approached the stream, Edward appeared as if from nowhere. Vanessa bit back her annoyance. There was nothing unusual about running into another member of the household when they were out riding. Cutsdean had several pleasant rides, but this was surely the most appealing. Vanessa had noted at the stables that Harley's horse was not in its customary stall and had been relieved that Edward was out: his habit of trying to insinuate himself on their rides was irritating.

What happened next was a little difficult for Vanessa to sort out in her mind afterward. Edward greeted them, riding up to place his horse on the opposite side of John's pony from her. His spirits were high, she could tell by the way his eyes glowed.

"Perfect day!" he proclaimed, beaming on the two of them. "And you'll never guess what I've just seen down along the stream. There, in the largest oak. Can you make it out? A leather jerkin hanging from the branch. However do you suppose it got there?"

Intrigued, Vanessa could indeed see some item of apparel swinging in the breeze. She was interested enough to consider riding in that direction when her son's pony suddenly bucked and bolted, lunging into the water. John's grip on the reins had slackened as he, too, looked toward the large oak and he was barely able to maintain his seat on the animal. Rollo plunged downstream, frantically trying to rid himself of his rider.

For a moment, Vanessa sat frozen on her horse. Then instinct took over and she followed the maddened horse through the water. She was not aware of Edward. Her concentration was purely on reaching her son before some harm befell him. Even as she gave chase, her astonishment at Rollo's behavior fuddled her mind. The pony had never shown the least sign of unruly conduct. And there he was, wildly swinging his head, shaking his body, stomping in the shallow stream so that sprays of water went in every direction.

Frightened, little John was calling for her while desperately attempting to keep his position on the pony. Vanessa could see his small body jerked one way and then another, his arms flailing for balance. As she finally came abreast of him, she reached across to grab the bridle, but Rollo was lunging too wildly for her to catch hold. Instead, she was forced to try for her son. His feet had long since lost the stirrups and only one hand held tightly to the reins. Half the time his body seemed to float above the horse, only to crash back down and drive Rollo to renewed excesses of body contortion.

Vanessa steadied her own mount, which was made nervous by his distraught neighbor. Holding the reins in one hand as firmly as she could, she strained to grasp her son about his waist. When she felt her hold was secure enough, she swung him bodily to her, badly wrenching her shoulder but maintaining her grip. John clung to her as she directed her horse onto the grassy bank. His face was white and terrified, his hands like claws digging into her flesh.

"There, it's all right," she murmured into his hair where his head was buried against her shoulder. "You're all right now, John." She tried to lift her hand to soothe him but a sharp pain ran through it and she allowed it to fall again at her side. "You'll have to climb down by yourself, love. I can't use my arm."

Shaken out of his own anxiety by his concern for her, he did as he was told, sliding to the bank to stand on visibly shaking legs. Vanessa awkwardly lowered herself from the sidesaddle, wincing when she had to put any pressure on her right arm. Rollo was still thrashing in the stream, further away now, but as they watched he rolled in the water, dislodging the saddle when the girth broke. Abruptly, his struggles ceased and he stood shuddering in the shallow water, his head hanging down in exhaustion. John called to him and he raised his head and whinnied before trotting over to the bank and thrusting his muzzle against John's chest.

Still bewildered, John looked up at his mother. "Why did he do it?" he whispered. "He scared me, Mama. I didn't want to fall off."

Before Vanessa could answer, Edward had come pounding up to them, on foot, swearing every inch of the way. "The damned horse wouldn't go in the water! The ———son of a———wouldn't set one of his———feet in a little———stream."

It was obvious that Edward had been bested in his struggles with the dilapidated nag. His clothes were once again tattered from a rough fall and his boots were scuffed. There were grass stains on his buckskins, and though he had chosen them purposely for the expedition he had in mind, he frowned at the stains with unmitigated disgust. He showed no concern for Vanessa or her son, groping about his waistcoat pocket for one of his fobs which was missing. "I'll kill the beast," he roared. "I'll slice his————throat."

"That's enough, Edward," Vanessa commanded. "John is shaken and I can't move my arm. Would you please retrieve Rollo's saddle from the stream?"

Edward regarded her with complete astonishment. As if he hadn't been through enough without wading into the icy water and permanently ruining his boots. "It's beyond reclaiming by now," he snapped. "And how would you get it back to the stables? *I* don't intend to ride with it dripping in my lap."

The situation, to his mind, was irretrievable and his mood was by now so foul he didn't care what she thought of him. All his work, all his plans, ruined. How clever he had been to hang the leather jerkin in the tree to capture their attention while he shoved the burr under Rollo's blanket! John had even unknowingly aided him by standing up in his stirrups to look. But there was no one to appreciate his cleverness. Edward gave her one glance of uncompromising dislike and stalked off to find his horse. His language, when he found that the beast had taken off, was only slightly worse than previously, but Vanessa and John were too far away to catch all its intricacy.

"Pantywaist!" John snickered, his courage somewhat restored.

"Worse," Vanessa said bitterly. "Come along, John. You'll have to ride Rollo bareback. We'll send someone back for the saddle later." She found that she was unable to remount her horse and smiled up at his worried frown. "I think I'll be more comfortable walking anyway, love."

"His back is all bloody!" John exclaimed as Rollo moved restlessly under him. "I'll walk, too."

Since Edward had disappeared somewhere (possibly to avenge himself on Harley's hapless nag), mother and son trudged back to the stables alone, leading their mounts and discussing what might have caused Rollo's injury. Vanessa didn't mention the shooting pains in her arm which even walking caused, and John was surprised, later, to see her arm resting in a sling.

"It's not broken," she assured him as Catherine stared wide-eyed. "Dr. Brinkworth says the shoulder is wrenched and I must keep my arm immobile. It's only for a few days."

"Does it hurt?" Catherine asked, her eyes filling with tears of empathy.

"Not if I don't jar it," Vanessa assured her. "And I'm being very careful about that." They didn't need to know that almost anything one did jarred it.

Vanessa felt sure her mother-in-law looked upon it as a righteous judgment on her.

SIXTEEN

The long-awaited letter finally came the next day, and it was a stunning disappointment. Not in the news he had about his brother. Alvescot wrote to say that Charles had regained consciousness soon after he returned home, and that the boy was slowly mending. There had been some concern about the extent of the head injury for about a week, but their fears had finally been allayed. Charles was beginning to speak normally again and his appetite was returning, but he would need careful nursing for some time yet. Alvescot thanked her again for her hospitality and said he had every confidence in her ability to manage Cutsdean with Paul Burford. It was a polite note, friendly, but it told her nothing she wanted to hear.

Vanessa read the letter three times, though it was awkward holding it in her left hand. One is given to reading between the lines when desperate for some morsel of affection. He did call her "My dear Vanessa," but that might well have been his usual form of salutation. Certainly signing himself her "devoted servant" was no more than standard practice. He excused his long silence by his anxiety for his brother's welfare and some pressing business at St. Aldwyns. "I shall be tied here for some weeks," he said, in regard to the continuing care Charles needed, but as this was not followed by any suggestion of what he might do after that, Vanessa could not find it encouraging. He hoped to hear from her soon about the status of her household.

Well, she couldn't very well write with her aching arm, and she had no intention of asking someone to act her scribe. Even eating with her left hand was difficult; she would not make the hopeless attempt to write with it. There seemed little hurry in answering the kind but uninvolved letter. She would, when she was able, convey her happiness in his brother's recovery and mention the fiasco of William Oldcastle. By then, too, she would know if Hortense intended to leave. It was impossible to tell at this point, for Hortense spoke to her only when spoken to.

Nothing else was changed in the household, except that Louisa frequently sat with her, reading from any book which Vanessa chose. There were so few things she could comfortably do that this was a blessing, but Louisa remained low-spirited and seemed grateful for something useful to do.

Paul Burford came to sit with her in the Library and go over the estate books. His presence always cheered her, and he took time from his work to substitute for her on rides with John. But the time passed slowly. It was a week and a half before she was able to use her arm with any degree of comfort. The pain was still there, but much diminished. With some effort she was able to make entries in the books and she knew it was time to write to Alvescot but she continued to delay the inevitable. What, after all, did she have to say to him?

When a month had slid past since his departure, she did not feel she could delay any longer. Simple courtesy demanded a response to his letter. Vanessa left the breakfast table that morning with the firm resolve to go straight to the Morning Room and pen her reply. The day was overcast and chilly, so she allowed the draperies to remain closed and seated herself at her desk, pulling a shawl closer about her shoulders.

Should she address him as "My dear James"? It would be in keeping with his own letter, though somehow coming from her pen it sounded a little too forward. She decided on "Dear Lord Alvescot." After that the first few sentences were easy, expressing her relief that his brother was recovering. But from that point on she had to worry about every word, trying not to sound as though she expected him to be particularly interested in her small problems, making them, in fact, sound like no trouble at all.

She had very nearly finished the painstaking letter when there was a tap at the door. Any interruption was a welcome relief and she called, "Come in." It could only be a footman, of course, and she finished the word she was writing before glancing toward the door.

Alvescot stood there, looking rather larger than she remembered him, and a great deal more forbidding. "May I?" he asked, his voice crisp.

The moment of stunned surprise passed and she rose haltingly from her chair. "Of course. Is something wrong? Why have you come?"

"What else was I to do when I didn't hear from you?" he demanded. "I imagined all sorts of wretched things happening here at Cutsdean. Why else wouldn't you have written?"

"I was writing you just now," she murmured, waving toward the single sheet lying on the desk. "I . . . I couldn't write for a few weeks. There didn't seem to be any hurry." And then, belatedly, "Won't you sit down?"

"May I see the letter?"

"Of course." Suddenly she felt a little embarrassed about the letter. It didn't seem to take into account his apparently real concern, somehow. But how was she to know his interest was genuine? The letter he had written could as well have come from any distant relation. Vanessa watched as he scanned the sheet, a puzzled frown drawing his brows together. When he had finished it, he folded it and stuck it in his pocket, but he said nothing, just standing there regarding her with unwavering eyes.

"I . . . I injured my shoulder just before I received your letter . . . James. My arm was in a sling for more than a week."

The sling was, of course, gone now, and he looked skeptical. "How did you injure yourself?"

"It's rather a long story."

"I expected long stories when I came all the way from St. Aldwyns to find out what was amiss here," he told her in a remarkably level voice. "Tell me about it."

"If you would sit down. . . ."

He joined her on the sofa, his hands planted firmly over his crossed knees. Vanessa described John's adventure on Rollo as best she was able under his intent gaze. When she had finished, he asked, "Did you come to any conclusion about what caused the pony to bolt?"

"Well, yes, I did, but my suspicions are unconfirmed. I wouldn't want to speak of them."

"Hogwash! You know as well as I do that Edward had to have been to blame. He put something irritating under the pony's blanket when you and John were looking toward the tree."

"Yes, but why would he do it? It seems so pointless."

"Don't be naive, Vanessa!" he retorted. "To win your regard, of course, by acting the brave knight who rescues your son. The idiot actually thinks you would consider marrying him."

"He *cannot* be that oblivious," she contradicted. "Perhaps he wanted to work his way up in my estimation so I would allow him the use of the stables again. But to take such a course! To endanger John's life!"

"He probably thought it was safe enough in the stream bed. But he has to go, Vanessa."

It was so easy for him to say, she thought rebelliously. He had made no remark on the parts of her letter about Oldcastle and Hortense, and now he was insisting that she take on one more of her household, and the least able to fend for himself, regardless of his unscrupulous behavior. Exasperated, she asked, "How do you suggest I get rid of him? Slice his throat, like he planned to do with Harley's horse?"

A grin appeared briefly on his lips. "Not a bad idea, but I'm afraid you couldn't get away with it, my dear. I think I have a better idea."

"Don't just tell me to ask him to leave! I'm not even sure Hortense is going, though I've asked her. She likes keeping me in suspense. And Edward, fine fellow that he is, would simply laugh and say, 'You don't mean that, Vanessa. Where would I go?' They are the most obstinate, selfish, inflexible bunch of people I've ever met!"

Her cheeks were flushed with anger and he raised one

hand to her face, brushing the glowing skin with a gentle fingertip. "You didn't use to let them upset you so much. When I first came here you knew what they were and that they were imposing on you, but you took it all in stride, regarding them with amusement and an uncommon tolerance. What changed all that?"

"You did," she muttered, defiant. "Coming and telling me I was a fool to let them stay, insisting it wasn't my duty, saying that Frederick wouldn't have wanted it. I would have put up with them because my parents thought I should. I regarded it as an act of Christian charity, not an idiocy. Even after you came I might have succeeded in keeping to my resolve, if your very presence hadn't made them all start behaving like a group from Bedlam: Mabel pushing Louisa on you and William sulking, Hortense aggrieved by your aristocracy and Edward forcing more attention on me. It would have been better if you'd never come!"

Abruptly he withdrew his hand, a startled look in his eyes. Alvescot had come to believe that Vanessa was as attracted to him as he was to her. Since he'd left Cutsdean not a day had gone by when he didn't think of her and wish that he could be with her. The emergency at St. Aldwyns had required his spending a lot of time sitting by his brother's bed, unoccupied, and he had gone over their interactions carefully, looking for signs of her interest. And he was sure he had found them. She had not rejected his tentative advances, though admittedly they were not so glaring as to call forth any decisive action.

Was it possible he'd been deluding himself? Vanessa was his cousin's widow and it was only two years since her husband had died. What he had taken for interest might have been mere loneliness, a desire to have someone to talk to who wasn't as reprehensible as most of her household. Certainly she had needed a friend, and had every incentive to rub along with him as co-trustee.

But she had let him kiss her, that last afternoon. Yes, and then he had purposely left her without any promise to return. Thinking back on his letter to her, he realized that he had assumed too much in it, after all those hours of considering their time together. By the time he wrote her,

he had settled in his mind that he wanted to marry her—
and he had not doubted that it was a mutual desire. How
could he have been so conceited?

Alvescot regarded her now with wary eyes. She had
turned her face away from him, toward the window. Her
hands lay clenched in her lap. Before he could speak, she
said softly, "I don't really mean that, James. You had every right to come and it was not your fault that everyone
was disturbed by your visit. I'd gotten accustomed to
running things here and I may at first have resented your
interference, but I came to understand you were only trying to help. So many people here are determined to un-
dermine what little authority I have that I cling to it
rather tenaciously, I fear. Your . . . friendship was most
welcome."

Still, she didn't look at him and he sat unmoving, and
unsure how to proceed. Slowly, he decided. It would be
all too easy to break the tenuous thread that joined them.
If she called it friendship that was better than nothing. In
fact, it was a great deal stronger bond than he had begun
to fear. Perhaps the strongest that any enduring partnership could be based on.

"I hope it still is welcome—my friendship," he said
lightly as he put a hand on her clasped ones, which he
found were very cold.

"Of course it is," she replied, meeting his gaze with her
clear, unreadable eyes.

"And may I, as a friend, make a suggestion about Edward?"

"Please do."

"I had a letter from my solicitor yesterday, just before
I left St. Aldwyns. He's made thorough inquiries into Mr.
Curtiss's disappearance and has discovered what may be a
trace of him, though it is by no means certain."

"He's alive?"

"Almost assuredly alive. His present location is more
dubious." Alvescot smiled at her, a slowly widening grin.
"I think it would not be altogether necessary to inform
Edward of the tentative nature of my solicitor's findings.
If he were, perhaps, told that his father was running a
gambling establishment, quite successfully, in northern

Italy, I think he would in all probability be willing to seek him out. It would be essential to give Edward a reasonable traveling fund, but I'd be willing to see to that."

"Don't be absurd. Edward is my financial responsibility, if he's anyone's." But her eyes sparkled. "A gambling establishment? Is that true?"

"Yes, as far as Hobart can tell. Apparently Curtiss has shifted the location from time to time, but there's little doubt that it's he. Hobart wanted to know if I wished a man sent to confirm the most recent location. All his information has come from travelers, most of whom didn't know Curtiss, but there was one man, a former friend, who confirmed the whole story, thinking it a marvelous jest."

"How bizarre! But exactly what one might expect of the Curtisses," she remarked, her expression slowly becoming more serious. "James, I don't mind if you tell Edward. In fact, I wish you would. On the other hand, I've come to be quite fond of Louisa and I think I would prefer that she and her mother didn't know, at least not yet. Mabel would want to hound him down, and she would drag poor Louisa halfway across the Continent to find him. What sort of life would that be for Louisa, even if Mr. Curtiss accepted them, which you may be sure he wouldn't want to do? I've already done enough damage in Louisa's life."

Alvescot squeezed her hand. "Don't be feeling guilty about that. Oldcastle needed a little push."

"Yes, but I gave him a shove." Vanessa sighed, nestling her hand in his. "Do you know, Louisa told me yesterday that she'd never been apart from him this long since they met? Even when he made infrequent trips to his home, he was never gone more than three weeks. She misses him dreadfully."

"I'll look him up next time I'm in London and see what I can do, but don't expect much. Finding out her father's running a gambling establishment won't further endear the family to him, especially when the old devil was supposed to be dead." Unconsciously he had begun to rub the soft flesh between her thumb and forefinger. "So you wish me just to tell Edward? I don't think he'll mind keeping it a secret from his mother and sister."

"If you would. I don't care about Mabel, but I'd rather spare Louisa any unnecessary pain if possible."

He nodded. This seemed as good a moment as any to advance his cause. Go slowly, he reminded himself. "I told my mother about your unusual household." There was a wry light in his eyes, inviting her to share his amusement. She responded with a hesitant smile, so Alvescot continued, "She thought you and John and Catherine needed a vacation from them and suggested you might come for a visit to St. Aldwyns when Charles is fully recovered. She's anxious to meet you."

Vanessa was shaken by the invitation. It had been phrased in such a way that it told her very little. If he had said, "I want you to come to St. Aldwyns and meet my mother," she would have known a little better how he felt. And yet there was no reason for him to convey such a message if he. . . .

There was a tap on the door and she gently withdrew her hand from his as she called, "Come in."

A footman entered to hand her a letter. "A boy's just brought it from the village, ma'am. He's awaiting a reply."

Vanessa broke the seal and quickly scanned the short note. "My word!" She turned to Alvescot to ask, "Did you stay at the inn in the village last night?"

"No, in Basingstoke. Why?"

She made a gesture indicating she would explain in a moment and rose to go to her desk. Her writing equipment was still lying there from her previous exertions and she quickly penned an answer, folding it carefully before handing it to the footman. "Have the boy take this, Thomas, and see that he has a coin, please."

When the footman had left, she remained sitting at her desk frowning thoughtfully at the closed door. Alvescot cleared his throat to gain her attention, his brows raised with curiosity.

"It was from William," she explained. "He's at the inn in the village. Just passing through, he said, and wondered if he might stop in for a short visit."

Alvescot laughed. "On his way from London to Suffolk, no doubt. What did you say?"

"I said we would be pleased to have him, and that I hoped he would spend the night. Poor soul! He must be missing Louisa as much as she misses him." Vanessa couldn't resist a small chuckle. "Passing through! I daresay he'll have some story concocted about how he's on his way to Andover or Salisbury. Don't press him, if you please. Louisa will be so happy, and Mabel. . . . Oh, my God!"

She looked stricken for a moment and he rose to come and stand behind her, placing one hand on her shoulder. "Whatever is the problem? I thought this was just what all of you wanted."

"But you're here!" she groaned. "Mabel will think you've come to offer for Louisa, and William . . . Heaven knows what William will think."

"Shall I leave?" he asked stiffly.

Vanessa turned to look up at him, a smile flickering on her lips. "No, of course not. I shall give you the Chinese Chippendale bedroom, James. I know you've longed to have it. William can have the Blue Velvet. But I must go and arrange for everything. This will take a bit of handling. We'll talk later . . . if that's all right?"

"Certainly," he agreed. His disappointment came out only in his flat statement. "You have more important things to do right now."

"Not more important, James. More immediate."

SEVENTEEN

The interview, Alvescot decided as he left the Morning Room after her, had not followed quite the course he had expected. On the drive from St. Aldwyns the previous day, he had pictured them firmly engaged within ten minutes of his seeing her. Of course, his excuse of coming because she hadn't written was not much better than Old-castle's "passing through," but it had seemed sufficient at the time. He *had* been worried about her and he *had* intended to take her to task for her silence, but he had also expected all that to vanish in a moment and to hold her in his arms, where she most decidedly belonged.

He had come with his valet in the traveling carriage and now sent for Bibury to bring his two valises to the Chinese Chippendale bedroom. After all this time, he was eager to see if it was worth the wait, and her teasing him about it. Not that he minded her teasing—he considered it a very good sign. She could just as easily, however, tease him when he was holding her in his arms.

The walls of the room were hung with Chinese painting on silk, with mirror paintings on either side of the fire-place. It was a spacious suite, with a dressing room at-tached, and various pieces of Chinese porcelain were displayed around the two rooms. The carved mahogany four-poster was decidedly English, however, with needle-work hangings, and the painted chimneypiece bore no trace of Chinese inspiration. As elsewhere in the house, the chimneypiece was carved in a fable motif, this one of bears and bees, which was so unoriginal as to be similar to one Alvescot had at St. Aldwyns. His mother had once told him it illustrated the Spanish proverb, "Take what you want, says God. Take it, and pay for it." Well, he would be perfectly willing to buy off Hortense, Mabel, Edward, Louisa, Oldcastle, and anyone else, if he could simply have the right to hold Vanessa in his arms.

Bibury leisurely unpacked and put away his clothing, while the earl stood at the window looking out over the park. In the distance he could see the village and he wondered just how Oldcastle *would* react to his being there. It was the most infernal luck that William hadn't come the previous day. Then perhaps Louisa would be engaged to him and Mabel would be satisfied. Alvescot did not look forward to meeting any of the household members, but he decided it behooved him to seek out Edward as soon as possible. That one thing he could do for Vanessa, and she might be so grateful she would rush into his waiting arms.

God, he was too old for this half-witted daydreaming. There was plenty of time to court Vanessa. She wasn't going to disappear. It bothered him that she'd looked so confused about the offer to visit St. Aldwyns, and even though they'd been interrupted, she could have said something about it before she left him. Had he put it wrong? He was trying to be so careful not to rush her. His arrival had come as a surprise, and he wanted to give her sufficient time to recover before he asked her to consider how she wished to spend the rest of her life.

He'd given it a great deal of thought. John had to know Cutsdean as his ancestral home, but Alvescot could not totally neglect St. Aldwyns. And what if they had children of their own? There was no solution but to share the two estates as their residence, going from one to the other during the course of a year. It was not ideal, but it would have to do. Almost anyone she married would expect at least as much of her. Alvescot was willing to make quite a few concessions if Vanessa was willing to marry him.

And why shouldn't she be? He had a lot to offer her, didn't he? She would become a countess and mistress of St. Aldwyns as well as Cutsdean. He would take some of the burden of management from her shoulders. The children would become his responsibility as well as hers.

Somehow, he wasn't sure all these things held the attraction for her that they might have held for another woman, but he realized that was part of her appeal to him. She was a strong, self-sufficient woman, with a beauty and intelligence to match. But he knew, as surely as he stood there by the window, that she wouldn't marry him unless she loved him. And about that he could not be sure.

"Thank you, Bibury. I won't be needing you until later," he said, dismissing the valet.

First he would find Edward and take care of that problem. It had begun to seem a rather insignificant problem, actually. If not the least of his concerns, Edward seemed rather low on the list right now, especially because Alvescot considered the matter more or less settled.

Edward proved, however, not only elusive but, when finally tracked down to the Orangery, of all places, to be in an obstinately foul mood. The earl wondered if it had continued unabated since the staged accident with the pony.

"I see you're back," Edward said with his customary sneer. "You take your obligations as co-trustee rather seriously."

"True." Alvescot watched the young man peel an orange and carelessly toss the skin on the ground. "I have some news I thought might interest you."

"I doubt it."

There was no sense allowing the fellow to irritate him, but Alvescot could feel the muscles in his jaw tighten. "Probably not," he said levelly, "if you don't consider it of any importance that your father's alive."

"What are you talking about?" Edward demanded. "My father killed himself over a year ago."

"He tried to make it look as though he had. What he did was turn all his property into ready cash and take off for the Continent."

"You're lying," the young man snarled. "Why would he do that?"

There was a gleam in Alvescot's eyes, but he said, "I could only speculate on that, Edward. What I do know is that he's been running various gambling establishments in northern Italy, and doing very well at it."

Edward tossed the uneaten orange toward the rear of the building, wiping his hands fastidiously on a linen handkerchief. His eyes were hooded now, but Alvescot could see that his cupidity had won over his disbelief. "Where in northern Italy?"

"He's been in Turin and Milan, but the latest information places him in Genoa, where he's using the name Como. By all accounts, he's living very well, has grown a beard, and changes his name each time he moves. I shouldn't think it would be difficult to track him down."

"No, but it would be expensive," Edward said, with a shrewd look at the earl. "How did you happen to gather all this information?"

"I was curious," Alvescot replied, indifferent. "Your sister couldn't 'feel' that your father was dead, you know, and it started me to wondering. I had my solicitor check it out."

His show of indifference did not fool Edward for a moment. In Edward's experience, one did not go to the time and expense of such an action without a definite goal in mind. And he considered it highly unlikely that the earl was going to all this effort for his feather-brained sister, so it must be Vanessa who had captured his interest. No wonder she wouldn't come around for Edward! He was not in a position to compete with Alvescot's title and wealth, and it was just like Vanessa to overlook Edward's inordinate good looks for the craggy-faced earl. He was determined to make them both suffer for this slight.

"I haven't the wherewithal to travel to Italy on some wild goose chase," he said, caustic now. "There's no guarantee I would find my father, in any case. Your information could very well be wrong. I think it just as likely my father is dead and someone has mistaken a similar-looking man for him. Running a gambling establishment is not the sort of thing a gentleman does."

Alvescot shrugged and turned away. "Believe what you wish. Actually, I think it's wise to be skeptical in instances such as this." He paused with his hand on the door. "Perhaps I won't bother telling your mother and sister. Mrs. Curtiss would undoubtedly make a mad dash for Italy to find her husband and enjoy the benefits of newly-acquired wealth. On the other hand, I might be remiss in withholding the information."

As he started to let himself out, he felt Edward move forward and grab his arm. "No, don't tell them. It would only be upsetting if the tale proved false. The thing to do is for me to go and see, now I think of it. That would save my mother and sister unnecessary false hope," he said virtuously. "But I'll need money for the trip. I can't tolerate traveling in a shabby way. And it may take time to track my father down, if it is my father."

"I would be willing to advance you a reasonable sum," Alvescot offered.

Edward didn't like the word "advance," but, since he never bothered to pay anyone back the money he borrowed, it didn't unduly bother him. "I'll need at least five hundred pounds."

Alvescot's brows lifted in skeptical amusement. "I would have thought three hundred would suffice for a single traveler. More than suffice. That's the figure I had in mind."

His voice had a "take it or leave it" quality which galled Edward, but he was not about to refuse the offer, either. If his father was indeed involved in a profitable gambling enterprise, Edward felt sure a partnership was in order. Strange he'd never thought of doing something on that order himself. Like most of the idle young men of his acquaintance, he was continually at the tables, finding more excitement there than in the rest of his uneventful life. Of course, it wouldn't do to have such an establishment in England, but in Italy. . . .

With a frown, he accepted Alvescot's offer of three hundred pounds. He didn't bother to thank the earl, or offer to sign a note. Accepting money was something he did automatically rather than graciously. Edward was convinced he should have been born into a wealthier family and acted, when the opportunity arose, as though he had been. On this occasion, he was irritated by Alvescot's condescending attitude, but three hundred pounds was three hundred pounds. He agreed to come to the earl's room later to get part of the money in cash and accept a bank draft for the remainder. Edward felt sure that if he had as much money at his disposal as Alvescot, he would carry a far greater sum on his person.

Alvescot was aware of Edward's irritation; the younger man made no attempt to disguise it. But when Edward had tried to play games with him, he'd resolved not to be a party to the rascal's childish tricks. There was never the least doubt in either man's mind that Edward would go to Italy. The only question was how much Edward would try to get, and Alvescot considered three hundred pounds the limit he was willing to expend, especially when it had occurred to him it was Edward's fault Vanessa had injured her shoulder.

What Edward did not fully comprehend, perhaps, was that he might not have the opportunity to return to Cutsdean if his mission in Italy didn't succeed. There was no chance Alvescot would allow him to take up residence at Cutsdean if *he* had anything to say about it, and he was still hopeful that he would. Vanessa had at least assumed he was going to stay with her for a while. That in itself could be counted a good sign, when there were few enough others.

The midday meal was fast approaching, so Alvescot went directly to his room to change. Oldcastle must have arrived by now, he realized, and the group that would assemble in the Saloon was likely to be keyed to a fine pitch. Hortense was not going to like the earl's being back; Mabel was going to love it. Louisa would be confused and despairing about the coincidence; William was likely to find it the final straw. Edward would consider the whole situation amusing; Vanessa . . . well, it was hard to tell how Vanessa would feel.

He met her in the hall on his way to the Saloon and she smiled apologetically at him. "I haven't told them you're here, James. Do forgive me, but I wanted William to have his moment of glory before . . . well, you know what I mean."

Yes, he knew what she meant. Still, it was rather discouraging to find she put the comfort of her other guests above his. Alvescot was in the habit of having things arranged for his own convenience. Her loyalty was admirable, no doubt, but it hardly soothed his wounded pride. Would she be as loyal to him when (and if) they married?

"Edward knows," he said. "I've spoken to him and agreed to advance him three hundred pounds for his journey."

"Three hundred pounds! James, he'll never pay it back."

"Oh, I know. He asked for five."

Vanessa laid a hand on his sleeve, gazing up at him with worried eyes. "I don't want you to be out of pocket, James. Please allow me to reimburse you."

"We'll discuss it later, my dear. Let's see him away from Cutsdean first. He won't tell his mother and sister about Mr. Curtiss. If there's a bonanza to be had, he wants to be the only one to have it."

"Naturally." She withdrew her hand from his arm as he opened the door to the Saloon and her assembled guests.

It was apparent by their expressions when they saw Alvescot that Edward hadn't told them about the earl's arrival. Whether this was out of his desire not to let escape anything concerning their conversation, or mere maliciousness, Vanessa didn't spend any time contemplating. There was a chorus of astonished reactions.

Hortense glared at him and demanded, "What are *you* doing here?"

Quite the opposite greeting from Mabel, who was seated beside William on the sofa but immediately rose to come forward with outstretched hand. "I *knew* you would return. I told them you had every intention of returning. There was never a doubt in my mind. Who could see Louisa and not be enchanted with her? She shall play the pianoforte for you directly after luncheon."

Poor Louisa looked sick. Her gaze traveled from William to Alvescot and back. The earl nodded politely to her but William glared at both of them. He had stood at Vanessa's entry and now strode to Louisa's chair, muttering, "Why didn't you tell me he had come back? Why did you pretend to be so glad to see me?"

"I *am* glad to see you, William, and I didn't know his

lordship had returned." Her voice was little more than a whisper.

"Very likely," he sniffed, turning on his heel and stalking to the window. Louisa followed him, going so far as to pluck at his sleeve to get his attention. "I won't play for him after luncheon, no matter what Mama says," she breathed, agitated. "It may be necessary for me to play this evening, if Vanessa wishes it, but I won't play before then, I promise you."

William was only slightly mollified. It had been difficult enough for him to work up the courage to return to Cutsdean after his contretemps with Vanessa. To find Alvescot here was decidedly too much. For one hour, when he had first arrived, everything had seemed to be going his way. Mabel had courted him and Louisa had gazed at him with her limpid blue eyes full of devotion. Her eyes, he noted now, were full of desperation, or something, but it was not devotion. William would have liked to announce, to the whole crowd of them, that he and Louisa were going to walk in the garden. Right then, when they should be going into luncheon. But Hortense was watching them with her cold, sharp eyes, and Edward was sneering at them. Mabel didn't look at him at all, but came and dragged her daughter away without a word.

Luncheon was an uncomfortable meal. But then, as Alvescot recalled, it usually was. William spoke to no one, and Mabel insisted that Louisa sit next to the earl. Hortense likewise was silent, regarding him with disdainful eyes. Since Vanessa was at the opposite end of the table from him, he could not speak with her, but made polite conversation with Louisa, assuring her (as she was the only one to ask) that his brother was progressing nicely. After the meal he stated firmly to Mabel that he intended to see his godchildren and would be pleased to hear Louisa perform on the pianoforte after dinner.

"I didn't bring them anything," he told Vanessa as they climbed the stairs together to the nursery floor. "I left St. Aldwyns in rather a hurry, once my mind was made up to come here. Do you think they'll mind?"

"No, of course not. They never had the opportunity to

thank you for your gifts before you left. You wouldn't want to spoil them . . . the way I do," she teased.

"I wouldn't mind," he murmured, not quite loud enough for her to be sure she heard. And then, in a normal tone, "I like your children, Vanessa. My sister says all children are demanding when they're young, and what you should look for is a good disposition and forthrightness. John and Catherine are possessed of both, thank heaven. Even if they can be disconcerting at times."

Vanessa very much wanted to ask him if he had discussed her children in particular with his sister, but found she hadn't the nerve. "Does your sister have children of her own?"

"Yes, two of them, but she and her husband have been living in Ireland for the last few years and I haven't seen them very often. Janine's at St. Aldwyns now for a visit while her husband confers with government officials in London. He has an appointment in Ireland which is rather tricky to handle and I think she's glad to be back at St. Aldwyns for a few weeks. I hope she'll still be there when you come to visit."

"I'm surprised you were willing to leave when she was there, if she comes so seldom."

Alvescot was following her down the hall to the schoolroom now and couldn't see her face. "The first time I came she had left to visit her husband's family for a while. This time . . . she understood the necessity of my leaving."

In the open doorway she turned to study him. There was no mistaking the fondness in his eyes, the conspiratorial half-smile that played about his lips. Vanessa felt her heart rate speed slightly and suffered a moment's shortness of breath. Alongside the excitement was a trace of fear. Was this what she wanted? For herself, undeniably yes. But was it best for her children? She glanced into the room where they played easily together.

"Catherine, John, look who's here," she called.

At sight of him looming behind her in the doorway, they squealed with delight. Vanessa wondered when he'd had the time to so capture their enthusiasm. She watched as they ran to him and he caught one in each arm. Both children spoke at once, asking questions, telling him their latest adventures. It was as if they'd known him all their lives, but had been separated from him for a long time.

Vanessa was willing to concede that they liked him, which was not the same thing as saying they would want him as a stepfather. He was like a favorite uncle to them, now. But how would they feel if he uprooted them, took them away to a place they'd never known and didn't want to know? They weren't particularly timid children, but such an upheaval in their lives was bound to upset them. And Alvescot would expect a great deal of her time, time which might have to be taken from that set aside for the children.

For an hour he stayed with them and talked, about his home and about theirs. Frequently he glanced up at Vanessa to see how she was reacting to this ploy, but her face was guarded. When John asked him how long he was staying, he said, "I don't know yet, but this time I'm sure I won't have to leave without saying good-bye. You'll know when I'm going to leave as soon as I do."

"Stay," Catherine insisted, working her little fist inside his large one. "Everyone stays."

"Yes," he agreed, laughing. "I've noticed that."

"Mr. Oldcastle is here, too," Vanessa told them, but they showed not the least interest.

EIGHTEEN

"Will you ride with me?" Alvescot asked as they left the schoolroom.

"Yes," Vanessa said, though her shoulder still gave her a little trouble on horseback.

"I'll have to borrow one of your animals. I only brought the carriage team."

"Of course. We have several horses who will carry your weight." They were on the first floor landing and he stood so close she could have touched him by lifting a hand. "Shall we meet at the stables in a quarter of an hour?"

Alvescot repressed a desire to touch her glorious hair or brush her cheek with a loving finger. Patience, he schooled himself. She does like you, she's simply not sure if this is a wise step to take. He did expect to be able to convince her that it was. "Quarter of an hour," he confirmed, watching as she walked away from him toward her corner suite at the other end of the hall. From the way she moved, not quite so gracefully as usual, he knew she was aware of his scrutiny and he turned reluctantly to his room.

When she arrived at the stables a few minutes after him, she wore a royal blue riding habit with a foam of lace at the collar and cuffs. He'd never seen the outfit before and knew without being told that it was her best.

"Your groom suggested Winterfrost for me. I've had your mare saddled." He allowed the groom to assist her onto her horse, though he would have preferred to do it himself. It turned out best that he didn't, though, because this way he was able to watch her mount and he saw the slight wince as she twisted to arrange herself in the side-saddle. Apparently her shoulder was not so well mended as she would have him believe. Alvescot felt a rush of anger toward Edward, but shoved it aside. They were going to be rid of Edward for good and what was important was they he keep his eye on Vanessa to see she didn't tire herself.

As they rode, the sun beat down on them and sparkled off the metal on the horses' harness. Alvescot spoke of his family, of St. Aldwyns, of Frederick. They encountered Paul Burford, whose eyes widened in surprise when he recognized the earl, but who greeted him warmly and inquired after his brother. Burford did not stay with them long, leaving with a jaunty, expectant smile. *He* knows why I'm here, Alvescot thought, slightly disgruntled. Perhaps it was time to make his visit more explicit to Vanessa.

They had ridden into a leafy glade where the luscious green grass was inviting and a profusion of wildflowers poked their blossoms toward the afternoon sunlight. Primrose and wood sorrel were interspersed with wood anemone and bluebells, each looking fragile but courageously gay. Alvescot reined in his horse. "Shall we?"

Even the short ride had made her shoulder ache, but Vanessa was half afraid to leave the safety of her mount. His eyes were softly caressing, squinting in the bright light. Behind him she saw a bird flash in the tree branches, its flight an easy escape. "All right."

With that muscular simplicity of motion she had grown to admire, he dismounted and tied his horse to a tree, turning to grasp her about the waist and ease her descent. His hands remained at her sides for a moment, steadying her, before he asked, "Your shoulder's hurting, isn't it?"

Vanessa dismissed the pain lightly. "Only the least bit. I haven't ridden much since the accident."

Taking her hand as though it were the most natural thing in the world, he led her to a tree where he sat and patted the ground beside him. "Lean against me and I'll massage it, my dear. Sometimes it takes a while for that kind of injury to heal properly. Is the doctor satisfied?"

He was leaning back against the tree, looking up at her with one brow lifted questioningly. Vanessa hesitated before seating herself a little apart from him, but he moved so his legs lay alongside hers, barely touching. Immediately, she could feel his strong hands come to rest on her shoulder, unmoving, waiting. "The doctor thinks it will be a few more weeks before the pain is entirely gone, but he said that's only to be expected." She kept her gaze on the patch of bluebells at her booted feet.

The hands started to move, gently kneading her shoulder and upper arm. "Tell me if that's too much," he urged. "Do you have your maid massage it?"

"No, I hadn't thought of it."

"Does it feel good?"

"Yes," she admitted.

"When I was wounded at Waterloo, I wouldn't let anyone touch me except the doctor. Even my valet had to practically beg me to let him change the dressing. I knew I was being unreasonable, but I didn't feel like being reasonable at the time. Do you know what I mean?"

"Yes."

"I thought you would. Don't misunderstand me. I don't think I'm a particularly unreasonable man most of the time, but there are moments when everything seems to come in on you all at once and you aren't quite ready to cope with it. Decisions are like that, too. When there are a lot of extraneous matters littering up your mind, you would sometimes rather not have to consider a large issue that will affect your whole future."

"That's true," she murmured.

"On the other hand," he continued gently, his hands still steadily working, "sometimes making the larger decision is the solution to the smaller problems. I've noticed that you, for instance, Vanessa, like to take charge of a situation. You like to get to the bottom of the matter, find out all the facts, consider all the possibilities, and then act. That's an admirable trait. Most people are prone to acting on their instincts, with the relevant facts only partially digested. Your handling of the estate shows a wholesome regard for having the proper information and taking a long-range view of a problem."

He shifted one hand so it touched her chin, lightly turning her face toward him. "I'm not accustomed to thinking of myself as a large problem, but I can see that you might think I am. The fact is, my dear, I've grown to love you, and I want to marry you. I realize that would mean a certain amount of disruption for you and the children, but I think we could overcome the worst of that. We could live part of the year at Cutsdean and part of the year at St. Aldwyns. It's not ideal, but it's possible."

Alvescot waited for her to say something. Her eyes had become large with emotion, but when she spoke, her question was almost irrelevant. Almost.

"Why did you leave without speaking of this? Why didn't you write something in your letter?"

"I needed to be away from you to consider the matter, my love. Marriage is not a step I take any more lightly than you do, though I'm not so encumbered with family as you are." It was the truth, every word of it. And yet he could have said more. He chose not to, which was a mistake. Vanessa, tuned to every nuance of his speech, sensed that he was not being completely frank with her.

She waited for him to say more. Instead, he kissed her. He drew her tenderly into his arms, lowered his lips to touch her forehead, her eyelids, her lips. Vanessa was conscious that he cradled her body so as to protect her sore shoulder, barely conscious, but it was important to her, his thoughtfulness. His kisses were long and tender, inadvertently drawing her into participation. She responded to the firm pressure on her mouth, hopeful but undemanding. Her lips craved the contact, sought the reassurance that his nearness brought.

One of her hands stole up to twine in his hair. How long ago it seemed when she'd first thought how she would like to feel the texture of his hair. It was soft and smooth, the individual strands teasing between her fingers. She could feel one of his hands in her own hair, nestling her head against his shoulder. His touch was confident, relaxed. This was the love he offered—gentle, even as his physical involvement grew. Vanessa opened her eyes to look into his. They were touched with desire and he smiled apologetically as he eased himself fractionally away from her.

"No," she whispered. "I want you to hold me, to touch me, but not. . . ."

"Of course not," he murmured, smiling. "I'm a gentleman, my love. That must wait for when we're married. You *are* going to marry me, aren't you?"

"I don't know, James."

Alvescot was stunned by her words. There had been little hesitation in her response to his kisses. She had even invited him to continue, nay to progress in his lovemaking. Her smokey eyes didn't waver for a second from his gaze, though they were filled with a strange mixture of sadness and desire.

When he didn't speak, and showed no sign of renewing his amorous advances, she flashed him a brief, uncertain smile and shifted away from him. "I'm very fond of you, James. If I had no one but myself to consider, I wouldn't hesitate. But there are the children, and there's Cutsdean. Have you thought about children of our own? I conceive rather readily, I'm afraid," she admitted with a deprecatory wave of her hand. "If I had a son. . . ."

"I've thought about it." He leaned back against the tree, wrapping his hands about his bent knees and not looking at her. "It would be difficult for John, of course, having a younger half-brother who would inherit the title one day, and even for Catherine to have a half-sister who bore a title with her name. That can't be changed, and I'd want to have children. You have to weigh that against your children's acquiring a man to give them the attention they can never have from their own father. John's situation doesn't really change. He inherits Cutsdean whether you marry me or not. I don't think you can let his peace of mind dictate your decision, Vanessa, especially when there's no way to tell how much it would affect him."

"Perhaps not." She rose, dusting the skirts of her riding habit. What they were discussing was a concern, certainly, but not what really pressed on her mind. She couldn't shake the idea that he wasn't telling her everything. "I don't mean to be difficult, James. As you said before, I like to consider all the facts before I make a decision. Sometimes it feels as though a piece were missing, and it's harder to reach a resolution."

Alvescot had risen when she did and now stood staring down at her. His thoughts were tangled with a variety of threads: hurt at the possibility she would reject him, confusion about what she wanted from him, surprise at her behavior. The last was uppermost in his mind. "Do you consider the missing piece to be your physical response to me, Vanessa?"

"No," she said sadly. "Did I shock you? I'm lonely, James, and I've built your few gestures of closeness out of all proportion. All I needed to know was that you would be gentle, and I already knew that. I wanted you to touch me because your touch makes me feel wonderful. It's not just the excitement; it's the feeling of being joined with you. I've stood on my own for some time now, and I intend to continue doing that, but having someone to make me feel like a woman again . . . I'm afraid I can't explain it, James. You're the only one who seems to accept me as the mistress of Cutsdean as well as a woman."

"I'm sure Paul Burford does."

"Yes, well, that's where it's confusing, I suppose. I don't regard him in the same way I do you."

"I'm glad to hear it." His voice was gruff and he reached down to pick up his riding crop. "But if you decided not to marry me, any intimate contact we had would embarrass you, my dear."

"No, it wouldn't," she retorted, walking to her mare and turning to watch his expression. "It would be something I would treasure, James, something I would look back on with wonder and pleasure. One of my memories to store up against the empty nights. I'm sorry if that upsets you, but it's how I feel. I've had to learn to be proud of my accomplishments here, even when they seemed sometimes to be at the expense of my womanhood. It's only fair I should be allowed some pride in my womanhood itself."

"For God's sake, Vanessa, nothing you've done here makes you less of a woman. You've done what you had to, and you've done it well."

Her faint smile didn't warm her eyes. "You don't quite understand, James. I'm not the same person I was when I married Frederick. Then I thought of myself as a woman, with a woman's obligations, and a woman's second-place role. I don't feel that way any longer. I've had all the aggravation and few of the rewards from taking a first-place role, but I can never revert to my former position." She eyed him shrewdly as he came to stand beside her. "I think perhaps that's why you left Cutsdean without speaking to me, and why, later, when you'd been able to block out some of the memory of my abrasive independence, you wrote such a casual letter. You were pretending to yourself that I was no different than other women. But I am, James, and I think it's something you haven't come to terms with yet."

Alvescot didn't know how to respond. In some ways he even thought she might be right. He *had* managed to forget that she expressed herself so strongly and acted so forcefully. Not imperiously, like his aunt Damery, but with a different sort of personal dignity, an air of assurance that one seldom saw in a woman when she was in company with a man. He could call to mind several occasions on which she had insisted on her right to control events at Cutsdean when he had offered to release her from the burden. Had he fallen in love with her because of, or in spite of, this attribute?

Though he continued to hold her gaze, Vanessa could tell that he was abstracted. With a smile she asked, "Will you hand me up, James? I'm afraid I haven't the height to mount by myself."

"But you would if you could," he said, trying to make his tone teasing.

"Precisely."

He made a foot hold with his hands and she swung herself gracefully into the saddle. Vanessa arranged the folds of blue cloth to a comfortable position as he mounted. But neither of them made any move to urge their horses forward. As they sat regarding one another, she impulsively reached out and touched his hand. "I haven't been totally honest with you, either, James. I'm more than fond of you. My whole being longs to be with you, but it may not be the right thing to do. Can you accept that?"

"In principle, my dear," he said softly, covering her hand. "But in practice it seems foolish and wasteful. I'm sure we could work out any differences between us. I admire what you've done here; I've told you that before. And I think, Vanessa, that as much as you've accomplished, it doesn't make your life feel complete. You told me you were lonely, and yet you have the children and Paul Burford's friendship. You want a man to share your love with, and forge that bond which gives strength and purpose to an otherwise unintelligible existence. Even the strongest among us need the replenishment that having someone love us gives. I won't try to change you, and I don't think you would try to change me. Society's conventions needn't apply to us in our private lives."

"But they will in our public lives, James, and you cannot help but lead a public life. Your friends would think me a very strange sort of woman."

"They would think you adorable . . . and a trifle eccentric, perhaps," he admitted with a grin. "Promise me you won't reject my offer out of hand, Vanessa. Think about it."

"I will if you will, my dear. I don't want it to be easier for you to love me from a distance."

Alvescot realized she was wholly serious about this request, and though at the moment he was feeling it wouldn't be possible to love her any more than he did right then, he said, "I will, but don't expect me to change my mind."

"I just want you to feel you can," she replied, finally removing her hand and urging the mare forward.

All through dinner Alvescot thought about what she'd said, since Hortense would not deign to speak with him and Louisa politely but firmly indicated she would rather not, given William's scowling face on her other side. Mabel, fortunately, wasn't close enough to distract him and Edward hadn't bothered to come to dinner at all.

Down the length of the table Vanessa smiled at him frequently, the old rueful gleam in her eyes. He remembered the first night he'd sat there, thinking that Vanessa was in need of male guidance. As it turned out, she was in need of no guidance at all and he tried to analyze whether that bothered him. There was a certain self-esteem to be gained from a woman's dependence on a man's opinion, of course, but look how ridiculous William and Louisa made such an exchange seem. Where neither opinion carried any weight, talk of guidance was nonsense, and where vanity demanded a flattering degree of attention, it was a hollow sort of victory.

Alvescot knew Vanessa would accord his opinions a proper respect, and what she asked in return was a similar understanding. Not, perhaps, the rule of the day, but an entirely logical arrangement between two intelligent and capable people. Now he came to think of it, he wasn't at all sure he would be comfortable with a subservient, dutiful wife. Earning your bolstered ego at someone else's expense was not exactly his idea of an honest way to conduct affairs. A comfortable wife started to look like the worst possible type of woman he could choose!

When the ladies left them alone, he and William eyed each other with a marked lack of enthusiasm. Alvescot took a sip from his glass and settled back in his chair, saying, "I understand you've spent some time in London, Oldcastle. Was it pleasant?"

"Reasonably," William muttered. "I thought you were settled in Sussex."

"I have been, but I became worried when I didn't hear from Mrs. Damery. As it happens, she had a shoulder injury which prevented her from writing."

William threw him a startled glance. "I didn't hear anything of an injury. How did she sustain it?"

"Rescuing little John. Apparently his pony ran away with him."

"Was Edward anywhere around?" William asked.

"Yes."

"Might have known. That man is a hazard."

"Fortunately, he will be leaving tomorrow. Permanently, I believe, for the Continent." Alvescot didn't find it necessary to inform him that the older Curtiss was alive and running a gambling establishment. It was not the sort of encouragement William needed.

"Oh? I hadn't heard that. His sister didn't mention it."

"I don't believe she knows yet. Edward can be rather secretive."

"Permanently, you say? He won't be coming back to England?"

"I shouldn't think so. It's a matter of a business opportunity."

"Something illegal, or I miss my bet," William snorted. "The man has no character." But the idea caught his imagination. Alvescot could tell by the way he pursed his lips and stared at the amber fluid in his glass, oblivious to the earl's presence. After a while, when he didn't say anything, Alvescot suggested they join the ladies.

NINETEEN

It had been a long evening, Alvescot decided as he slipped into his nightshirt and extinguished the candle by his bed. Louisa had played, and played, and played—at her mother's request. Alvescot had sat with Vanessa on the sofa despite Mabel's attempts to divert him. This had encouraged William, but Mabel had made sure he didn't get close enough to Louisa to have a private word with her. They both played at cards with the two older women, and exchanged wistful glances, but at the end of the evening Mabel rushed her daughter off to her room with hardly a nod in William's direction.

She *had* said, "I expect you will be leaving early," to poor Oldcastle.

Lord, the woman doesn't know when she's well off, Alvescot thought as he climbed into the luxurious bed with its lovely needlework hangings. He had tried to make it as evident as possible that his interest was in Vanessa and not Louisa, but Mabel persisted in her folly. And Edward. Edward had returned and followed him up the stairs so closely Alvescot had felt hounded. The young man had grumbled at only fifty pounds in cash, and took the bank draft for the remainder with a long-suffering groan. Alvescot had felt like snatching back the paper and ripping it to shreds before Edward's eyes.

For some time he lay there in the dark considering various methods of convincing Vanessa to marry him. It might be possible to speak with the children, but he thought she wouldn't be pleased with that. If she wanted to speak with them, she would do it herself. Perhaps already had, when she had left for a while to say good-night to them.

He had just settled himself for sleep when he heard the knob of his door turn. His first thought was a rather wondering joy that Vanessa would come to him like this and his body responded accordingly.

"William?"

Oh, for God's sake, he shuddered under the covers. She had let herself through the door and was carrying a candle which glowed warmly on her nakedness. Not again! "This is not William's room," he said firmly.

"But it must be!" Louisa exclaimed, a catch in her voice. "I made very sure I had the direction right this time. I counted how many steps it was from my room in broad daylight. I could not be mistaken."

"William has the Blue Velvet room this time. *I* have the Chinese Chippendale."

"No one said!" The candle swung crazily as she tossed her hands about in despair. "I don't know where the Blue Velvet room is."

Sighing, Alvescot threw his feet over the side of the bed and rose. "Why don't you at least wear something on your way to his room?" he asked in exasperation. "Lord, Louisa, you're going to catch your death of cold."

"I don't think you can have anything on and still be considered in a Compromising Position," she informed him, almost sternly. "They did say 'not fully clothed,' but how is one to know just how much clothing one may wear and still have it right? I don't want to take any chances."

He pulled a blanket from the bed as she spoke and now approached to drape it about her shoulders. "I'll see you back to your room."

"No! I shan't go to my room! Don't you see? This is the only opportunity I will ever have. He's going to go away tomorrow and I won't ever see him again. It's not fair," she wailed. "Just tell me where the Blue Velvet room is."

Alvescot was torn. In order to avoid a minor scandal, he really should see her back to her own room, but he could understand her despair. Mabel was too blind to know where her own benefit lay, and he *had* promised

Louisa some time ago that he would do what he could to promote her happiness with William. The Blue Velvet room was only two doors down the hall. Really, one shouldn't be put in this sort of position in a well-run household.

"All right," he said at length. "But, Louisa, you don't have to go to him naked. I'm sure simply talking to him is all you need to do to set aside any misunderstanding. It's obvious he's fond of you, and I should think all you have to do is let him know your sentiments and everything will work out to your satisfaction."

"My mother wouldn't accept it if we simply decided to get married. Surely you can see that! No, we have to be found in a Compromising Position so we *have* to get married."

"And who's going to find you in a compromising position in William's room?" he demanded. "People don't just walk in there in the middle of night."

This problem had never occurred to her. It had seemed enough to engineer the situation without actually deciding who would be the one to discover them. "Well," she said, the candle wavering in her hand, "I shall just have to scream or something to bring one of the servants."

Alvescot groaned. "You can't do that. Surely you don't want one of the servants walking in on you naked, Louisa."

"Hmm. Well, then it will have to be you, Lord Alvescot. That can't do any harm. You've already seen me naked."

"Never! What excuse would I have for barging into William's room at this time of night?" he demanded, feeling slightly unnerved. "Listen to me, Louisa. You're of age. All you have to do is *talk* to William. I'm sure he wants to marry you, and then you simply marry him. Mabel can't stand in your way."

In the urgency of their discussion they hadn't bothered to lower their voices. Now there was an inarticulate roar from the hall and Alvescot's door was flung open, just grazing past Louisa, but catching the blanket as it passed to slam against the wall. Louisa was once again left in all her blond nakedness staring in surprise at a fully clothed and frothing William.

"I knew it!" he yelped. "I knew it! I knew I would find you here! For shame, Louisa! I had thought you had more propriety. To think I ever considered making you my wife. I cringe to contemplate it!"

His histrionics were not carried on in a low voice and Alvescot attempted to hush him, to close the door, and to cover Louisa all at the same time. Louisa had burst into tears and was not the least concerned about her natural state. She shrugged off the corner of the blanket Alvescot had managed to toss over her shoulder and gasped, "You don't understand, William."

"I understand. There is nothing wrong with my understanding." His pompous stance was marred by his widening eyes as he at last seemed to realize she was completely naked. He tried not to look at her, he struggled to keep his eyes on her face, but they refused to obey his split inclinations. "My God!" he breathed, unaware he had spoken.

"I meant to come to you," she explained earnestly. "I thought you had the Chinese Chippendale bedroom as you did when you were here before. How was I to know Vanessa had given it to Lord Alvescot?"

Mention of the earl's name revived all William's outrage. "Cad!" he cried. "Bounder! Seducer of innocents! And in a respectable household! How dare you? I shall gouge out your eyes! I shall slit your throat! I shall break your arms and hack off your legs!"

"Oh, William," Louisa giggled, "don't be absurd. Lord Alvescot was just bringing me to your room."

"My room! Is that the way it's done in your circles, my lord?" he asked, overflowing with contempt. "Taking pure young innocents and passing them from man to man? You deserve to be hung!"

Alvescot could hear hurrying footsteps in the hall now and he gave a resigned sigh. In a moment Vanessa appeared in the doorway, taking in the scene with perplexed and sleepy eyes. "What has happened?" she demanded.

They all attempted to answer her at once, but Alvescot, strained now beyond endurance by her arrival, rudely told his two companions to be still. Then, making one final attempt to settle the blanket about Louisa's shoulders, he said, "Miss Curtiss mistook her direction. She was seeking Mr. Oldcastle's room and assumed him to be in this room, as he was on his previous stay. Being unable to gain his attention any other way, she had resolved to place the two of them in a compromising position so they would have to be married. As she didn't know how much clothing a delicately nurtured young woman must remove in order to be compromised, she arrived naked, just to be on the safe side, you understand." His eyes held Vanessa's for a long moment, during which her lips began to twitch. "Just so," he murmured.

William had been forced to listen to this recital, but he didn't have to believe it. He was tempted not to believe it, but he found it such a flattering, attractive idea, that he chose to accept it as truth. "Did you really?" he asked, eyes wide with admiration. "You wanted to marry me that much?"

"Yes," Louisa replied, her eyes now shyly dropped.

"Well, I say, it wasn't exactly a *proper* thing to do, you know," he informed her judiciously, "but you meant well. Actually, it wasn't proper of me to go to your room tonight, either, but dash it all, Louisa, there's no getting past your dragon of a mother."

"You went to my room?"

"Ah, yes. But I had no intention of seducing you!" he assured her. "I thought we would just have a moment to talk alone, don't you know. Without Mabel and Alvescot and the lot of them hanging around. But you weren't there."

"No."

"So I was going back to my room, thinking Mabel had locked you away somewhere, when I heard your voice coming from here. I was that angry! Yes, well, you know about all that."

Vanessa interrupted their exchange, which stood some chance of continuing for quite a while, by suggesting, "Why don't you both go along to Louisa's room to talk? It's not fair to keep Lord Alvescot from his rest."

Obediently they wandered out into the hall together,

hardly aware of the other two. Louisa tripped on the dragging blanket and William solicitously rearranged it about her shoulders. Vanessa watched until they were out of sight, then turned to say to Alvescot, "I'm sorry about that. It must have been rather embarrassing."

"I'm no more easily embarrassed than you are, my dear," he retorted, "and it's not the first time it's happened."

"It isn't?"

"No. Louisa came wandering into my room the last time I was here, when I had that little closet, you remember."

"I remember," she laughed. "Was she looking for William then?"

"Oh, yes, no one ever comes looking for me."

Their eyes held for a moment and Vanessa gently closed the door behind her. "It had never occurred to me to wander about the halls naked."

"I'm glad." He opened his arms to her and she came into them in a soft swirl of cotton fabric. He could feel her breasts pressed against his chest, the length of her body touching his. "I'll remember what you said this afternoon," he whispered into her ebony hair. "I won't ask you to consummate our bond. Just to hold you, to touch you, is all I can ask of you now."

"Thank you, James. It's not prudishness, you know," she said, looking up at him with her gray-brown eyes, wanting him to understand. "It's a matter of prudence. I've wanted you, and I would willingly give myself if it weren't taking such a chance."

"I know."

And then his lips met hers, warm and inviting, and she released herself to the sensation of being loved and desired. It was a mutual feeling. Her hands traced the contours of his head and shoulders, his back and his buttocks through the nightshirt. He felt so solidly male under her exploring hands, so gloriously firm and exciting. She wanted to feel the texture of his skin, to stroke it with loving fingers, to call forth the rich sensations she was experiencing as he stroked her breasts through the layers of cotton. Slowly he unfastened the buttons on her dressing gown and slid it off onto the floor, leaving her in only her thin cotton nightdress.

"Lie with me," he urged, pressing her softly to him.

Vanessa climbed onto the bed. She thought briefly of discarding the nightdress but decided it would remind them both of the limitation she had imposed and he accepted. He lay down beside her, drawing her once more into his arms. At first he merely stroked her hair, murmuring beside her ear the beautiful nonsense of love. She could feel the steady pulse of his manhood against her, as unrelenting and undemanding as waves pounding on the shore. Her fingers were slightly unsteady as she pushed her nightdress up about her waist, and then did the same with his nightshirt. The beat of his heart against hers echoed their increased desire. And still he held her, assuring her by his control, that she needn't fear he could not contain his passion.

With warm, sure fingers he untied the bow at her neck and slid a hand inside to cup her breast. On the tender flesh his hand felt firm but gentle, caressing the sensitive, taut nipple with infinite care. Waves of pleasure spread through her body, and with his other hand he traced their progress, unknowing and yet perfectly attuned, stroking her thighs, easing between her legs. The sensations were so exquisite that almost unconsciously her own hand went to touch him, to give the pleasure that he gave. She had never done it before without being asked. And she had never before felt such a rush of joy in the giving.

His mouth came to encircle her breast with a sigh, his tongue moist and teasing on her nipple. Gentle, and yet excruciatingly arousing. Her body felt awash with eroticism, engulfed. She could feel the soaring crisis, the breathless, shattering pinnacle . . . and the pulsating waves of satisfaction. She experienced his release with hers, apart but bound in gratitude. Vanessa kissed his forehead, his lips, enclosed him tightly in her arms. "I love you," she whispered.

He smoothed back the dark curls that had fallen across her forehead and cheeks. "Then marry me, Vanessa. You've given me more than I dared hope for tonight, but I want to share the full richness of love with you. Not just physically, but in every way. Your children would want you to be happy. There's no sense in sacrificing yourself for no reason. I promise you they'll love St. Aldwyns almost as much as Cutsdean, and I think you will, too, my dear."

The room was dark but her eyes had grown accustomed to it and she touched his lips, running a finger over the tender width of his mouth. "I'll speak to them in the morning, James." Then she sat up and carefully tied the bow at her neck. "It won't be their decision, though; it will be mine. If I decide against marriage, I will always have this memory."

"There's no need for memories when you can have daily doses," he said lightly, squeezing her hand and climbing out of bed to find her dressing gown on the floor. He held it for her and fastened the buttons before once more kissing her softly. "I'll see you to your room."

"No, thank you," she laughed. "I shouldn't want to find myself in a compromising position with you, James. Think of our reputations."

"To hell with our reputations."

But she shook her head. "I know Cutsdean in the dark my dear. There's no need, honestly. All it would take was our running into William as he returned to his room. Please."

"Very well." As she slipped out the door, he said, "I love you," to her retreating back but she didn't respond.

Alvescot lay awake for some time puzzling over her real reason for this hesitation. What an extraordinary woman to stay with him out of love and desire, and yet feel that she wasn't ready to accept his offer of marriage! Vanessa stirred a wondering admiration in him; her behavior was not bound by normal convention. No other woman he knew would have allowed such intimacy before marriage, and yet he could accept—no, even respect—her decision to lie with him even if she might decide not to marry him. Alvescot realized, too, that she would have allowed a consummation of their intimacy if she hadn't had to consider the possibility of conceiving. There was no doubt in his mind that she loved him; it was her reason for staying with him. But the children didn't seem excuse enough not to marry him. Their problems were real but solvable. Bemused, and slightly worried, he decided that any further action would have to wait until morning, and he drifted off to sleep.

TWENTY

Edward was ready to leave. With the money he'd gotten from Alvescot he intended to travel post chaise to London, and spend a few days there enjoying himself before he went on to Europe. There was really no hurry, if one didn't count the possibility his father would move his establishment in the meantime, and Edward felt certain he would have no trouble finding him again if he did. For the first time in years he had sufficient money to indulge himself for a few days, and he was determined to do it.

His parting with his mother, who was only half awake in her bedchamber, was much as he expected. She wept and pleaded with him not to abandon her, but she also managed to let fall that Louisa had come in early that morning to tell her she was marrying William Oldcastle.

"I shall have to go and live with them, and he doesn't like me above half, Edward," she moaned. "Oh, what hopes I had of Alvescot, but Louisa tells me he has always been interested in Vanessa. Imagine! What can she offer him that my poor Louisa cannot? Vanessa isn't half so good on the pianoforte, and she only sings passably! I told Louisa she could not marry William, and she said, 'I'm of age, Mama.' Have you ever? Talking to her own mother that way! But if you were to stay at Cutsdean," she said slyly, "then I think it would be only right for me to stay here with you."

"I'm not staying," Edward informed her bluntly. "I have business in Italy and I have no intention of returning any time in the near future."

"What business?"

"Something has come up," he said, vague. "You'd best go with Louisa and William and make the best of it, Mama. I'm not surprised William doesn't like you, the way you've been behaving toward him."

It was a family trait to give dig for dig, and Mabel, even in her hour of distress, was not to be deterred. "And you," she rasped, "had best not plan on being able to come back to Cutsdean, Edward. If Vanessa and Alvescot are contemplating matrimony, you may be sure neither of them has any intention of allowing you to hang on them for the rest of your life."

Edward hadn't given the matter any thought, but he was grateful for her warning. Not that he told her so. What he did was ask for any money she had available, and as always she came through from her meager resources. She sighed as he closed the door behind himself, trying to accustom herself to this double tragedy. At least William was well-heeled, and without Edward's drain on any allowance she might receive, she would be in a position to indulge herself a little. The thought made her feel better, but not so enthusiastic as to leave her bed. There was plenty of time to face her radiant daughter and her gloomy-faced prospective son-in-law when she was adequately rested.

What she had said was perfectly true, Edward thought as he closed the door. If he left now, with a budding romance underway, there was every chance he wouldn't have Cutsdean to return to should the necessity arise. It even occurred to him that Alvescot had been lying, but that conjecture was immediately put aside. The earl had waved about his solicitor's letter and jotted down the information Edward would need from it. He couldn't imagine anyone going to the trouble of having a letter available if it weren't the real thing.

In the recesses of his mind Edward stored every bit of information which might prove useful to him at present or in the future. This, too, was a Curtiss habit which he had improved upon over the years, acquiring great ability at eavesdropping and snooping through other people's correspondence. He paused now in the hall, trying to remember a scrap of conversation he had overheard in the stables. Alvescot's groom had been talking with his coachman on their first sojourn at Cutsdean, and the little he had heard was not enough to put any pressure on the earl, so he had regretfully dismissed it from his mind.

But lovers were notoriously high-strung, he knew from experience, and it wouldn't do the least harm to embellish a little on what he had heard, to put the cat among the pigeons. Something about a woman, he recalled, an acquaintance of the earl's in Spain. Alvescot's groom had been there at the time to take care of his horses and he was telling the coachman, apropos what appeared to him a new affair of the heart with Vanessa, perhaps, that only once before had he seen his employer show such interest in a young woman. "A regular beauty, she was," the man had said. "Had his lordship doing the pretty every minute he had to spare, and I promise you there weren't many. Came to nothing, though. Her family wasn't interested in an English lord. Had their sights on someone a little more influential in their own country, I shouldn't doubt. Bothered him a lot, you know. He kept to himself for months and, by God, I've always thought he never quite got over it. Him such an outgoing gentleman till then, if you take my meaning."

That was all Edward had heard, but perhaps it was enough. Try as he would, he could not dredge up a name for the woman. Possibly it hadn't been given, or even known. But as far as Edward was concerned, all Spanish beauties were named Maria, in one form or another, and he chose it to make his story seem more legitimate. If it was wrong, Alvescot wasn't going to have much of a chance to refute it, if Edward knew anything about women, and he was sure he did. They took off with the bit between their teeth at the slightest hint of scandal, never stopping to listen to a perfectly reasonable explanation. Jealousy was what did it, he thought smugly. And Vanessa was too proud by far to accept a man whose integrity wasn't intact. That was what he would have to stress.

Edward couldn't be bothered to say good-bye to his sister, in spite of the engagement which might prove of use to him in the future. William, he knew, was not particularly inclined to lend him money, but once they were married he might be induced to part with a little of the ready. Not that Edward had much hope of putting pressure on Louisa; the woman was as stubborn as they came and she had complained for the last year that Edward kept her from having two pennies to rub together in her pocket.

So Edward went directly to Vanessa to purchase his insurance policy. If he could, without seeming to, dissuade her from marrying Alvescot, it might be possible for him to return to Cutsdean one day. As a gambler, Edward would have said the odds were vastly in his favor for the success of his plan, and he approached her in the Library with his jaunty smile.

"I'm off," he declared, dropping into a chair across from her desk. "Alvescot said you know all about my father being in Italy and I'm going to confirm it. I think it's best if we don't say anything to my mother and sister at present. No use getting their hopes up." He offered his most sincere countenance for her inspection. "I've told them it's business. My mother says Louisa insists on marrying Oldcastle, so I'm sure the two of them will be kept too busy to notice I'm gone."

"I daresay," she agreed.

"I'd like the carriage, if I might. Just into Basingstoke, you know. I'll hire a post chaise there."

"Of course."

"Alvescot gave me a draft, but he didn't have much in the way of ready cash," he suggested.

"I'm sure you'll manage as far as London."

Just like her to ignore his needs, Edward thought as he prepared for his master stroke. She deserved a bit of a disappointment. Look what she already had! There was a definite justice about her not becoming a countess, with all the extra wealth Alvescot could provide. Vanessa had had things too easy for too long. While he! Edward mused about the difficulties of his life for a moment, letting them work him into enough of a rage to deliver his parting blow.

"You'll have to watch out for Alvescot," he said casually.

Vanessa had studied the handsome face opposite her as

he worked his way toward his announcement. She allowed her eyes to widen. "Oh? Why?"

"I know he seems the perfect gentleman." Edward had trouble refraining from sneering when he said it, but he knew that would be the wrong thing to do. "But I've heard things to the contrary." Here he paused, giving her a chance to absorb the possibility of wrongdoing, to wonder what the earl could have done to cause talk about himself. Edward decided it would be best to make her ask, but Vanessa merely stared at him, a disconcerting sort of stare, though one couldn't have called it disbelief, exactly.

Finally he said, "I heard it from his own groom, you know." This sounded a bit defensive, and was perhaps open to misinterpretation, so he added, "I just happened to overhear him speaking to the coachman one day."

Even this intriguing information did not bring a response from her. She sat at her ease, one hand resting on the desk and the other out of his range of vision. Edward convinced himself the other hand was clenched tightly in her lap.

"You are a trusting sort of woman, Vanessa," he explained, patient with her anxiety. "Because a man is an aristocrat, and a cousin of your late husband's, you're willing to accord him a belief in his innate decency. I merely thought I should warn you to be on your guard. This man is not as he appears!" he announced with all the drama of a player on the stage.

Vanessa said nothing but she was beginning to wonder if Edward, too, had been wandering about the house the previous evening. Had he seen her come out of Alvescot's room late at night? It didn't seem likely, or he would have pressed for money for his silence. She did wish he'd get on with what he intended to tell her, but she wouldn't give him the satisfaction of prompting him.

"It seems," Edward said, his voice now hushed with conspiracy as he leaned toward her, "that his lordship is taken to seducing young ladies of good birth. There was a woman in Spain, apparently from a superior family, whom he ravaged and left to fend for herself. The name was Maria, I believe. Now, the Spaniards may in general be a group of blood-thirsty villains, but their best families have a claim to an Englishman's respect." He sat back, self-righteous, and frowned at her. "It was not an honorable thing to do, Vanessa. Any man who could do such a dastardly deed is not an acquaintance you would want to have. I warn you for your own good."

"I see. Well, thank you for telling me, Edward, but I don't think it would be advisable for you to spread such a story. I can't think Lord Alvescot would allow such a slander to pass." She rose to dismiss him.

"No, no!" he protested, leaping to his feet. "*You* are the only one I would tell, because you've been so good as to allow him to trespass upon your hospitality. A woman isn't likely to hear these truths, and consequently is unguarded against any man who might attempt to take advantage of her. Many a sorry lady would have benefited from some timely advice. You know it is only my great admiration for you that prompts me to indulge in such a distasteful task."

"I'm sure," she replied, noncommittal. "As you are off, Edward, I'll bid you a pleasant journey. I hope you find your father and that your reunion with him will be all you could wish."

Though she didn't appear moved by his story, Edward felt sure he had planted a kernel of doubt that would sprout into full-blown outrage by the time he reached Basingstoke. He mumbled his farewells, appropriately subdued after his grave announcement, and strode from the room.

Vanessa went to stand at the Library window, where she had a view of the carriage drive. It was a good twenty minutes before the carriage was prepared and Edward's luggage was strapped to the roof. She didn't know how he thought he was going to convey all those valises in a post chaise, but she didn't bother to remind him of the limited capacity of one of those smaller vehicles. Perhaps he'd have them transported separately. It no longer mattered to her; she was simply glad to be rid of him.

When the carriage had vanished from sight, she went up to the nursery floor to see the children. She had promised Alvescot she would talk to them, but this wasn't the right time. First, there was a need to talk to him, again, in light of Edward's disclosures. Not that she believed for a moment the allegations made against him, but she was familiar enough with Edward's methods of operation that she suspected there was some grain of fact amidst his fiction. And it might be just the element that was eluding her, the reticence she detected in him that made her hesitate to commit herself.

On her way to the Morning Room she asked Tompkins to find his lordship if he was in the house, and ask him if he would spare her a moment of his time.

"In the Morning Room?" he asked, disbelieving his own hearing.

"Yes," she laughed, "in the Morning Room. I'm letting down standards right and left, aren't I, Tompkins? But I would appreciate your keeping us from being interrupted."

"Of course, ma'am."

The draperies had been opened and sunlight streamed into the room, mellowing the soft colors of the carpet and sofa. Vanessa wandered about the room, restlessly moving the fire screen and rearranging the ornaments on the mantel. It was *her* room, her private sanctuary, symbolic of her independence . . . and her loneliness. Having it proclaimed her position as mistress of Cutsdean, her right to direct her own affairs and those of the household over which she presided. If she married James, things would never be the same again.

But they would be different than they had been with Frederick. Vanessa couldn't imagine Alvescot's taking off and leaving her for long stretches of time. He didn't have Frederick's wanderlust, or his craving for adventure. James was a considerate, tender man who would share his life with her and offer her the love she would find it difficult to live without, now she had come to love him. She could, of course, continue to live as she had, carrying out her responsibilities and continually plumbing her resources for the courage to act as forcefully as she needed to run Cutsdean properly. But it would be much more comfortable if she had someone's approval, someone's love to help replenish those resources.

And what did she have to offer him? Her love. Little enough beside the negative qualities which might disrupt his life: her insistence on being treated as an equal; her determination to maintain her control over Cutsdean; her two fatherless children. Really, she wasn't much of a bargain. More of a liability.

She was standing beside the sofa when he rapped on the door. He had been at breakfast while she was there, but she hadn't had a chance to speak with him, as William had been there, too, pontificating on how he would handle Mabel if she objected to his marrying Louisa. Vanessa had excused herself, apologetically smiling at James for leaving him to such boredom. Now he regarded her with an amused half-smile, saying, "Unfair to leave me with that fellow. Did you really have accounts to do?"

"They may not have been pressing, but I went directly to the Library and worked on them." She waved him to a seat on the sofa as she sat down. "Edward found me there—to say good-bye."

"He's left? Excellent!" He reached for her hand, pressed it, and maintained his hold.

"He did have something else to say. It seems to have occurred to him to damage your reputation before he left. You have to credit him with never letting an opportunity slip by."

"What did he say?" Alvescot was perfectly relaxed, since there was no episode in his life that could be considered particularly damaging, if one didn't count a few youthful escapades that were long forgotten. But he felt annoyed that he hadn't considered the possibility of Edward's getting a little revenge as he left.

"It was a story of your ravaging a well-born young lady in Spain. Maria, he said her name was."

Alvescot sat perfectly still for a moment, his gaze steadily on her. "You didn't believe him, did you?"

"No, but I did think there might be . . . some truth to 'Maria's' existence. Edward isn't clever enough to have thought of the setting. He'd have invented some connection here in England, no doubt, if he'd been pressed. Apparently, he overheard your groom talking to your coachman some time ago."

Absently he began to stroke her hand, gazing now at

the fire screen a few feet away. "There was a young woman named Maria. When I was on the Peninsula, I fell desperately in love with her."

Vanessa could feel an ache grow inside her, but she said nothing.

"She was from a prominent family, but one which needed to ally itself with wealth and influence. Spanish influence, you understand. They considered my English influence of less than no use to them, though the wealth they wouldn't have minded. So they let me court her for a while, until someone more promising came along. Then they refused my offer for her, though I believed her to be as much in love with me as I was with her. She was only twenty at the time and a rather shy, biddable girl. Stunningly beautiful."

He turned to smile at her, moving his hand to touch her cheek. "I tell you that to explain my infatuation, Vanessa, not to compare you with her. To me you are the more beautiful because your beauty is underlaid with a strength of character I don't think she could ever possess. Maria wasn't strong enough to oppose her parents, and I don't think she really wanted to. It's more customary there for an arranged marriage than it is in England now. She was young enough to see something romantic about unrequited love. Lord, I shouldn't blame her. I've moped around for years cursing my fate that I couldn't marry her."

"Do you still?" Vanessa asked gently.

"I did when I came to Cutsdean," he admitted. "I can remember thinking of her the first day I was here. And being astonished at myself on the last day that all thought of her had vanished."

"Why didn't you tell me about her?"

"What was there to say?" He shrugged his shoulders helplessly. "I didn't know, until I met you, that my longing for her was slightly ridiculous. You loved Frederick when you married him, but you came to terms with his death, and here I was mourning a pretty young woman who has probably grown to love her husband and produced a parcel of children for him. Our different religions, our different countries, could have made a marriage between us uneasy at best. When I first met you, and you told me you allowed all Frederick's relatives to stay here because your parents thought you should, I was tempted to compare you with her. A dutiful daughter. It didn't take long to see quite a difference between the two of you."

The ache had eased somewhat in her chest, but she had to know just a little more. "And when you left here to go to your brother?"

"I didn't trust my new emotions, Vanessa. For years I've been accustomed to considering Maria the ideal of womanhood." He gave her a rueful smile. "I don't think I actually thought what it would be like married to her, a fragile, almost helpless woman. When I spoke of her to my mother and sister, after Waterloo, telling them about my grave disappointment, they exchanged glances that I took at the time to be sorrow for me."

He laughed and twisted a lock of her hair about his fingers. "Do you know what they told me when I was at St. Aldwyns this time? They told me they had thought then that it was a great blessing she hadn't married me. Not because she was Spanish, but because, according to my mother, I kept describing her as 'a delicate, innocent flower.' They had a great laugh about it."

"I don't wonder," Vanessa said, her eyes sparkling. "What did you tell them about me?"

"I told them you were a little obstinate, but capable. That you were used to doing things your own way. That you were a handsome woman, but not fashionable. That you weren't likely to bow and scrape to anyone. And that I loved you dearly."

Vanessa swallowed past the lump in her throat. "Do they mind that I'm a bit strong-willed, James?"

"Mind? Lord, no. My mother sighed and said, 'Thank God you found the right one this time, James. Bring her here as soon as Charles is well.' Mother's not particularly used to bowing and scraping herself, Vanessa."

"No, I don't suppose she is. But do you think they'll like me?"

"Only if you agree to marry me, my love. Otherwise, they're likely to be quite put out with you."

His smile was so warmly loving she felt a momentary,

and absurd, pricking of tears at her eyes. She blinked them back, saying, "I thought there was something you weren't telling me, James. I thought perhaps you weren't sure you wanted me, with all my determination and my stubbornness, even though you loved me."

"I'm sure I want you, with all your determination and stubbornness, my dear," he laughed. "I didn't tell you about Maria because I didn't want you to think I was an absolute fool."

"We all make mistakes about the type of person we're best suited to," she admitted, not meeting his eyes. "Different things are important to you when you're younger, and they're not always the qualities that strengthen a marriage in the long run. I think sometimes that people shouldn't marry until they're older."

James bent to kiss her, his arms enfolding her in a snug embrace. "I see," he said, pressing for no details. He could feel her shiver and snuggle closer to him, her warm body trusting against his. "And do you think you're old enough to marry me?"

"Yes," she admitted, lifting her head to meet his eyes. "I'm quite sure I want to marry you, James. You don't think I'm a bit loose after last night, do you?"

"Not at all, my love. I think you're exactly the sort of woman I want to marry. A very sensuous, almost proper, and exceedingly lovely lady."